AS THEY ENTERED THE FOREST, THE DRUG TOOK EFFECT.

Alarm filled him momentarily, coupled with a vivid picture of Mary's face. Then the image and the alarm vanished.

Now he was sprinting, his men beside him. A searchlight burst into life, sweeping its beam among the tree trunks. As it caught Group Three, the colonel opened fire.

He had acted fast, hardly realizing he was firing. The guns they carried had special light-touch trigger actions to respond to their new tempo.

A burst of firing answered his shot, but it fell behind them. They were moving faster. They wove rapidly among the stegor trees. Dawn gave them light to see by. Opposition, as Briefing had forecast, was scattered. They ran without stopping. They passed camouflaged vehicles, tanks, tents, some containing sleeping men. All these they skirted. They shot anything that moved. A fifty per cent acceleration of perception and motion turned them into supermen.

Also by Brian Aldiss

Fiction
The Brightfount Diaries
The Primal Urge
The Male Response
The Hand-Reared Boy
A Soldier Erect
A Rude Awakening
The Malacia Tapestry

Science Fiction
Non-Stop
Galaxies Like Grains of Sand
Equator
Hothouse
The Dark Light Years
Greybeard
Earthworks
The Saliva Tree
Cryptozoic
Barefoot in the Head
The Eighty-Minute Hour: A Space Opera
Enemies of the System
Helliconia Spring
Helliconia Summer
Helliconia Autumn

Fantasy
Report on Probability A
Frankenstein Unbound
Brothers of the Head

Stories
Space, Time and Nathaniel
The Best SF Stories of Brian Aldiss
Intangibles Inc., and Other Stories

The Moment of Eclipse
Comic Inferno
Last Orders

Non-fiction
Cities and Stones
The Shape of Further Things
Billion Year Spree
Hell's Cartographers (with Harry Harrison)
Science Fiction Art (Editor)

Anthologies and Series (as Editor)
Best Fantasy Stories
Introducing Science Fiction
The Penguin Science Fiction Omnibus
Space Opera
Space Odysseys
Evil Earths
Galactic Empires 1 & 2
Perilous Planets

with Harry Harrison
Nebula Award Stories 2
Farewell Fantastic Venus!
The Year's Best Science Fiction (annually from 1968)
The Astounding-Analog Reader (2 volumes)
Decade 1940s
Decade 1950s
Decade 1960s
The SF Master Series

BRIAN W. ALDISS
STARSWARM

BAEN
SCIENCE FICTION
BOOKS

STARSWARM

Copyright © 1985 by Brian W. Aldiss

A Baen Book

Baen Enterprises
260 Fifth Avenue, 3S
New York, N.Y. 10001

First Baen printing, December 1985

ISBN: 0-671-55999-0

Cover art by Joe Bergeron

Printed in the United States of America

Distributed by
SIMON & SCHUSTER
MASS MERCHANDISE SALES COMPANY
1230 Avenue of the Americas
New York, N.Y. 10020

Contents

Sector Vermilion

The most simple statement you can make is also the most profound: Time passes. A million centuries—give or take a dozen—have elapsed since the human family began to move from one planet to another.

Directly, little is known about the first primitive men or the worlds they conquered. Indirectly, we know a great deal. The classical Theory of Multigrade Superannuation helps us.

The Theory was formulated in Starswarm Era 80, and with it we, forty-four eras later, can deduce more about both past and present than we should otherwise be able to do.

The fifth postulate of the Theory states that "the progress factors that intelligent beings cause, as well as the factors stimulating their intelligence, are both independent of the universal progression factor, within certain limits." These limits are defined in the remaining postulates, but the statement as it stands is adequate.

Put simply, it means this: The Universe is similar to a cosmic clock; the civilizations of man are not mere cogs but infinitely smaller clocks, ticking in their own right.

Shorn of its intellectual clothes, the idea stands forth naked and exciting. It means that at any one time, the inhabited solar systems of Starswarm—our

1

galaxy—will exhibit all the characteristics through which a civilization can pass.

So it is fitting that in this anniversary of star flight we should survey a handful of the myriad civilizations, all contemporary in one sense, all isolated in another, that go to make up our galactic cluster. Perhaps we may find a hint that will show us why the ancients launched their frail metal spores into the expanses of space.

Our first survey comes from the remote part of Starswarm designated as Sector Vermilion. There, far from the accepted routes of our interstellar societies, you will find a culture with some unity that embraces two hundred and fifteen thousand planets.

Among those planets is Abrogun—a planet with a long history, tenanted now by a few hermit-like families. Among those families . . .

I

A giant rising from the fjord, from the grey arm of sea in the fjord, could have peered over the crown of its sheer cliffs and discovered Endehabven there on the edge, sprawling at the very start of the island.

Derek Flamifew/Ende saw much of this sprawl from his high window; indeed, a growing restlessness, apprehensions of a quarrel, forced him to see everything with particular clarity, just as a landscape takes on an intense actinic visibility before a thunderstorm. Although he was warmseeing with his face, yet his eye vision wandered over the estate.

All was bleakly neat at Endehabven—as I should know, for its neatness is my care. The gardens are made to support evergreens and shrubs that never flower; this is My Lady's whim, who likes a sobriety to match the furrowed brow of the coastline. The building, gaunt Endehabven itself, is tall and lank and severe; earlier ages would have found its structure impossible: its thousand built-in para-gravity units ensure that column, buttress, arch and wall support masonry the mass of which is largely an illusion.

Between the building and the fjord, where the garden contrives itself into a parade, stood by My Lady's laboratory and My Lady's pets—and, indeed, My Lady herself at this time, her long hands busy with the minicoypu and the squeaking atoshkies. I stood with her, attending the animals' cages or passing her instruments or stirring the tanks, doing always what she asked. And the eyes of Derek Ende looked down on us; no, they looked down on her only.

Derek Flamifew/Ende stood with his face over the receptor bowl, reading the message from Star One. It played lightly over his countenance and over the boscises of his forehead. Though he stared down across that achingly familiar stage of his life outside, he still warmsaw the communication clearly. When it was finished, he negated the receptor, pressed his face to it, and flexed his message back.

"I will do as you message, Star One. I will go at once to Festi XV in the Veil Nebula and enter liaison with the being you call the Cliff. If possible, I will also obey your order to take some of its substance to Pyrylyn. Thank you for your greetings; I return them in good faith. Goodbye."

He straightened and massaged his face: warm-looking over great light distances was always tiring, as if the sensitive muscles of the countenance knew that they delivered up their tiny electrostatic charges to parsecs of vacuum and were appalled. Slowly his boscises also relaxed, as slowly he gathered together his gear. It would be a long flight to the Veil, and the task that was set him would daunt the stoutest heart. Yet it was for another reason he lingered; before he could be away, he had to say a farewell to his mistress.

Dilating the door, he stepped out into the corridor, walked along it with a steady tread—feet covering mosaics of a pattern learned long ago in his childhood—and walked into the paragravity shaft. Moments later, he was leaving the main hall, approaching My Lady as she stood, gaunt, with rodents scuttling at breast level before her and Vatya Jokatt's heights rising behind her, grey with the impurities of distance.

"Go indoors and fetch me the box of name rings, Hols," she said to me; so I passed him, My Lord, as he went to her. He noticed me no more than he noticed any of the other parthenos, fixing his sights on her.

When I returned, she had not turned towards him, though he was speaking urgently to her.

"You know I have my duty to perform, Mistress," I heard him saying. "Nobody else but a normal-born Abrogunnan can be entrusted with this sort of task."

"This sort of task! The galaxy is loaded inexhaustibly with such tasks! You can excuse yourself forever with such excursions."

He said to her remote back, pleadingly: "You can't talk of them like that. You know of the nature of the Cliff—I told you all about it. You know this isn't an excursion: it requires all the courage I have. And you know that in this sector of Starswarm only Abrogunnans, for some reason, have such courage . . . don't you, Mistress?"

Although I had come up to them, threading my subservient way between cage and tank, they noticed me not enough even to lower their voices. My Lady stood gazing at the grey heights inland, her countenance as formidable as they; one boscis twitched as she said, "You think you are so mighty and brave, don't you?"

Knowing the power of sympathetic magic, she never spoke his name when she was angry; it was as if she wished him to disappear.

"It isn't that," he said humbly. "Please be reasonable, Mistress; you know I must go; a man cannot be forever at home. Don't be angry."

She turned to him at last.

Her face was high and stern; it did not receive. Her warmvision was closed and seldom used. Yet she had a beauty of some dreadful kind I cannot describe, if kneading together weariness and knowledge can create beauty. Her eyes were as grey and distant as the frieze of the snow-covered volcano behind her. She was a century older than Derek, though the difference showed not in her skin—which would stay fresh yet a thousand years—but in her authority.

"I'm not angry. I'm only hurt. You know how you have the power to hurt me."

"Mistress—" he said, taking a step towards her.

"Don't touch me," she said. "Go if you must, but don't make a mockery of it by touching me."

He took her elbow. She held one of the minicoypus quiet in the crook of her arm—animals were always docile at her touch—and strained it closer.

"I don't mean to hurt you, Mistress. You know we owe allegiance to Star One; I must work for them, or how else do we hold this estate? Let me go for once with an affectionate parting."

"Affection! You go off and leave me alone with a handful of miserable parthenos and you talk of affection! Don't pretend you don't rejoice to get away from me. You're tired of me, aren't you?"

Wearily, he said, as if nothing else would come, "It's not that—"

"You see! You don't even attempt to sound sincere. Why don't you go? It doesn't matter what happens to me."

"Oh, if you could only hear your own self-pity!"

Now she had a tear on the icy slope of one cheek. Turning, she flashed it for his inspection.

"Who else should pity me? You don't, or you

wouldn't go away from me as you do. Suppose you get killed by this Cliff, what will happen to me?"

"I shall be back, Mistress," he said. "Never fear."

"It's easy to say. Why don't you have the courage to admit that you're only too glad to leave me?"

"Because I'm not going to be provoked into a quarrel."

"Pah! You sound like a child again. You won't answer, will you? Instead you're going to run away, evading your responsibilities."

"I'm not running away!"

"Of course you are, whatever you pretend. You're just immature."

"I'm not, I'm not! And I'm not running away! It takes real courage to do what I'm going to do."

"You think so well of yourself!"

He turned away then, petulantly, without dignity. He began to head towards the landing platform. He began to run.

"Derek!" she called.

He did not answer.

She took the squatting minicoypu by the scruff of its neck. Angrily she flung it into a nearby tank of water. It turned into a fish and swam down into the depths.

II

Derek journeyed towards the Veil Nebula in his fast lightpusher. Lonely it sailed, a great fin shaped like an archer's bow, barnacled all over with the photon cells that sucked its motive power from the dense and dusty currencies of space. Midway along the trailing edge was the blister in which Derek lay, senseless over most of his voyage, which stretched a quarter way across the light-centuries of Vermilion Sector.

He awoke in the therapeutic bed, called to an-

other day that was no day by gentle machine hands
that eased the stiffness from his muscles. Soup
gurgled in a retort, bubbling up towards a nipple
only two inches from his mouth. He drank. He
slept again, tired from his long inactivity.

When he woke again, he climbed slowly from
the bed and exercised. Then he moved forward to
the controls. My friend Jon was there.

"How is everything?" Derek asked him.

"Everything is in order, My Lord," Jon replied.
"We are swinging into the orbit of Festi XV now."
He gave Derek the coordinates and retired to eat.
Jon's job was the loneliest any partheno could have.
We are hatched according to strictly controlled
formulae, without the inbred organizations of DNA
that assure true Abrogunnans their amazing longevity; five more long hauls and Jon will be old
and worn out, fit only for the transmuter.

Derek sat at the controls. Did he see, superim-
posed on the face of Festi, the face he loved and feared? I
think he did. I think there were no swirling clouds
for him that could erase the clouding of her brow.

Whatever he saw, he settled the lightpusher into
a fast low orbit about the desolate planet. The sun
Festi was little more than a blazing point some
eight hundred million miles away. Like the riding
light of a ship it bobbed above a turbulent sea of
cloud as they went in.

For a long while, Derek sat with his face in a
receptor bowl, checking ground heats far below.
Since he was dealing with temperatures approaching absolute zero, this was not simple; yet when
the Cliff moved into a position directly below, there
was no mistaking its bulk; it stood out as clearly
on his senses as if outlined on a radar screen.

"There she goes!" Derek exclaimed.

Jon had come forward again. He fed the time
coordinates into the lightpusher's brain, waited,
and read off the time when the Cliff would be
below them once more.

Nodding, Derek began to prepare to jump. Without haste, he assumed his special suit, checking each item as he took it up, opening the paragravs until he floated and then closing them again, clicking down every snap-fastener until he was entirely encased.

"395 seconds to next zenith, My Lord," Jon said.

"You know all about collecting me?"

"Yes, sir."

"I shall not activate the radio beacon till I'm back in orbit."

"I fully understand, sir."

"Right. I'll be moving."

A little animated prison, he walked ponderously into the air lock.

Three minutes before they were next above the Cliff, Derek opened the outer door and dived into the sea of cloud. A brief blast of his suit jets set him free from the lightpusher's orbit. Cloud engulfed him as he fell.

The twenty surly planets that swung round Festi held only an infinitesimal fraction of the mysteries of the Starswarm. Every globe in the universe huddled its own secret purpose to itself. On some, as on Abrogun, the purpose manifested itself in a form of being that could shape itself, burst into the space lanes, and rough-hew its aims in a civilized, extraplanetary environment. On others, the purpose remained aloof and dark; only human beings, weaving their obscure patterns of will and compulsion, challenged those alien beings to wrest from them new knowledge that might be added to the store of old.

All knowledge has its influence. Over the millennia since interstellar flights had become practicable, mankind was insensibly moulded by its own findings; together with its lost innocence, its genetic stability disappeared. As man fell like rain over other planets, so his family lost its original hereditary design; each centre of civilization bred new ways of thought, of feeling, of shape—of—life itself. In Sector Vermilion, the man who dived headfirst to meet an entity called the Cliff was human more in his sufferings than his appearance.

The Cliff had destroyed all the few spaceships or lightpushers landing on its desolate globe. After long study from safe orbits, the wise men of Star One evolved the theory that the Cliff attacked any considerable source of power, as a man will swat a buzzing fly. Derek Ende, alone with no power but his suit motors, would be safe—or so the theory went.

Riding down on the paragravs, he sank more and more slowly into planetary night. The last of the cloud was whipped from about his shoulders, and a high wind thrummed and whistled around the supporters of his suit. Beneath him, the ground loomed. So as not to be blown across it, he speeded his rate of fall; next moment he sprawled full length on Festi XV. For a while he lay there, resting and letting his suit cool.

The darkness was not complete. Though almost no solar light touched this continent, green flares grew from the ground, illumining its barren contours. Wishing to accustom his eyes to the gloom, he did not switch on his head, shoulder, stomach or hand lights.

Something like a stream of fire flowed to his left. Because its radiance was poor and guttering, it confused itself with its own shadows, so that the smoke it gave off, distorted into bars by the bulk of the 4G planet, appeared to roll along its course like burning tumbleweed. Further off were larger sources of fire, most probably impure ethane and methane, burning with a sound that came like frying steak to Derek's ears, spouting upward with an energy that licked the lowering cloud race with blue light. At another point, a geyser of flame blazing on an eminence wrapped itself in a thickly swirling pall of smoke, a pall that spread upward as slowly as porridge. Elsewhere, a pillar of white fire burned without motion or smoke; it stood to the right of where Derek lay, like a floodlit sword in its perfection.

He nodded approval to himself. His drop had been successfully placed. This was the Region of Fire, where the Cliff lived.

To lie there was pleasant enough, to gaze on a scene never closely viewed by man fulfilment enough—until he realized that a wide segment of landscape offered not the slightest glimmer of illumination. He looked into it with a keen warmsight, and found it was the Cliff.

The immense bulk of the thing blotted out all light from the ground and rose to eclipse the cloud over its crest.

At the mere sight of it, Derek's primary and secondary hearts began to beat out a hastening pulse of awe. Stretched flat on the ground, his paragravs keeping him level to 1G, he peered ahead at it; he swallowed to clear his choked throat; his eyes strained through the mosaic of dull light in an endeavour to define the Cliff.

One thing was sure: it was huge! He cursed the fact that although photosistors allowed him to use his warmsight on objects beyond the suit he wore, this sense was distorted by the eternal firework display. Then in a moment of good seeing he had an accurate fix: the Cliff was still some distance away! From first observations, he had thought it to be no more than a hundred paces distant.

Now he realized how large it was. It was enormous!

Momentarily he gloated. The only sort of tasks worth being set were impossible ones. Star One's astrophysicists held the notion that the Cliff was in some sense aware; they required Derek to take them a sample of its flesh. How do you carve a being the size of a small moon?

All the time he lay there, the wind jarred along

the veins and supporters of his suit. Gradually it occurred to Derek that the vibration he felt from this constant motion was changed. It carried a new note and a new strength. He looked about, placed his gloved hand outstretched on the ground.

The wind was no longer vibrating. It was the earth that shook, Festi itself that trembled. The Cliff was moving!

When he looked back up at it with both his senses, he saw which way it headed. Jarring steadily, the Cliff bore down on him.

"If it has intelligence, then it will reason—if it has detected me—that I am too small to offer it harm. So it will offer me none, and I have nothing to fear," Derek told himself. The logic did not reassure him.

An absorbent pseudopod, activated by a simple humidity gland in the brow of his helmet, slid across his forehead and removed the sweat that had formed there.

Visibility fluttered like a rag in a cellar. The forward surge of the Cliff was still something Derek sensed rather than saw. Now the masses of cloud blotted the thing's crest, as it in its turn eclipsed the fountains of fire. To the jar of its approach even the marrow of Derek's bones raised a response.

Something else also responded.

The legs of Derek's suit began to move. The arms moved. The body wriggled.

Puzzled, Derek stiffened his legs. Irresistibly, the knees of the suit hinged, forcing his own to do likewise. And not only his knees, but his arms too, stiffly though he braced them on the ground before him, were made to bend to the whim of the suit. He could not keep still without breaking his bones.

Thoroughly alarmed, he lay there flexing contortedly to keep rhythm with his suit, performing the gestures of an idiot.

As if it had suddenly learned to crawl, the suit

began to move forward. It shuffled over the ground; Derek inside went willy-nilly with it.

One ironic thought struck him. Not only was the mountain coming to Mohammed; Mohammed was perforce going to the mountain . . .

III

Nothing he did checked his progress; he was no longer master of his movements; his will was useless. With the realization rode a sense of relief. His Mistress could hardly blame him for anything that happened now.

Through the darkness he went on hands and knees, blundering in the direction of the oncoming Cliff, prisoner in an animated prison.

The only constructive thought that came to him was that his suit had somehow become subject to the Cliff; how, he did not know or try to guess. He crawled. He was almost relaxed now, letting his limbs move limply with the suit movements.

Smoke furled about him. The vibrations ceased, telling him that the Cliff was stationary again. Raising his head, he could see nothing but smoke— produced perhaps by the Cliff's mass as it scraped over the ground. When the blur parted, he glimpsed only darkness. The thing was directly ahead!

He blundered on. Abruptly he began to climb, still involuntarily aping the movements of his suit.

Beneath him was a doughy substance, tough yet yielding. The suit worked its way heavily upward at an angle of something like sixty-five degrees; the stiffness creaked, the paragravs throbbed. He was ascending the Cliff.

By this time there was no doubt in Derek's mind that the thing possessed what might be termed volition, if not consciousness. It also possessed a power no man could claim; it could impart that volition to an inanimate object like the suit. Helpless inside it, he carried his considerations a stage further. This power to impart volition seemed to have a limited range; otherwise the Cliff surely would not have bothered to move its gigantic mass at all, but would have forced the suit to traverse all the distance between them. If this reasoning were sound, then the lightpusher was safe from capture in orbit.

The movement of his arms distracted him. His suit was tunnelling. Giving it no aid, he lay and let his hands make swimming motions. If it was going to bore into the Cliff, then he could only conclude he was about to be digested: yet he stilled his impulse to struggle, knowing that struggle was fruitless.

Thrusting against the doughy stuff, the suit burrowed into it and made a sibilant little world of movement and friction that ceased the moment it stopped, leaving Derek embedded in the most solid kind of isolation.

To ward off growing claustrophobia, he attempted to switch on his headlight; his suit arms remained so stiff he could not bend them enough to reach the toggle. All he could do was lie there in his shell and stare into the featureless darkness of the Cliff.

But the darkness was not entirely featureless. His ears detected a constant *slither* along the outside surfaces of his suit. His warmsight discerned a meaningless pattern beyond his helmet. Though he focused his boscises, he could make no sense of the pattern; it had neither symmetry nor meaning for him ...

Yet for his body it seemed to have some meaning. Derek felt his limbs tremble, was aware of pulses and phantom impressions within himself that he had not known before. The realization percolated through to him that he was in touch with powers of which he had no cognizance; conversely, that something was in touch with him that had no cognizance of his powers.

An immense heaviness overcame him. The forces

of life laboured within him. He sensed, more vividly than before, the vast bulk of the Cliff. Though it was dwarfed by the mass of Festi XV, it was as large as a good-sized asteroid. . . . He could picture an asteroid, formed from a jetting explosion of gas on the face of Festi the sun. Half-solid, half-molten, the matter swung about its parent in an eccentric orbit. Cooling under an interplay of pressures, its interior crystallized into a unique form. Thus, with its surface semi-plastic, it existed for many millions of years, gradually accumulating an electrostatic charge that poised . . . and waited . . . and brewed the life acids about its crystalline heart.

Festi was a stable system, but once in every so many thousands of millions of years the giant first, second, and third planets achieved perihelion with the sun and with each other simultaneously. This happened coincidentally with the asteroid's nearest approach; it was wrenched from its orbit and all but grazed the three lined-up planets. Vast electrical and gravitational forces were unleashed. The asteroid glowed: and woke to consciousness. Life was not born on it: it was born to life, born in one cataclysmic clash!

Before it had more than savoured the sad-sharp-sweet sensation of consciousness, it was in trouble. Plunging away from the sun on its new course, it found itself snared in the gravitational pull of the 4G planet, Festi XV. It knew no shaping force but gravity; gravity was to it all that oxygen was to cellular life on Abrogun; though it had no wish to exchange its flight for captivity, it was too puny to resist. For the first time, the asteroid recognized that its consciousness had a use, for it could to some extent control the environment outside itself. Rather than risk being broken up in Festi's orbit, it sped inward, and by retarding its own fall performed its first act of volition, an act that brought it down shaken but entire on the surface of the planet.

For an immeasurable period, this asteroid—the Cliff—lay in the shallow crater formed by its impact, speculating without thought. It knew nothing except the inorganic scene about it, and could visualize nothing else but that scene it knew well. Gradually it came to some kind of terms with the scene. Formed by gravity, it used gravity as unconsciously as a man uses breath; it began to move other things, and it began to move itself.

That it should be other than alone in the universe had never occurred to the Cliff. Now that it knew there was other life, it accepted the fact. The other life was not as it was; that it accepted. The other life had its own requirements; that it accepted. Of questions, of doubt, it did not know. It had a need; so did the other life; they should both be accommodated, for accommodation was the adjustment to pressure, and that response was one it comprehended.

Derek Ende's suit began to move again under external volition. Carefully it worked its way backward. It was ejected from the Cliff. It lay still.

Derek himself lay still. He was barely conscious. In a half-daze, he pieced together what had happened.

The Cliff had communicated with him; if he ever doubted that, the evidence of it lay clutched in the crook of his left arm.

"Yet it did not—yet it could not communicate with me!" he murmured. But it had communicated: he was still faint with the burden of it.

The Cliff had nothing like a brain. It had not "recognized" Derek's brain. Instead, it had communicated directly to his cell organization, and in particular, probably, to those cytoplasmic structures, the mitochondria, the power sources of the cell. His brain had been by-passed, but his own cells had taken in the information offered.

He recognized his feeling of weakness. The Cliff

had drained him of power. Even that could not drain his feeling of triumph; for the Cliff had taken information even as it gave it. The Cliff had learned that other life existed in other parts of the universe.

Without hesitation, without debate, it had given a fragment of itself to be taken to those other parts of the universe. Derek's mission was completed.

In the Cliff's gesture, Derek read one of the deepest urges of living things: the urge to make an impression on another living thing. Smiling wryly, he pulled himself to his feet.

Derek was alone in the Region of Fire. An infrequent mournful flame still confronted its surrounding dark, but the Cliff had disappeared. He had lain on the threshold of consciousness longer than he thought. He looked at his chronometer and found that it was time he moved towards his rendezvous with the lightpusher. Stepping up his suit temperature to combat the cold beginning to seep through his bones, he revved up the paragrav unit and rose. The noisome clouds came down and engulfed him; Festi was lost to view. Soon he had risen beyond cloud or atmosphere.

Under Jon's direction, the space craft homed onto Derek's radio beacon. After a few tricky minutes, they matched velocities and Derek climbed aboard.

"Are you all right?" the partheno asked, as his master staggered into a flight seat.

"Yes—just weak. I'll tell you all about it as I do a report on spool for Pyrylyn. They'll be pleased with us."

He produced a yellow-grey blob of matter that had expanded to the size of a large turkey and held it out to Jon.

"Don't touch this with uncovered hands. Put it in one of the low-temperature lockers under 4Gs. It's a little souvenir from Festi XV."

IV

The Eyebright in Pynnati, one of the planet Pyrylyn's capital cities, was where you went to enjoy
yourself on the most lavish scale possible. This
was where Derek Ende's hosts took him, with Jon
in self-effacing attendance.

They lay in a nest of couches that slowly re-
volved, giving them a full view of other dance and
couch parties. The room itself moved. Its walls
were transparent; through them could be seen an
ever-changing view as the room slid up and down
and about the great metal framework of the Eyebright. First they were on the outside of the structure, with the brilliant night lights of Pynnati
winking up at them as if intimately involved in
their delight. Then they slipped inward in the slow
evagination of the building, to be surrounded by
other pleasure rooms, their revellers clearly visible as they moved grandly up or down or along.

Uneasily, Derek lay on his couch. A vision of his
Mistress's face was before him; he could imagine
how she would treat all this harmless festivity:
with cool contempt. His own pleasure was consequently reduced to ashes.

"I suppose you'll be moving back to Abrogun as
soon as possible?"

"Eh?" Derek grunted.

"I said, I suppose you would soon be going home
again." The speaker was Belix Ix Sappose, Chief
Administrator of Star One; as Derek's host of the
evening, he lay next to him.

"I'm sorry, Belix, yes—I shall have to."

"No 'have to' about it. You have discovered an
entirely new life form, as I have already reported
to Starswarm Central; we can now attempt communication with the Festi XV entity, with goodness knows what extension of knowledge. The
government can easily show its gratitude by award-
ing you any post here you care to name; I am not

without influence in that respect, as you are aware. I don't imagine that Abrogun in its present state of political paralysis has much to offer a man of your calibre. Your matriarchal system is much to blame."

Derek thought of what Abrogun had to offer; he was bound to it. These decadent people did not understand how a human contract could be binding.

"Well, what do you say, Ende? I do not speak idly." Belix Ix Sappose tapped his antler system impatiently.

"Er . . . oh, they will discover a great deal from the Cliff. That doesn't concern me. My part of the work is over. I'm a field worker, not an intellectual."

"You don't reply to my suggestion."

He looked at Belix with only slight vexation. Belix was an unglaat, one of a species that had done as much as any to bring about the peaceful concourse of the galaxy. His backbone branched into an elaborate antler system, from which six sloe-dark eyes surveyed Derek with unblinking irritation. Other members of the party, including Jupkey, Belix's female, were also looking at him.

"I must return," Derek said. What had Belix said? Offered some sort of post? Restlessly he shifted on his couch, under pressure as always when surrounded by people he knew none too well."

"You are bored, Ende."

"No, not at all. My apologies, Belix. I'm overcome as always by the luxury of Eyebright. I was watching the nude dancers."

"May I signal you a woman?"

"No, thank you."

"A boy perhaps?"

"No, thank you."

"Ever tried the flowering asexuals from the Cephids?"

"Not at present, thank you."

"Then perhaps you will excuse us if Jupkey and I remove our clothes and join the dance," Belix said stiffly.

As they moved out onto the dance floor to greet the strepent trumpets, Derek heard Jupkey say something of which he caught only the words "arrogant Abrogunnan." His eyes met Jon's; he saw that the partheno had overheard the phrase, too.

To conceal his mortification, Derek rose and began to pace around the room. He shouldered his way through knots of naked dancers, ignoring their complaints.

At one of the doors, a staircase was floating by. He stepped onto it to escape from the crowds.

Four young women were passing down the stairs. They were gaily dressed, with sonant-stones pulsing on their costumes. Their faces were filled with happiness as they laughed and chattered. Derek stopped and beheld the girls. One of them he recognized. Instinctively he called her name: "Eva!"

She had already seen him. Waving her companions on, she came back to him, dancing up the intervening steps.

"So the hero of Abrogun climbs once more the golden stairs of Pynnati! Well, Derek Ende, your eyes are as dark as ever, and your brow as high!"

As he looked at her, the trumpets were in tune for him for the first time that evening, and his delight rose up in his throat.

"Eva! ... your eyes as bright as ever ... and you have no man with you."

"The powers of coincidence work on your behalf." She laughed—yes, he remembered that sound! —and then said more seriously, "I heard you were with Belix Sappose and his female; so I was making the grandly foolish gesture of coming to see you. You remember how devoted I am to grandly foolish gestures."

"So foolish?"

"So devoted! But you have less ability to change, Derek Ende, than has the core of Pyrylyn. To suppose otherwise is foolish; to know how unalterable you are and still to see you is doubly foolish."

He took her hand, beginning to lead her up the staircase; the rooms moving by them on either side were blurs to his eyes.

"Must you still bring up that old charge, Eva?"

"It lies between us; I do not have to touch it. I fear your unchangeability because I am a butterfly against your grey castle."

"You are beautiful, Eva, so beautiful! And may a butterfly not rest unharmed on a castle wall?" He fitted into her allusive way of speech with difficulty.

"Walls! I cannot bear your walls, Derek! Am I a bulldozer that I should want to come up against walls? To be either inside or outside them is to be a prisoner."

"Let us not quarrel until we have found some point of agreement," he said. "Here are the stars. Can't we agree about them?"

"If we are both indifferent to them," she said, looking out and impudently winding his arm about her. The staircase had attained the zenith of its travels and moved slowly sideways along the upper edge of Eyebright. They stood on the top step with night flashing their images back at them from the glass.

Eva Coll-Kennerley was a human, but not of any common stock. She was a velure, born of the dense y-cluster worlds in Vermilion Outer, and her skin was richly covered with the brown fur of her kind. Her mercurial talents were employed in the same research department that enjoyed Belix Sappose's more sober ones; Derek had met her there on an earlier visit to Pyrylyn. Their love had been an affair of swords until her scabbard disarmed him.

He looked at her now and touched her and could say not one word. When she flashed a liquid eye at him, he essayed an awkward smile.

"Because I am oriented like a compass towards strong men, my lavish offer to you still holds good. Is it not bait enough?" she asked him.

"I don't think of you as a trap, Eva."

"Then for how many more centuries are you going to refrigerate your nature on Abrogun? You still remain faithful, if I recall your euphemism for slavery, to your Mistress, to her cold lips and locked heart?"

"I have no choice!"

"Ah yes, my debate on that motion was defeated—and more than once. Is she still pursuing her researches into the transmutability of species?"

"Oh yes, indeed. The medieval idea that one species can turn into another was foolish at that time; now, with the gradual accumulation of cosmic radiation in planetary bodies and its effect on genetic stability, it is correct to a certain definable extent. She is endeavouring to show that cellular bondage can be—"

"Yes, yes, and this serious talk is an eyesore in Eyebright! Do you think I can hear of her when I want to talk of you? You are locked away, Derek, doing your sterile deeds of heroism and never entering the real world. If you imagine you can live with her much longer and then come to me, you are mistaken. Your walls grow higher about your ears every century, till I cannot—oh, it's the wrong metaphor!—cannot scale you!"

Even in his pain, the texture of her fur was joy to his warmsight. Helplessly he shook his head in an effort to brush her clattering words away.

"Look at you being big and brave and silent—even now! You're so arrogant," she said—and then, without perceptible change of tone, "Because I still love the bit of you inside the castle, I'll make once more my monstrous and petty offer to you."

"No, please, Eva!"

"But yes! Forget this tedious bondage of Abrogun and Endehabven, forget this ghastly matriarchy, live here with me. I don't want you for ever. You know I am a eudemonist and judge by standards of pleasure—our liaison need be only for a century or two. In that time, I will deny you nothing your senses may require."

"Eva!"

"After that, our demands will be satisfied. You may then go back to the Lady Mother of Endehabven for all I care."

"Eva, you know I spurn this belief, this eudemonism."

"Forget your creed! I'm asking you nothing difficult. Who are you to haggle? Am I fish, to be bought by weight, this bit selected, that rejected?"

He was silent.

"*You* don't really need me," he said at last. "You have everything already: beauty, wit, sense, warmth, feeling, balance, comfort. *She* has nothing. She is shallow, haunted, cold—oh, she needs me, Eva."

"You are apologizing for yourself, not her."

She had already turned with the supple movement of a velure and was running down the staircase. Lighted chambers drifted up about them like bubbles.

His laboured attempt to explain his heart turned to exasperation. He ran down after her, grasping her arm.

"Listen to me!"

"No one in Pyrylyn would listen to such masochistic nonsense! You are an arrogant fool, Derek, and I am a weak-willed one. Now release me!"

As the next room came up, she jumped through its entrance and disappeared into the crowd.

V

Not all the drifting chambers of Eyebright were lighted. Some pleasures come more delightfully with the dark, and these were coaxed and cosseted into fruition in halls where illumination cast only the gentlest ripple on the ceiling and the gloom was sensuous with perfumes. Here Derek found a place to weep.

Sections of his life slid before him as if impelled by the same mechanisms that moved Eyebright. Always, one presence was there.

Angrily he related to himself how he always laboured to satisfy her—yes, in every sphere laboured to satisfy her! And how when that satisfaction was accorded him it came as though riven from her, as a spring sometimes trickles down the split face of a rock. Undeniably there was satisfaction for him in drinking from that cool source— but no, where was the satisfaction when pleasure depended on such extreme disciplining and subduing of self?

"Mistress, I love and hate your needs!"

And the discipline had been such ... so long ... that now when he might enjoy himself far from her, he could scarcely strike a trickle from his own rock. He had walked here before, in this city where the hedonists and eudemonists reigned, walked among the scents of pleasure, walked among the ioblepharous women, the beautiful guests and celebrated beauties, with My Lady always in him, feeling that she showed even on his countenance. People spoke to him; somehow he replied. They manifested gaiety; he tried to do so. They opened to him; he attempted a response. All the time he hoped they would understand that his arrogance masked only shyness—or did he hope that it was his shyness that masked arrogance? He did not know.

Who could presume to know? The one quality holds much of the other. Both refuse to come forward and share.

He roused from his meditation knowing that Eva Coll-Kennerley was again somewhere near. She had not left the building!

Derek half-rose from his position in a shrouded alcove. He was baffled to think how she could have traced him here. On entering Eyebright, visitors were given sonant-stones, by which they could be traced from room to room; but judging that no one would wish to trace him, Derek had switched his stone off even before leaving Belix Sappose's party.

He heard Eva's voice, its unmistakable overtones not near, not far . . .

"You find the most impenetrable bushels to hide your light under—"

He caught no more. She had sunk down among tapestries with someone else. She was not after him at all! Waves of relief and regret rolled over him . . . and when he paid attention again, she was speaking his name.

With shame on him, he crouched forward to listen. At once his warmsight told him to whom Eva spoke. He recognized the pattern of the antlers; Belix was there, with Jupkey sprawled beside him on some elaborate kind of bed.

". . . useless to try again. Derek is too far entombed within himself," Eva said.

"Entombed rather within his conditioning," Belix said. "We found the same. It's conditioning, my dear—all conditioning with these Abrogunnans. Look at it scientifically: Abrogun is the last bastion of a bankrupt culture. The Abrogunnans number mere thousands now. They disdain social graces and occasions. They are served by parthenogenically bred slaves. They themselves are inbred. In consequence, they have become practically a species apart. You can see it all in friend Ende. A tragedy, Eva, but you must face up to it."

"You're probably right," Jupkey inserted lazily. "Who but an Abrogunnan would do what Derek did on Festi?"

"No, no!" Eva said. "Derek's ruled by a woman, not by conditioning. He's—"

"In Ende's case they are one and the same thing, my dear, believe me. Consider their social organization. The partheno slaves have replaced all but a handful of true men. They live on their great estates, ruled by a matriarch."

"Yes, I know, but Derek—"

"Derek is caught in the system. They have fallen into a mating pattern without precedent in Starswarm. The sons of a family marry their mothers, not only to perpetuate their line but because a productive female has become rare by now. Derek Ende's 'mistress' is both mother and wife to him. Add the factor of longevity and you ensure an excessive emotional rigidity that almost nothing can break—not even you, my sweet Eva!"

"He was on the point of breaking tonight!"

"I doubt it," Belix said. "Ende may want to get away from his claustrophobic home, but the same forces that drive him off will eventually lure him back."

"I tell you he was on the point of breaking—but I broke first."

"Well, as Teer Ruche said to me many centuries ago, only a pleasure-hater knows how to shape a pleasure-hater. I would say you were lucky he did not break—you would only have had a baby on your hands."

Her answering laugh did not ring true.

"My Lady of Endehabven, then, must be the one to do it. I will never try again—though he seems under too much stress to stand for long. Oh, it's really immoral! He deserves better!"

"A moral judgement from you, Eva!" Jupkey exclaimed amusedly.

"My advice to you, Eva, is to forget all about the fellow. Apart from everything else, he is scarcely articulate—which would not suit you for a season."

The unseen listener could bear no more. A sudden rage—as much against himself for hearing as against them for speaking—burst over him. Straightening up, he seized the arm of the couch on which

Belix and Jupkey nestled, wildly supposing he could tip them onto the floor.

Too late, his warmsight warned him of the real nature of the couch. Instead of tipping, it swivelled, sending a wave of liquid over him. The two unglaats were lying in a warm bath scented with essences.

Eva shouted for lights. Other occupants of the hall cried back that darkness must prevail at all costs.

Leaving only his dignity behind, Derek ran for the exit, abandoning the confusion to sort itself out as it would. Burningly, disgustedly, he made his way, dripping, from Eyebright. The hastening footsteps of Jon followed him like an echo all the way to the space field.

Soon he would be back at Endehabven. Though he would always be a failure in his dealings with other humans, there at least he knew every inch of his bleak allotted territory.

ENVOI

Had there been a spell over all Endehabven, it could have been no quieter when My Lord Derek Ende arrived home.

I informed My Lady the moment his lightpusher arrived and rode at orbit. In the receptor bowl I watched him and Jon come home, alighting by the very edge of the island, by the fjord with its silent waters.

All the while the wind lay low as if under some stunning malediction, and none of our tall arborials stirred.

"Where is my Mistress, Hols?" Derek asked me, as I went to greet him and assist him out of his suit.

"She asked me to tell you that she is confined to her chambers and cannot see you, My Lord."

He looked me in the eyes as he did so rarely. "Is she ill?"

"No. She simply said she could not see you."

Without waiting to remove his suit, he hurried on into the building.

Over the next two days, he was about but little, preferring to remain in his room while My Lady insisted on remaining in hers. Once he wandered among the experimental tanks and cages. I saw him net a fish and toss it into the air, watching it while it struggled into new form and flew away until it was lost in a jumbled background of cumulus; but it was plain he was less interested in the riddles of stress and transmutation than in the symbolism of the carp's flight.

Mostly he sat compiling the spools on which he imposed the tale of his life. All one wall was covered with files full of these spools—the arrested drumbeats of past centuries. From the later spools I have secretly compiled this record; for all his unspoken self-pity, he never knew the sickness of merely observing.

We parthenos will never understand the luxuries of a divided mind. Surely suffering as much as happiness is a kind of artistry?

On the day that he received a summons from Star One to go upon another quest, Derek met My Lady in the Blue Corridor.

"It is good to see you about again, Mistress," he said, kissing her cheek. "To remain confined to your room is bad for you."

She stroked his hair. On her nervous hand she wore one ring with an amber stone; her gown was of olive and umber.

"Don't reproach me! I was upset to have you go away from me. This world is dying, Derek, and I fear its loneliness. You have left me alone too often. However, I have recovered and am glad to see you back."

"You know I am glad to see you. Smile for me

and come outside for some fresh air. The sun is shining."

"It's so long since it shone. Do you remember how once it always shone? I can't bear to quarrel anymore. Take my arm and be kind to me."

"Mistress, I always wish to be kind to you. And I have all sorts of things to discuss with you. You'll want to hear what I have been doing, and—"

"You won't leave me alone anymore?"

He felt her hand tighten on his arm. She spoke very loudly.

"That was one of the things I wished to discuss— later," he said. "First let me tell you about the wonderful life form with which I made contact on Festi."

As they left the corridor and descended the paragravity shaft, My Lady said wearily, "I suppose that's a polite way of telling me that you are bored here."

He clutched her hands as they floated down. Then he released them and clutched her face instead, cupping it between his palms.

"Understand this, Mistress mine, I love you and want to serve you. You are in my blood; wherever I go I never can forget you. My dearest wish is to make you happy—this you must know. But equally you must know that I have needs of my own."

"I know those needs will always come first with you, whatever you say or pretend."

She moved ahead of him, shaking off the hand he put on her arm. He had a vision of himself running down a golden staircase and stretching out that same detaining hand to another girl. The indignity of having to repeat oneself, century after century.

"You're being cruel!" he said.

Gleaming, she turned. "Am I? Then answer me this—aren't you already planning to leave Ende-habven again?"

He said haltingly, "Yes, yes, it's true I am thinking. . . . But I have to—I reproach myself. I could be kinder. But you shut yourself away when I come back; you don't welcome me—"

"Trust you to find excuses rather than face up to your own nature," she said contemptuously, walking briskly into the garden. Amber and olive and umber, and sable of hair, she walked down the path, her outlines sharp in the winter air. In the perspectives of his mind she did not dwindle.

For some minutes he stood in the threshold, immobilized by antagonistic emotions.

Finally he pushed himself out into the sunlight.

She was in her favourite spot by the fjord, feeding an old badiger from her hand. Only her increased attention to the badiger suggested that she heard him approach.

His boscises twitched as he said, "I'm sorry."

"I don't mind what you do."

Walking backward and forward behind her, he said, "When I was away, I heard some people talking. On Pyrylyn this was. They were discussing the mores of our matrimonial system."

"It's no business of theirs."

"Perhaps not. But what they said suggested a new line of thought to me."

She put the badiger back in his cage without comment.

"Are you listening, Mistress?"

"Do go on."

"Try to listen sympathetically. Consider all the history of galactic exploration—or even before that, consider the explorers of worlds without space flight. They were brave men, of course, but wouldn't it be strange if most of them only ventured into the unknown because the struggle at home was too much for them?"

He stopped. She had turned to him; the half-smile was whipped off his face by her look of fury.

"And you're trying to tell me that that's how you see yourself—a martyr? Derek, how you must

hate me! Not only do you go away, but you secretly blame me because you go away. It doesn't
matter, that I tell you a thousand times I want you
here—no, it's all my fault! I drive you away! That's
what you tell your charming friends on Pyrylyn,
isn't it? Oh, how you must hate me!"

Savagely he grasped her wrists. She screamed to
me for aid and struggled. I came near but halted,
playing my usual impotent part. He swore at her,
bellowed for her to be silent, whereupon she cried
the louder, shaking furiously in his arms, both of
them tumultuous in their emotions.

He struck her across the face.

At once she was quiet. Her eyes closed almost, it
would seem, in ecstasy. Standing there, she had
the pose of a woman offering herself.

"Go on, hit me! You want to hit me!" she
whispered.

With the words, with the look of her, he too was
altered. As if realizing for the first time her true
nature, he lowered his fists and stepped back, staring at her, sick-mouthed. His heel met no resistance. He twisted suddenly, spread out his arms as
if to fly, and fell over the cliff edge.

Her scream pursued him down.

Even as his body hit the waters of the fjord, it
began to change. A flurry of foam marked some sort
of painful struggle beneath the surface. Then a seal
plunged into view, dived below the next wave, and
swam towards the open sea, over which an already freshening breeze blew.

Sector Grey

Originality is far to seek in Era 124. Diversity is everywhere, originality nowhere. As a humorist put it, "Every day someone somewhere is inventing gunpowder."

All this chimes well with the Theory of Multigrade Superannuation, which allows for identical events occurring on different worlds at different times. Men evolve, family characteristics alter; the ancient mythic Adam remains unregenerate. Hence the persistence of aggression patterns that lead to war.

A volume such as this, which tries to scan Starswarm at one particular moment in time, must allow latitude for at least a campaign, if it is to be representative.

There are many conflicts to choose from.

Perhaps one of the most notable is now being waged in the strange formation known as the Alpha Wheel, beyond the Rift in Sector Grey. We have not the time, nor the sensory ability, to describe war on the largest scale it is ever likely to attain, fought bitterly between two races of telesensual beings.

We understand much more today about the Alpha Wheel than we did. The Wheel, quite simply, failed to develop. It remains a region only a light year and a half across, retaining within its borders many strange materials and even its own physical laws.

One instance of this: the disproportion in this

embryo universe's chemical composition has resulted
in an enormous quantity of free oxygen. Its abundance is so great that it fills what we would call
interplanetary space, held there by the high gravitational and centrifugal forces of the system. Thus, the
eight hundred planets that comprise the Wheel share
one common atmosphere.

It is hard not to see a parallel between this oddity
and the fact that the Jakkapic races, alone in Starswarm, are telesensual. As they share their ambient
air, so they share certain sensory perceptions. And
they have been at war, one planet with another, ever
since man first made contact with them.

We know many men who are divided against themselves, for all that psyche-healing can do. The Jakkapic
races suffer in the same way. Their wars are the
more terrible because every blow struck against the
enemy hurts the friend and the self equally.

The movements of Jakkapic machines are as pre-
dictable to an enemy as the movements of their troops.
Their minds are shared; thus, their machines, being
in essence but extensions of their minds, can never
be secret. Deadlock in this murderous chess game
would have been reached aeons ago, were it not for
the element of mortality. Hearts and engines alike
undergo failures. At the moment of failure, which is
unpredictable, disorganization occurs. Then the enemy strikes. The vast search systems that blink out
across the blizzards of the Wheel are looking not for
success but failure.

The hearts and engines that concern us here must
be human ones. If we want a war in human terms,
we have not far to go from the Wheel. The planet
Drallab in the Eot system is also in Grey Sector.

There, a war has been raging for ten standard
years. It is a mere tiff on a galactic scale, and is
chiefly of interest because such is the rigid code of
honour of the military juntas which rule Drallab

*that, although they are well launched into their Early
Technological Age, they allow no weapon that cannot be carried by one man. Nation after Drallabian
nation has exerted itself not to breaking the rule but
to breeding stronger men to carry larger weapons. We
shall see how the rule is circumvented in a different
way, by the use of drugs.*

*Some of these drugs were superseded in Starswarm
Central a thousand millennia ago. On Drallab, they
are new, revolutionary. Every day someone somewhere is inventing gunpowder.*

Sergeant Taylor lay in a hospital bed and dreamed
a dream.

He was a certain colonel. He had inherited the
rank from his father and his father's father. He
had spent the first tender night of his life lying in
the swamps of As-A-Merekass. Since he had survived being eaten by hydro-monitors and alliga-
tors, he was allowed to begin the military up-
bringing suitable to his family status. The parade
ground had never been distant from his adoles-
cence. All the women who had care of his earlier
years possessed iron breasts and faces like army
boots. The pulpy fruit of success would one day be
his.

He was a certain colonel whose barracks during
this war year were below ground. In the mess the
Special Wing was making merry. The place was
overcrowded, with long trestle tables full of food
and wine and with soldiers and the women who
had been invited to attend. Despite the Spartan
aspect of the mess, the atmosphere was one of
festival—that especially hectic kind of festival held
by men whose motto is the old one: Eat, drink,
and be merry, for tomorrow we die.

The colonel was eating and drinking, but he was
not yet merry. Although it pleased him to see his
men carousing, he was cut off from their merri-
ment. He still knew what they had forgotten, that

at any moment the summons might come. And then they would leave, collect their equipment, and go above to face whatever dark things had to be faced.

All this was a part of the colonel's profession, his life. He did not resent it, nor did he fear it; he felt only a mild attack of something like stage fright.

The faces around him had receded into a general blur. Now he focused on them, wondering idly who and how many would accompany him on the mission. He also glanced at the women.

Under duress of war, all the military had retreated underground. Conditions below were harsh, mitigated, however, by generous supplies of the new synthetic foods and drinks. After a decade of war, plankton brandy tastes as good as the real thing—when the real thing has ceased to exist. The women were not synthetic. They had forsaken the ruined towns above for the comparative safety of the subterranean garrison towns. In so doing, most of them had saved their lives only to lose their humanity. Now they fought and screamed over their men, caring little for what they won.

The colonel looked at them with both compassion and contempt. Whichever side won the war, the women had already lost it.

Then he saw a face that was neither laughing nor shouting.

It belonged to a woman sitting almost opposite him at the table. She was listening to a blurry-eyed, red-faced corporal, whose heavy arm lay over her shoulder as he spun a rambling tale of woe. Mary, the colonel thought; she must be called something simple and sweet like Mary.

Her face was ordinary enough, except that it bore none of the marks of viciousness and vulgarity so common in this age. Her hair was light brown, her eyes an enormous blue-grey. Her lips were not thin, though her face was.

Mary turned and saw the colonel regarding her. She smiled at him.

Moments of revelation in a man's life always come unexpectedly. The colonel had been an ordinary soldier; when Mary smiled, he became something more complex. He saw himself as he was—an old man in his middle twenties who had surrendered everything personal to a military machine. This sad, beautiful, ordinary face spoke of all he had missed, of all the richer side of life known only to a man and woman who experience each other through love.

It told him more. It told him that even now it was not too late for him. The face was a promise as well as a reproach.

All this and more ran through the colonel's mind, and some of it was reflected in his eyes. Mary, it was clear, understood something of his expression.

"Can you get away from him?" the colonel said, with a note of pleading in his voice.

Without looking at the soldier whose arm lay so heavily over her shoulders, Mary answered something. What she said was impossible to hear in the general hubbub. Seeing her pale lips move, in an agony at not hearing, the colonel called to her to repeat her sentence.

At that moment the duty siren sounded.

The uproar redoubled. Military police came pouring into the mess, pushing and kicking the drunks onto their feet and marching them out of the door.

The colonel rose to his feet. Leaning across the table and touching Mary's hand, he said, "I must see you again and speak to you. If I survive this mission, I will be here tomorrow night. Will you meet me?"

A fleeting smile. "I'll be here," she said.

Hope flooded into him. Love, gratitude, all the secret springs of his nature poured forth into his veins. Then he marched towards the doors.

Beyond the doors, a tube truck waited. The Special Wing staggered or was pushed into it. When all were accounted for, the doors closed and the tube moved off, roaring into the tunnel on an upward gradient.

It stopped at Medical Bay, where orderlies with alcoholometers awaited them. Anyone who flipped the needle was instantly given an antitoxic drug. The colonel, though he had drunk little, had to submit to an injection. The alcohol in his blood was neutralized almost at once. Within five minutes everyone in the room was stone cold sober again. To wage war in its present form would not have been possible without drugs.

The party, quieter now and with set faces, climbed back into the tube. It rose on an ascending spiral of tunnel, depositing them next to Briefing. They were now on the surface. The air smelled less stale.

Accompanied by five under-officers and NCOs, the colonel entered Information Briefing. The rest of his men—or those picked for this particular mission—went to Morale Briefing. Here, animations would prepare them by direct and subliminal means for the hazards to come.

The colonel and his party faced a brigadier who began speaking as soon as they sat down.

"We have something fresh for you today. The enemy is trying a new move, and we have a new move to counteract it. The six of you will take only eighteen men with you on this mission. You will be lightly armed, and your safety will depend entirely on the element of surprise. When I tell you that, if all goes well, we expect to have you back here in ten hours, I do not want you to forget that those ten hours may vitally affect the whole outcome of the war."

He went on to describe their objective. The picture was simple and clear as it built up in the colonel's mind. He discarded all details but the key ones. Where the forty-eighth parallel crossed the sea, the enemy was gathered in some strength in a stegor forest. Beyond the forest stood unscalable cliffs. On the clifftop, surrounded by the forest, was an old, circular, wooden building, five storeys high. On the top storey of this building, looking over the treetops, was a weather station. It commanded the narrow strait of sea that separated enemy from enemy.

The weather station watched for favourable winds. When they came, the signal would be given to gliders along the coast. The gliders would be launched and flown over enemy territory. They contained bacteria.

"We stand to have a major plague on our hands if this setup is not put out of action at once," the brigadier said. "Another force has been given the task of wiping out the gliders. We must also put the weather station out of action, and that is your job.

"A high-pressure area is building up over us now. Reports show that conditions should be ideal for an enemy launching in ten to twelve hours. We have to kill them before that."

He then described the forces to be met with in the forest through which the attackers must go. The defences were heavy, but badly developed. Only the paths through the forest were defended, since vehicular attack through the trees was impossible.

"This is where you and your men come in, Colonel. Our laboratories have just developed a new drug. As far as I can understand, it's the old hyperactivity pill carried to the ultimate. Unfortunately, it's still rather in the experimental stage, but desperate situations call for desperate remedies . . ."

With the briefing finished, the officers were joined by the men selected to accompany them. The twenty-four of them marched to the armoury, where they were equipped with weapons and combat suits.

Outside, in the open air, it was still night. In a land vehicle they rode over to an air strip, the ruins of an old surface town making no more than vague smudges in the darkness. They passed piles of defused enemy grenades. A vane awaited them. In ten minutes they were all aboard and strapped into positions.

A medical man entered. He would administer the new drug when they reached the enemy forest; now he administered a preparatory tranquillizer orally, like a sacrament.

The vane climbed upward with a bound. Twenty-four men subsided into a drugged coma as they hurtled high into the stratosphere. Below, out of the bowl of night, the enemy forest swam.

Descending vertically, they landed in an acre of bracken beneath the shadow of the first trees. The sedation period ended as the hatch swung open.

"Let's keep it quiet, men," the colonel said.

He checked his chronometer with the pilot's before leaving. It was dawn, and a chill breeze blew. The great cluster that contained Starswarm Central wheeled low in the sky.

The medico came around handing out boomerang-shaped capsules that fitted against the bottom teeth under the tongue.

"Don't bite on 'em until the colonel gives the word," he said. "And remember, don't worry about yourselves. Get back to your vane and we'll take care of the rest."

"Famous last words," someone muttered.

The medico hurried back to the vane. It would be off as soon as they were gone; the Special Wing had to rendezvous with another elsewhere when the mission was over. The party set off for the trees in single file, almost at once a heavy bore opened fire.

"Keep your heads down. It's after the vane, not us," the colonel said.

Worries came sooner than expected. A strobolight

came on, its nervous blink fluttering across the cléaring, washing everything in its path with white. At the same time, the colonel's helmet beeped, telling him a radio eye had spotted him.

"Down!" he roared.

The air crackled as they crawled into a hollow.

"We'll split into our five groups now," the colonel said. "One and Two to my left, Four and Five to my right. Seventy seconds from now, I'll blow my whistle; eat your pills and be off. Move!"

Twenty men moved. Four stayed with the colonel. Ignoring the racket in the clearing, he watched the smallest hand on his chronometer, his whistle in his left fist. As he expected, the fusillade had died as he blew his blast. He crunched his capsule and rose, the four men beside him.

They ran for the wood.

They were among the trees. The other four groups of five were also among the trees. Three of them were decoy groups. Only one of the other groups, Number Four, was actually due to reach the round building, approaching it by a different route from the colonel's.

As they entered the forest, the drug took effect. A slight dizziness seized the colonel, a singing started in his ears. Against this minor irritation, a vast comfort swept through his limbs. He began to breathe more rapidly, and then to think and move more rapidly. His rate of metabolism was accelerating.

Alarm filled him momentarily, although he had been briefed on what to expect. The alarm came from a deep and unplumbed part of him, a core that resented tampering with its personal rhythm. Coupled with it came a vivid picture of Mary's face, as if the colonel, by submitting to this drug, was somehow defiling her. Then the image and the alarm vanished.

Now he was sprinting, his men beside him. They flicked around dense bush, leaving a clearing behind. A searchlight burst into life, sweeping its beam among the tree trunks in a confusing pattern of light and shade. As it caught Group Three, the colonel opened fire.

He had acted fast, hardly realizing he was firing. The guns they carried had special light-touch trigger actions to respond to their new tempo.

A burst of firing answered his shot, but it fell behind them. They were moving faster. They wove rapidly among the stegor trees. Dawn gave them light to see by. Opposition, as Briefing had forecast, was scattered. They ran without stopping. They passed camouflaged vehicles, tanks, tents, some containing sleeping men. All these they skirted. They shot anything that moved. A fifty per cent acceleration of perception and motion turned them into supermen.

Absolute calm ruled in the colonel's mind. He moved like a deadly machine. Sight and sound came through with ultra-clarity. He seemed to observe movement before it began. A world of noise surrounded him.

He heard the rapid hammer of his heart, his breathing, the breathing of his fellows, the rustle of their limbs inside their clothes. He heard the crackle of twigs beneath their feet, faint shouts in the forest, distant shots—presumably marking the whereabouts of another group. He seemed to hear everything.

They covered the first mile in five minutes, the second in under four. Occasionally the colonel glanced at his wrist compass, but a mystic sense seemed to keep him on course.

When an unexpected burst of firing from a flank killed one of the group, the other four raced on without pause. It was as if they could never stop running. The second mile was easy, and most of the third. Normally, the enemy was prepared for any eventuality: but that did not include a handful of men running. The idea was too laughable to be entertained. The colonel's group got through only because it was impossible.

Now they were almost at destination. Some sort of warning of their approach had been given. The trees were spaced more widely, kirry-mashies were being lined up, gun posts manned. As the light strengthened, it began to favour the enemy.

"Scatter!" the colonel shouted, as a gun barked ahead. His voice sounded curiously high in his own ears.

His men swerved apart, keeping each other in sight. They were moving like shadows now, limbs flickering, brains alight. They ran. They did not fire.

The gun posts opened up. Missing four phantoms, they kept up their chatter in preparation for the main body of men who never arrived. The phantoms plunged on, tormented most by the noise, which bit like acid into their eardrums.

Again the phantoms grouped in a last dash. Through the trees loomed a round wooden building. They were there!

The four fired together as a section of the enemy burst from a nearby hut. They shot a gunner dead as he swung his barrel at them. They hurled explosives into a sandbagged strongpoint. Then they were in the weather station.

It was as Briefing had described it. The colonel leading, they bounded up the creaking spiral stair. Doors burst open as they mounted. But the enemy moved with a curious sloth and died without firing a shot. In seconds they were at the top of the building.

His lungs pounding like pistons, the colonel flung open a door, the only door on this storey.

This was the weather room.

Apparatus had been piled up in disorderly fashion, bearing witness to the fact that the enemy had only recently moved in. But there was no mistaking the big weather charts on the walls, each showing its quota of isobar flags.

Several of the enemy were in the room. The firing nearby had alarmed them. Beyond them was a glimpse of cliff and grey sea. One man spoke into a phone; the others, except for a man sitting at the central coordinating desk, stared out of the windows anxiously. The desk man saw the colonel first.

Astonishment and fear came onto his face, slackening the muscles there, dropping his mouth open. He slid around in his seat, lifting his hand at the same time to reach out for a gas gun on the desk. To the colonel, he appeared to be moving in ultra slow motion, just as in ultra slow motion the other occupants of the room were turning to face their enemy.

Emitting a high squeal like a bat's, the colonel twitched his right index finger slightly. He saw the bullet speed home to its mark. Raising both hands to his chest, the man at the desk toppled off his stool and fell beside it.

One of the colonel's men tossed an incendiary explosive into the room. They were running back down the spiral stairs as it exploded. Again doors burst open on them, again they fired without thought. There was answering fire. One man squealed and plunged headfirst down the stairs. His three companions ran past him out into the wood.

Setting his new course, the colonel led his two surviving men towards their rendezvous. This was the easiest part of their mission; they came to the scattered enemy from an unexpected quarter and were gone before he realized it. Behind them, the weather station blazed, sending its flames high into the new day.

They had four miles to go this way. After the second mile, the maximum effect of the drug began to wear off. The colonel was aware that the abnormal clarity of his brain was changing into deadness. He ran on.

Sunshine broke through in splinters onto the floor of the forest. Each fragment was incredibly sharp and memorable. Each noise underfoot was unforgettable. A slight breeze in the treetops was a protracted bellow as of an ocean breaking on rock. His own breathing was an adamantine clamour for air. He heard his bones grind in their sockets, his muscles and sinews swishing in their blood.

At the end of the third mile, one of the colonel's two men collapsed without warning. His face was black, and he hit the ground with the sound of a felled tree, utterly burned out. The others never paused.

The colonel and his fellow reached the rendezvous. They lay twitching until the vane came for them. By then there were twelve twitching men to carry away, all that was left of the original party. Two medical orderlies hustled them rapidly into bunks, sinking needles into their arms.

Seemingly without interval, it was twelve hours later.

Again the colonel sat in the mess. Despite the fatigue in his limbs, he had willed himself to come here. He had a date with Mary.

The junketing was getting into full swing about him, as the nightly tide of debauchery and drunkenness rose. Many of these men, like the colonel himself, had faced death during the day; many more would be facing it tomorrow on one minor mission or another. Their duty was to survive; their health was kept in capsules.

The colonel sat at the end of one long table, close to the wall, keeping a chair empty next to him as the room filled. His ears echoed and ached with the noise about him. Wearily he looked round for Mary.

After half an hour had passed, he felt the first twinge of apprehension. He did not know her real name. The events of the day, the rigours of the mission, had obliterated the memory of her face. She had smiled, yes. She had looked ordinary enough, yes. But he knew not a thing about her except the hope she had stirred in him.

An hour passed, and still the chair beside him was empty. He sat on and on, submerged in noise. Probably she was somewhere with the drunk who had had his arm around her yesterday. Boom boom boom went the meaningless din, and the chair remained empty beside him.

It was after two in the morning. The mess was emptying again. Then it became suddenly clear. Mary would not come. She would never come. He was just a soldier, there would be an empty chair beside him all his life. No Mary would ever come. In his way of life, the Drallabian way of life, there was no room for Marys. He pressed his face into his hands, trying to bury himself in those hard palms.

This was Sergeant Taylor's dream, and it woke him crying in his hospital bed.

He wept until the shouts of men in nearby beds brought him back to reality. Then he lay and marvelled about his dream, ignoring the pain of his shattered eardrums.

It was a wonderful mixture of reality and superreality. Every detail concerning the raid had been accurately reconstructed. Just like that, he had led his men to success a very few hours ago. The hyperactivity pills had behaved in the dream as in real life.

"What the hell was you dreaming about?" asked the fellow in the next bed. "Some dame stand you up or something?"

Sergeant Taylor nodded vaguely, seeing the man's

lips move. Well, they had said there might be after-effects. Perhaps even now someone was inventing a drug to grow you new eardrums ...

Only in two details had his dream transcended reality.

He had never seen nor consciously looked for any Mary. Yet the authority of the dream was such that he knew that through all his life, through all the empty discipline and the empty debauchery, a Mary was what he had been seeking. He knew too that the dream predicted correctly: given the conditions of this war, there would never be a Mary for him. Women there were, but not women like Mary.

The other detail fitted with the first one ...

"Or maybe the way you was squealing, you was above ground playing soldier again, eh?" suggested the fellow in the next bed.

Sergeant Taylor smiled meaninglessly and nodded at the moving lips. He was in a world of his own at present, and he liked it.

Yes, the other detail fitted with the first. In his dream he had promoted himself to colonel. It could be mere oneiric self-aggrandizement: but more likely it was something deeper than that, another slice of prediction matching the first.

Sergeant Taylor was a soldier. He had been a soldier since birth, but now he was realizing it all through. That made him soldier-plus. Mary was the softer side of life, the unfulfilled, the empty-chair side; now it was ruled out of being, so that he could only grow harder, tougher, more bitter, more callous. He was going to make a splendid soldier.

No love—but bags of promotion!

Sergeant Taylor saw it all now, clear as a ray of sunlight. It was good to have shed his sentimental side in a dream. Shakily, he started to laugh, so that the man in the next bed stared at him again.

They should be able to think up some really bizarre missions for a man who was stone deaf ...

Sector Violet

This episode concerns the will in man to preserve that which he finds beautiful and rare. As it happens, it also provides—but this indirectly—an illustration of what chance can do to our metabolisms.

What it does not concern itself with is the working of chance itself, and when and whether chance is really something with a darker name—Fate. Certainly there is a sense in which the fates of the two humans from Sector Violet, whom we shall meet presently, were sealed a million years before they were born. But in the same way, all our fates are decided to a great extent by the worlds to which we are born. Whether fate comes to mean a way of life or a way of death depends on the planet: whether we are blessed or cursed is a matter of environment.

As planetary beings, we are peculiarly aware of this principle. However we define man, we cannot define him in isolation, apart from his milieu. The warring telesensual races of the Alpha Wheel fully convince us of that.

This is a misfortune when the environment happens to be a hostile planet on which mankind is ill-equipped to survive.

Some planets are sunk too far into antiquity to support man. Though other factors seem congenial, the biosphere wears down, the soil dies, the inor-

*ganic conquers. Abrogun is on its way to becoming
such a world.*

*Other planets may be too unripe to support man-
kind. Such is Istinogurzibeshilaha, the world on which
the two we are about to meet were born.*

*If unripe planets can bear only unripe personali-
ties, what sort of duties do the privileged owe them?*

The announcement that trickled from a thousand
speech glands was as gentle as if it bubbled through
liquid.

"The first party to disembark will be the immigrant intake from Istinogurzibeshilaha. Will the
immigrant intake from Istinogurzibeshilaha please
assemble at their deck exit for departure to the
Dansson Immunization Centre as soon as possible.
Your luggage will be unloaded later. Your luggage
will be unloaded later."

The man with the slow pulse in his throat lay on
his bunk and listened to the repetition of this speech
without raising the lashless lids of his eyes. The
luxurious voice brought him back from a region
far beyond the grave, where shapeless things walked
among blue shadows. When he had reoriented himself, he allowed his eyes to open.

His mate Corbis huddled on the floor by the
door, trembling.

He sat up slowly, for the temperature in their
cabin was still too low for activity. But she was
less torpid than he, and came over to him to put
an arm round his shoulders before he was properly sitting up. She rested the edge of her mouth
against his.

"I'm afraid, Saton," she said.

The words raised no rational response from him,
though they conjured up a memory of the prod-
dings of fright he had experienced walking through
the tall wooden forests of his native planet.

"We've arrived, Saton. This is Dansson at last,

and they want us to disembark. Now I'm terribly afraid. I've been afraid ever since I came out of light-freeze. They promised us a proper revival temperature, but the temperature in here is only ten degrees. They know we are no good when it isn't warm enough."

Saton's mind was unstirred by her alarm. He huddled on the bunk, not moving except to blink his eyes.

"Suppose Dansson isn't the haven we were led to think it is," she said. "It couldn't be a trick of some sort, could it? I mean, suppose all those tests and examinations we underwent on Istinogurzibeshi-laha were just a bait to get us here . . . Oh, we hear that Dansson is so marvellous, but did we ever hear of one person who ever *returned* from Dansson? If they had some awful fate in store for us, we— why, we'd be completely helpless."

She listened to the tramp of strange feet in the corridor beyond their door. She too had had her frightening dreams during the long interstellar journey.

She had seen that time when her mother was a little girl, forty years ago, and the humans who roamed the galaxy at will had first arrived and found her people in their wooden villages, dotted about those few zones of Istinogurzibeshilaha which would support life. In her dreams humans had been taller than the sad sequoias, and had brought not benefits and wonders but gigantic metal cages and coffins. She had woken with the clang of steel doors about her ears.

"We shouldn't have come, Saton," she said. "I'm afraid. Let's not stay on Dansson."

The pulse came and went in his throat, and he said, "Dansson is one of the capital planets of the universe."

It was the first fact that drifted into his chilled mind. His system was functioning too slowly to respond to her, and by the same token he suspected that her mind was not working properly, was simply responding to subconscious fears.

Years of study at one of his home planet's new schools, established by men from Dansson, had led to his and Corbis's passing the series of examinations through which one could gain passage to the admired cynosure of Dansson—chief planet in Violet, principal sector of the galaxy. He remembered the ranks of unfamiliar machines, the sick excitement, and the flashing lights in the Danssonian embassy as the tests progressed, and the pleasure and surprise of learning that he had passed with honours. Now Corbis and he would be able to get work in Dansson and compete on more or less equal terms with the other families of humanity that congregated there. The challenge awed him.

The announcer spoke to them again, more pressingly.

Corbis was climbing into the clothes cupboard as the mellow voice began once more to urge them to the hatch.

"They're coming after us," she said. "They're coming to collect us. We must have been mad to let ourselves in for this."

He had no emotion, but it was clear he would have to go to her. He pulled himself out of bed and climbed into the single garment of polyfur he had been issued at the start of the journey. Then he went over and attempted to reason with her. He was still drowsy, and closed his eyes as he spoke.

"It's no good," she said. "I *know* we've been trapped and tricked, Saton. We shouldn't have trusted the Warms. They're bigger than us."

The beautiful yellow pupils of her eyes had contracted to slits in fear. As he looked at her, loving her, the fear suddenly enveloped him, too. He was overcome by the distrust the Istinogurzibeshilahans had for the races of humanity they called Warms. It was the distrust the underprivileged feel for those who have the advantages and, because it was instinctive, it went deep. Corbis might well be right. He climbed into the cupboard with her.

She clutched him in the dark, whispering into his aural holes. "We can wait till the ship is empty, then we can escape."

"Where to? Istinogurzibeshilaha is hundreds of thousands of light years from here."

"We were told of a special quarter where our kind live—Little Istino, wasn't it? If such a place exists, we can go there and find help."

"You are mad, Corbis. Let's get out of here. What has given you these ideas? For years we longed to get here."

"While we were under light-freeze, I dreamed there were Warms here in our cabin. They moved us about and examined us while we were helpless, carrying out experiments on us, sampling my blood. There's a tiny plaster on my wrist that was not there before. Feel!"

He ran his fingers over the soft and tiny scales on her arm. The feel of the plaster, a symbol of medical care, only reassured him.

"You had a bad dream, that's all. We're still alive, aren't we? . . ."

As he spoke, he heard someone enter their cabin. They froze into immobility, listening. Someone came into the centre of the room, stood there muttering under his breath, and went out again.

They lay there, huddled together for a long while, listening to the gentle flow of announcements over the speech glands. At last, the glands ceased, and silence filled the now-empty starship.

Saton and Corbis moved slowly through the streets, partly compelled by caution, partly because they had still not entirely overcome the effects of enforced hibernation.

It had been easy to dodge the few androids working in the corridors of the ship, and only slightly harder to escape from the immense complex of the space port. But now, in the city itself, they were entirely at a loss.

At first they did not recognize that it was a city. Its buildings, by the rough-hewn standards of Istinogurzibeshilahan architecture, were scarely recognizable as buildings. For here material had gone to create units that represented the essential nonsolidity of matter. Their shapes held enormous gaiety and ingenuity. Indeed, occasionally fantasy had been followed to the point of folly, but to the wondering eyes of Saton and Corbis all was beautiful.

Between the buildings were vast floral displays, terraced several storeys high. Some of these were dark with mighty trees much like the trees that grew in the fertile places of Istinogurzibeshilaha. The forbidding as well as the engaging was prominent, so that nature was not too sentimentally represented. There were also terraces on which wild animals prowled, and immense aviaries where birds flew almost free. The total effect was that of an endless zoo.

Saton and Corbis walked along a pedestrian way, anxious yet entranced. On sunken roads, formidably fast traffic slid through the city; overhead, air cars passed like missiles. On their own level, there were a great many people walking at leisurely paces, but both were too nervous to stop anyone and ask their way.

"If we had some money, we could get transportation to Little Istino," Corbis said. They had been issued Danssonian credit books on the ship, with the state of their finances entered into them. But by missing disembarkation, they had missed collecting currency.

"If we come to a café, we'll try to pick up some information," Saton said. Unfortunately, they saw nothing resembling shops or cafés—or factories for that matter, for all of the strange buildings seemed purely residential.

After some minutes of walking, they came to a halt. Avenues stretched interminably in all directions; they could go on walking forever. Saton clutched Corbis's hand, motioning her to silence. He was watching a Warm nearby.

To judge from his appearance, the Warm was a velure, mutated human stock from Vermilion Sector, with a rich coat of fur; presumably in deference to local mores, he wore a light garment over his body. He had stopped at one of the shapely pillars that Saton and Corbis had been passing ever since they left the space field. The pillars bulged a couple of feet from the ground, tapering again higher up and ending in a spike some nine feet above ground.

The velure slid open a panel in the bulge of the pillar, inserted something from his pocket, and dialled. He waited.

Well below the level of the air cars, a series of massive piano-shaped objects sailed overhead. One of these pianos moved off its course now, descended slightly, and settled on top of the pillar so that the spike of the pillar plugged into a hole in its underside.

Lights flicked on the object and the velure dialled again.

Faint humming sounds came from the piano. A scoop descended from it down to pavement level, and a red light on the scoop flicked on and off. A green light came on; the scoop opened. From it the velure took something and continued on his way.

By the time the scoop had retracted into the piano, removed itself from the pillar, and resumed its aerial circuit, the velure had disappeared.

It was at this point that Saton realized that the watchers were being watched. A man stood close by, surveying them quizzically.

"I believe you two are from out-system," he said, when they turned to look at him.

"What makes you think that?" Saton asked.

The man laughed gently. "I've seen people from out-system amazed at our microfab circuit before."

He came over to them. "Can I show you around or direct you anywhere? My time's my own this morning."

Saton and Corbis looked at each other.

The man put his hand out. "Name's Slen-Kater. Welcome to Dansson."

They hesitated until the hand was lowered.

"We are happy on our own, thank you," Corbis said.

Kater shrugged. He was a small, sturdy man with a wild mop of yellow hair, through which he now ran his rejected hand.

"The fact that I'm a Warm and you're a Cold makes no difference to me," he said, "if that's what you're thinking."

Corbis twisted her neck in her peculiar gesture of anger and Saton said, "Thank you. We should be glad of your help. You see, after we disembarked, my mate unfortunately lost her handbag. It contained all the money we possess."

At once Kater was all sympathy.

"You've walked some way from the field. No doubt you'd like a drink before we get on our way. Perhaps you'll give me the pleasure."

"We're very obliged to you," Saton said. He took Corbis's arm because she was still looking displeased.

"No bother. Of course, you can dial yourself a drink on the microfab circuit if you have a Danssonian credit book. Look, I'll show you."

From his pocket he produced a credit book much like the ones Saton and Corbis had been issued. He flipped open the panel in the pillar and inserted his book in a scanner. There was an illuminated directory at the back of the recess; Kater flicked it to the drinks section, read out the number of a synthop, and dialled it.

"That sends a general call to one of the fab

units," Kater said, pointing upwards. "Here comes
one. These units have antigravity devices to keep
them airborne. They're the factories of Dansson.
Each one is packed with processor-chips no bigger
than your body cells. As you may know, the speed
of really small electronic devices is terrifically high.
This would throw together my own private air car,
if I wished it, and assemble it right here on the
spot—in under five minutes."

The piano settled on the top of the pillar, and
Kater dialled again.

"How do you pay for what you get?" Corbis asked.

"There's a scale of charges. The charge is de-
ducted against my credit rating. My credit number goes through even before I dial—off the front
of my book. Ah, one synthop!"

The scoop came down from the piano, opened,
and revealed a beaker full of an amber liquid.
Kater picked it out, poured its contents onto the
ground, and flung the glass into a trash chute in
the base of the pillar.

"Now, let's go and get a sociable drink," he said.

They sat at a pleasant table, drinking. Saton had
chosen a warm liquid that went far towards fully
reviving him from the recent light-freeze, and yet,
somehow, he could not help feeling uneasy. Perhaps they should never have joined up with this
creature with the yellow hair, who was saying
cheerfully, "Oh, you'll be happy on Dansson."

"How do you know I will be happy on Dansson?"
Corbis asked. "Perhaps I will be miserable here.
Perhaps I will miss my home."

Kater smiled. "You'll be happy here," he said.
"It's unavoidable."

To soothe things over, Saton said, "My mate
really means that things seem very strange to us.
Even the layout of the city is different from anything we know at home. For instance, your habit
of building such massive big blocks and setting

them among parkland is new to us. Why, this building we're in is almost as big as a city."

"It is a city," Kater said. "Dansson is simply a nexus of cities, each interrelated with the others, but each with a function of its own. Since we managed to get all factory and distributive outlets mobile in the way you've seen, the old idea of a city has died. The result is that the distribution of population areas in Dansson is governed solely by social function."

The block they had entered to get to the café was shaped like an immense wedge standing with its tapering end towards the clouds. They sat looking down on an inner courtyard; gesturing out at it, Saton asked, "And what particular function has this building?"

"Well, we call it a classifornium. It's a—well, a museum-cum-zoo. Its contents come from all over the galaxy. I can show you around at least part of it, if you have the time."

Saton saw from the corner of his eye that Corbis was signalling to him that they should escape from this Warm as soon as they had learned from him where Little Istino was; he realized that this was prudent. But something else happened to him. He was seized by an intense intellectual curiosity. He wanted to look into that museum, whatever happened. He knew that overwhelming curiosity of old; it had been responsible for the years in which he had sweated and toiled to prepare himself for the tests which, when passed, would bring him to Dansson, away from his dark-green home planet. And it was more than curiosity; it was a craving for knowledge. It was this, rather than fear, that led him to dread death, for death would mean an end to knowing, an end to learning, an end to the piecing together of facts that would eventually lead to an understanding of the whole strange scheme of things.

"We've got the time," Saton said.

"Splendid," Kater said.

As he went to pay for their drinks, Corbis said, "We must get away now. Why do we stay with this man?"

Rationalizing, Saton said, "We are as safe with Kater as with anyone. If we are being sought for, isn't a museum a good hiding-place? Time enough to get to Little Istino later."

Despairingly, she turned away. Her gaze caught a newscast that a patron of the café had left on the next table. She reached over and picked it up, hoping that perhaps it might contain a reference to that part of the city where their kind lived, perhaps even a hint that would show them how to get there.

She could read the headlines, with their news of a food surplus in the southern hemisphere, clearly enough. But the ordinary print . . . in the distant epoch when her ancestors had become nocturnal, many of their retinal cones ceased to develop and had become rods for better night vision; as a result the focus of her eyes was too coarse to achieve definition. She threw the cast down in vexation.

When Kater returned to the table, they joined him and followed him into the immense wedge of the classifornium.

With a sure sense of what would fascinate anyone from out-system, Kater took them to the Inficarium, where they plunged into a strange and wonderful world. As they stopped to stare in awe at the huge main corridor of the Inficarium, Kater grinned at them. "Infectious disease has been wiped out on Dansson, and on most of the major planets in the sector," he said. "We are apt to forget that throughout the greater part of man's history disease was a common experience of everyday life. Nowadays, with infectious illness eliminated, many of the once-common bacteria and virus that caused disease are threatened with extinction. A few eras ago the IDPA—the Infectious Diseases Preservation Association—was set up, and many interesting strains were saved from dying out and brought here. This Inficarium, in its present form, is fairly recent."

Fascinated, Saton and Corbis went from gallery to gallery, peering through optical instruments that allowed them to view the various exhibits. In the Virus Hall they studied the groups of virus that once infested plants, the rare ones that infested fish and frogs and amphibians, and all the prolific varieties that once ranged almost at will throughout the phyla of animal life.

"You see how beautiful, how individual they are, and how wonderfully developed to survive in their particular environments," Kater said. "They make you realize what a small part of life-sensation man is able to apprehend direct. It is a sad commentary on our times that they were permitted to get so near to extinction."

In the next gallery they found some of the viruses, now grown on tissue cultures, which caused the diseases that once infested man. First came the general infectious diseases, such as yellow fever, dengue, smallpox, measles, and similar strains. They were followed by the viruses infecting a particular part of the body: the influenzas, the para-influenzas, adenoviruses, and enteroviruses, such as the three poliomyelitis viruses, and the lymphogranuloma inguinale present in venereal diseases.

Then they passed to the infections damaging the nervous system, and from there to the near relations of the viruses, the Rickettsiae, and from there into the Bacteria House, and so eventually, dazed, into the Protozoa House. By this time, the coarse-focus eyes of Corbis and Saton were exhausted, and they had to call a halt.

Leaving Kater to wait for them by one of the exits, they went to rinse their faces and cool their pupils. This gave Corbis the chance to insist that they make for Little Istino straight away.

Saton decided to ask Slen-Kater about the region. When he did, the velure said that it was not far—in fact, he would show them how to get there.

"First, before we leave here, you will have to have an inoculation."

"What for?"

"It's a precaution the governors of the Inficarium have to take—just in case any of the diseases escaped, you know," Kater explained. "It won't take a minute."

Saton was still remote, his mind taken up with the tremendous range of alien life they had seen. When Corbis started to protest, he cut her off. It was to see things like the Inficarium that he had worked to get to Dansson, and his patience with her fears grew less by the hour.

She sensed this. After they had received their inoculation in a little bay next to the exit, she turned to the Warm.

"We did not expect such kindness as you have shown us on our first day on Dansson," she said. "My mate is less anxious than I about adjusting to this planet. I feel that we are despised as an inferior species of man."

Unperturbed, Kater said, "That feeling will die very soon."

There was a silence as they walked along outside.

Saton said, "Do not embarrass Slen-Kater. Let him show us the way to Little Istino, and then we must take up no more of his time."

"Oh, I don't embarrass him; he would not mind what I said if he thought they were the words of an inferior breed. Would you like the history of us Colds who live on Istinogurzibeshilaha? You might find us as interesting as your rare diseases."

Kater smiled at that. "We have come to the station where you can catch a ground car for Little Istino—though I'm sure your history would have been very interesting."

As he turned to go, Saton said humbly, "Slen-Kater, you must forgive us—our manners are up-set after the light-journey. We still have one favour to ask you—"

"Please, Saton, ask someone else!" Corbis whispered, but as Kater turned towards them, Saton indicated the notice board by their side. "Our eyes cannot adjust to the fine print, and we cannot read our destination. Would you be kind enough to see us into the right car?"

"Certainly."

"And there's another thing—could you lend us the price of the fare? If we could have your credit number, we will repay you when we get established."

"By all means," Kater said.

"You may guess how unhappy we are at having to ask such degrading favours."

"Nobody stays unhappy on Dansson—don't worry!"

The business of obtaining a ticket from the com-plex of coin machines and then of descending to the right level looked very formidable to the strang-ers. The station was large and appeared to house a maze of alternative routes. Also, it was uncomfort-ably warm, and they could feel their body temper-atures rising. The pulses in their throats beat faster.

"This car will get you to Little Istino," Kater said, as a yellow polyhedron slid into the plat-form. "This is single-level service, so you will only have ten stops before you are there."

As they hesitated by the door, Saton grasped his hand. "You have been so hospitable, we cannot thank you enough. There is just one thing—where do we go when we get out at the other end?"

"Don't you think we can ask when we get there?" Corbis interjected.

Smiling, Kater got into the car with them.

"It's not all that much out of my way," he said.

As the car gathered speed, Corbis said, "I really

don't know why you have come along with us. Do you take us for interesting freaks?"

"We're all interesting freaks, if it comes to that. I just want to help you get to where you wish to go. Is that so strange?"

"And so all the while you must be thinking of us as poor cold-blooded creatures."

"I'm afraid my mate has rather a chip on her shoulder at present," Saton said. "The mere size of this city is so overwhelming—"

"Don't be silly," Corbis said. "Didn't you feel inferior when you saw that in this place they have to strive to protect from extinction diseases that hundreds of people on Istinogurzibeshilaha die of every year? And it is apparent we can't think so efficiently as this gentleman, or see so well, or read with the same facility—"

She broke off and turned to Kater. "I'm sure you will excuse my behaviour and put it all down to my natural inferiority. Perhaps you have time to learn something of the history of man on Istinogurzibeshilaha, since you are so interested in us?

"I'll give it you in a nutshell—we've lived through two million years of underprivilege.

"I don't remember how long there have been forms of space travel, but it's a long, long time. And about two million years ago, a big transvacuum liner got into trouble and had to put down on Istinogurzibeshilaha. Its drive was burned out or something. Do you know what the world was like that those men and women found? It was barren and desolate, without the amenities you take for granted on Dansson. Most of it consisted of bare and lifeless soil—there weren't enough earthworms and bacteria in the ground to render it fertile enough for plants. True, some vegetation did exist, but this was limited to primitive plants and trees—spore—and conebearing things like cycads and giant ferns, spruce and pine, and the giant sequoias.

"Oh, don't think such a dark-green world does

not possess a certain amount of grandeur. It does. But—no grass, no flowers, none of the angiosperms with their little seed pods that are embryo plants and afford nourishment for other plant life. You see what I mean. Istinogurzibeshilaha was at the beginning of its Lower Triassic period of evolutionary growth.

"Why do I say 'was?' It still is! In another thirty million years or so we shall just about graduate into the Jurassic.

"Can you imagine what an ordeal those first men and women went through? In those deserts and dark forests, what is there for a warm-blooded man? Nothing! Not even animals he can kill! The mammals have yet to arrive on our planet, because you don't get them until the higher-energy foods available in flowering plants materialize.

"The early reptiles roam about—stupid, inefficient, slowmoving, *cold-blooded* things—existing on what nourishment is available. And amphibians. Fish and crustaceans, of course. They provide food."

As she talked, her tone lost its earlier resentment. Her eyes rested on Kater's face as if it was merely an outcrop of that stern landscape she described. Saton sat looking out of the window, watching mile after mile of the galactic city flash by. Dusk was falling; the fantastic towers seemed to float in space.

"Those people—our ancestors—had to live off the land when their own supplies ran out. They had a fight, I can tell you. They had their own grain, but the grain failed when sown. It just wasn't the right environment. So the people lived off the lower foods that were available.

"It was quite a change of diet. And you know what happened? They didn't die out. They adapted. Maybe it would have been better if they had died out—we would not be here. Because to adapt meant that they slowly became cold-blooded. When life begins on a planet, it always starts cold-blooded;

in the circumstances, cold blood is a survival factor—did you know that, Slen-Kater? That way, life is lived slowly, and it can survive on the vitamin-poor diet available. Much later along the evolutionary path, you get chemical reactions in the bloodstream, which heat it, caused by eating new foods—the richer foods that follow in the wake of the seed-bearing plants.

"Evolution played a trick on our ancestors. It sent them backward down the path. They became— we are—reptiles."

"That's nonsense," Saton said. "We are still men, simply cold-blooded."

Corbis laughed.

"Oh, yes, there are worse than us. Our unhappy ancestors went feral when their blood started running cold. For thousands of years, they were nocturnal in habit. One group of them, about fifty strong, left the rest and took to a semi-aquatic life in the region of the Assh-hassis Delta. You should see *their* descendants today, Slen-Kater! Why, they aren't even viviparous! However alien I am to you, at least I don't lay eggs!"

She burst into ragged laughter, and Saton put his arms around her.

After a silence, Kater said, "I expect you know the history of Dansson. We—man—destroyed the seventy-seven nations of bipedal Danssonians before we took over the planet. I would think our history is more disgraceful than yours, if we are competing for disgrace."

Corbis turned and looked at him with interest.

"I hope you are feeling better now," he said to her. "We are just about to get out."

The ground car had stopped several times while she had been talking. Now it stopped again, and they alighted. When they climbed above-ground, it was to survey a part of the city much like the part they had left, except that here the great buildings were more conservative in shape and more riotous in colour. The microfab system floated over their heads, shuttling its piano-shaped objects through the dusk.

Kater halted and pointed out a scarlet building down the avenue to their left.

"That's Little Istino. You will feel at home among people from your own planet—but don't forget we are all basically of the same kind."

"I wish to apologize for being rude earlier," Corbis said. "I will make no excuses, but I was feeling very unhappy. Now I feel much more content."

"Strangely enough, so do I," Saton said. "It must be your company!"

Slen-Kater laughed. "No, it's not that. Perhaps I will walk along with you right to your door. You're finding it hard to get rid of me, aren't you? You see, there is a reason why you are feeling happier."

They walked by his side, looking curiously at him as he continued.

"I am an immigration officer. I was asked to follow you when you did not check in for your inoculations at the space field. No, no, don't look so alarmed. With every ship that comes in we run into the same problem of people who for one reason or another don't want to come and see us. They often prove to be the brightest and most interesting."

"After all this are you going to arrest us?"

"Certainly not. I have no need to. You will be peaceable and content here."

"You sound very confident," Corbis said.

"With reason. Everyone who lives on or comes to Dansson is inoculated against unhappiness. Oh yes, we have a serum. Happiness is purely a glandular state. There's no illness here, as you know. Give a man the right glandular balance, and he will be happy. You had your inoculation that you missed at the space field as we left the Inficarium."

"Wait a minute," Saton said, stopping abruptly.

"You said that was a routine shot to ensure we had not picked up any diseases."

"My dear Saton—there was no possible danger of that. Those dangerous little life forms are all sealed away safely. No, it seemed a good time to make you feel happier. It has worked already, hasn't it?"

Saton raised his fists, looked at them, and laughed. There was no force in them, no core to his anger, no dismay in his surprise. He seized Corbis's arm and hurried her along, excited at the feeling of pleasure that swept over him. They certainly knew how to live on Dansson.

"Do you have these injections too, Slen-Kater?" Corbis asked.

"Certainly. Only being resident, I don't need as much as . . . as visitors. Only the very eminent are allowed to be creatively miserable. As you're new here, you've had a stiff dose to tide you over the next few months."

She tried to feel vexed at this. Somehow she thought there was something in his statement that should have roused her apprehensions. Instead, she could only see what a joke he had played on them. She giggled, and was still giggling when they reached the scarlet structure, towering high above them.

"This is Little Istino, and you'll be fine here. There are plenty of your own kind within," Kater said. "And none of those egg-laying Assh-hassis to worry you. They have a separate block elsewhere in the city."

"You mean you have them here, too? What use can they be to a wonderful, modern planet like Dansson?"

Immigration Officer Kater stuck his hands in his pockets and looked down genially at them; they were nice little beings really.

"I admit the Assh-hassis aren't much *use*," he said. "But then neither are many of the thousands of lesser races of man we house here. You see, as true man spreads across this part of the galaxy, he is slowly wiping out those half-brothers who are no match for him. So they have to be preserved—for study and so on. It's roughly like the viruses, I suppose."

Corbis and Saton looked at each other.

"I never thought of the Assh-hassis as a virus," Saton said. "They'll be amused when we get back to Istinogurzibeshilaha and tell our people."

"Oh, you'll never go back there," Kater said. "No one ever leaves Dansson."

"Why not?"

He smiled. "You'll see. You'll be too happy to leave."

They were still laughing as they parted from him, the best of friends all around.

"That was a very comical remark he made," Corbis said, as they waved him farewell, "about parts of Dansson being reserved for inferior types of human—almost like a cage in a zoo, except I suppose the inhabitants don't notice the bars."

"Wouldn't the Assh-hassis be furious if they realized the truth?" Saton chuckled.

Arm in arm, they turned and hurried into the big scarlet cage.

Sector Diamond

In a great concourse of worlds such as ours, the extinction of species occurs frequently—as frequently as spacegoing man opens up another planet. Sometimes it is a backward human race, such as the inhabitants of Istinogurzibeshilaha, that is threatened. More often it is a species which has some kind of social organization but which lacks higher intelligence.

Colonization forms one of the main pressures operating against the survival of alien life. Every standard year, three new planets are opened up. Where possible, the colonists are assisted to fit into the network of life already established there. Sometimes the nature of this life is such that this cannot be done, in which case more drastic measures have to be taken.

Over the past four millennia, much good work has been carried out by the Planetary Ecological Survey, a Starswarmwide organization with headquarters on the populous pleasure world of Droxy, in Sector Diamond. PES sends out teams that land on planets ripe for development and assess how the local life can best be preserved—or eliminated.

It is never an easy job. Sometimes man himself may provide a complicating factor.

* * *

At other times of day, the pygmies brought the old man fish from the river, or the watercress he loved, but in the afternoon they brought him two bowls of entrails.

He stood to receive them, staring over their heads through the open door, looking at the blue jungle without seeing it. He dared not let his subjects see that he suffered or was weak—the pygmies had a short way with weakness. Before they entered his room, he forced himself to stand erect, using his stick for support.

The two bearers bowed their heads until their snouts were almost in the still steaming bowls.

"Your god gives you thanks. Your offering is received," the old man said.

Whether or not they really understood his clicking attempt to reproduce their tongue, he could not tell. They rose and departed with their rapid, slithering walk. In the bowls, the oily substance glistened, reflected from the sunshine outside.

Sinking back onto his bed, the old man fell into his usual fantasy; the pygmies came to him, and he treated them not with forbearance but with hatred. He poured over them the weight of his long-repressed loathing, striking them with his stick and driving them and all their race forever from this planet. They were gone. The azure sun and the blue jungles were his alone; he could live where nobody would ever find or worry him. He could die at last, as simply as a leaf falls from a tree.

The reverie faded, and he recognized it for what it was. He knotted his hands together and coughed a little blood. The bowls of intestines would have to be disposed of.

Next day, the rocket ship landed a mile away.

The overlander lumbered along the forest track. It made good speed with Barney Brangwyn at the wheel. On either side of the vehicle, the vegetation

was of the sombre blue-green type that character-
ized most living things on the planet Kakakakaxo.

"Neither of you looks in the pink of health!"
Barney observed, flicking his eyes from the track
to glance at the faces of his two companions.

The three members of the Planetary Ecological
Survey team had blue shadows shading every feature of their countenances. The shadows gave an
illusion of chill, yet in this equatorial zone, and
with the sun Cassivelaunus shining at zenith, it
was comfortably warm, if not hot. The surrounding jungle grew thickly; the bushes sagged under
the weight of their own foliage. They were heading
for a man who had lived in these surroundings for
almost twenty years. Now that they were here, it
became easier to see why he was universally regarded as a hero.

"There's plenty of cover here for any green pygmies who may be watching us," Tim Anderson
said, peering at the thickets.

Barney chuckled at the worried note in the younger man's voice.

"The pygmies are probably still getting over the
racket we made in landing," he said; "we'll be
seeing them soon enough. When you get as ancient
as I am, Tim, you'll become less keen to meet the
local bigwigs. The top dogs of any planet are generally the most obstreperous—ipso facto, as the
lawyers say."

He lapsed into silence as he negotiated a gulley,
swinging the big vehicle expertly up the far slope.

"By the evidence, the most obstreperous factor
on Kakakakaxo is the climate," Tim said. "Only
six or seven hundred miles north and south of
here, the glaciers begin, and go right on up to the
poles. I'm glad our job is just to inspect the
planet—I shouldn't want to live here myself, pygmies or no pygmies. I've seen enough already to
tell you that."

"It's not a question of choice for the colonists,"

Craig Hodges, leader of the team, remarked. "They come because of some kind of pressure: economic factors, oppression, destitution, or the need for *lebensraum*—the sort of grim necessities that keep us all on the hop."

"You're a cheerful couple," Barney exclaimed. "At least Daddy Dangerfield likes it here! He has faced Kakakakaxo for nineteen years, playing god, wet-nursing his pygmies!"

"He crashed here accidentally; he's had to adjust," Craig said.

"What a magnificent adjustment!" Tim exclaimed. "Daddy Dangerfield, God of the Great Beyond! He was one of my childhood heroes. I can hardly believe we're going to meet him."

"Most of the legends built around him originate on Droxy," Craig said, "where half the ballyhoo in the universe comes from. I am chary about the man myself, but he could prove informative."

"He'll be informative," Barney said, skirting a thicket of rhododendron. "He'll save us a load of field work. In nineteen years—if he's anything like the man he's cracked up to be—he should have accumulated a mass of material of inestimable value to us, and to Dansson."

When a PES team landed on an unexplored planet like Kakakakaxo, they categorized possible dangers and determined the nature of the opposition the superior species would offer colonists. The superior species might be mammal, reptile, insect, vegetable, mineral, or virus. Frequently it proved so difficult that it had to be exterminated—and exterminated so that the ecological balance of the planet was disturbed as little as possible. Disaster happened.

Their journey ended unexpectedly. They were only a mile from their ship when the jungle gave way to a cliff, which formed the base of a steep mountain. Rounding a high spur of rock, they saw a sort of settlement ahead. Barney braked and cut out the power, and the three of them sat for a minute in silence, taking in the scene.

Rapid movement under the trees followed their arrival.

"Here comes the welcoming committee," Craig said. "We'd better climb down and look agreeable, as far as that is possible. Heaven knows what they are going to make of your beard, Barney."

They were surrounded as soon as they jumped to the ground. The pygmies moved quickly; though they appeared from all quarters, it took them only a few seconds.

They were ugly creatures. They moved like lizards, and their skin was like lizard skin, green and mottled, except where it broke into coarse scales down their backs. None of them stood more than four feet high. They were four-legged and two-armed. Their heads, perched above their bodies on no visible neck, were like cayman heads fitted with long, cruel jaws and serrated teeth. These heads now swivelled from side to side, silently observing the visitors.

Once they had surrounded the ecologists, the pygmies made no further move. The initiative had passed from them. In their baggy throats, heavy pulses beat.

Craig pointed at a pygmy in front of him and said, "Greetings! Where is Daddy Dangerfield? We intend you no harm. We merely wish to see Dangerfield. Please take us to him."

He repeated his words in Galingua.

The pygmies stirred, opening their jaws and croaking. An excited clack-clack-clacking broke out on all sides. An overpowering odour of fish rose from the creatures. None of them volunteered anything that might be construed as a reply.

Their stocky bodies might have been ludicrous, but their two pairs of sturdy legs and their armoured jaws certainly gave no cause for laughter.

"These are only animals" Tim exclaimed. "They

possess none of the personal pride you'd expect in a primitive savage. They wear no clothes. Why, they aren't even armed!"

"Don't say that until you've had a good look at their claws and teeth," Barney said.

"Move forward slowly with me," Craig said to his comrades. "Dangerfield must be about somewhere, heaven help him."

Thigh-deep in clacking cayman-heads, the PES men advanced towards the settlement. This manoeuvre was resented by the pygmies, whose noise redoubled, though they backed away without offering opposition.

Bounded on one side by the cliff face, the village stood under trees. In the branches of the trees, a colony of gay-coloured birds had plaited a continuous roof out of lianas, climbers, leaves and twigs. Under this cover, the pygmies had their rude huts, which were no more than squares of woven reed, propped at an angle by sticks to allow an entrance.

Tied outside these dwellings were furry animals, walking in the small circles allowed by their leashes, and calling to each other. Their mewing cries, the staccato calls of the birds, the croaking of the cayman-heads, made a babel of sound. And over everything drifted the stench of decaying fish.

"Plenty of local colour," Barney remarked. "These tethered animals are an odd touch, aren't they?"

In contrast to this squalid scene was the cliff face, which had been carved with stylized representations of foliage mingled with intricate geometrical forms. The decoration rose to a height of some forty feet and was inventive and well-proportioned. Later, the ecologists were to find this work crude in detail, but from a distance its superiority to the village was marked. As they came nearer, they saw that the decorated area was the façade of a building hewn in the sheer rock, complete with doors and windows, from which pygmies watched their progress with unblinking curiosity.

"I begin to be impressed," Tim observed, eyeing the patterns in the rock. "If these little horrors can create something as elaborate as that, there is hope for them yet."

"Dangerfield!" Craig called, when another attempt to communicate with the pygmies failed.

Barney pointed to the far side of the clearing. Leaning against the dun-coloured rock of the cliff was a sizeable hut, built of the same flimsy material as the pygmy dwellings, but constructed with more care and of less crude design.

While the ecologists were looking at it, an emaciated figure appeared in the doorway. It was human. It made its way towards them, aiding itself with a stout stick.

"That's Dangerfield!" Barney exclaimed. "It must be Dangerfield. As far as we know, there's no other human being on this whole planet."

A warning stream of excitement ran through Tim. Daddy Dangerfield was a legend among the youth of Starswarm. Crash-landing on Kakakakaxo, nineteen years before, he had been the first man to visit this uninviting little world.

Although only eighty-six light years from Droxy, one of the great interstellar centres of commerce and pleasure, Kakakakaxo was off the trade lanes. So Dangerfield had lived alone with the pygmies for ten standard years before someone had arrived with an offer of rescue.

By then it was too late: the poison of loneliness had become its own antidote. Dangerfield refused to leave. He claimed that the pygmies had need of him. So he remained where he was, King of the Crocodile People, Daddy to the Little Folk—as the Droxy tabloids phrased it, with their affection for capital letters and absurd titles.

As Dangerfield approached the team, the pygmies fell back before him. It was hard to recognize, in the bent figure peering anxiously at them, the young, bronzed giant by which Dangerfield was represented in the comic strips. The thin, sardonic face with its powerful hook nose had become a caricature of itself. This was Dangerfield, but appearances suggested that the legend would outlive the man.

"You're from Droxy?" he asked, speaking in Galingua. "You've come to make another film about me? I'm pleased to see you here. Welcome to the untamed planet of Kakakakaxo."

Craig Hodges put out his hand. "We're from Droxy," he said. "But we are no unit come to make a film; our mission is more practical than that."

"You ought to shoot one—you'd make your fortune. What are you doing here, then?"

As Craig introduced himself and his team, Dangerfield's manner became notably less cordial. He muttered angrily to himself about invaders of his privacy.

"Come to our overlander and have a drink with us," Barney said. "You must be glad to have someone to talk to."

"This is my place," the old man cried, waving his stick over the tawdry clearing. "I don't know what you people are doing here. I'm the man who beat Kakakakaxo. If you had pushed your way in here twenty years ago as you did just now, the pygmies would have torn you to bits—right to little bits. I tamed 'em! No living man has ever done what I've done. They've made films about my life on Droxy—that's how important I am. I'm known throughout Diamond Sector. Didn't you know that?"

His sunken eye rested on Tim Anderson. "Didn't you know that, young man?"

"I was brought up on those films, sir. They were made by the old Melmoth Studios."

"Yes, yes, that was the name. You don't belong to them? Why don't they come back here anymore, eh, why don't they?"

Tim wanted to tell this gaunt relic that Dangerfield, the Far-flung Father, had been one of his boyhood heroes, a giant through whom he had first felt the ineluctable lure of space travel; he wanted to tell him that it hurt to have the legend defaced. Here was the giant himself—bragging of his part, and bragging, moreover, in a supplicatory whine.

They came up to the overlander. Dangerfield stared at the neat shield on the side, under which the words Planetary Ecological Survey were inscribed. After a moment, he turned on Craig.

"Who are you people? What do you want here? I've got troubles enough."

"We're a fact-finding team, Mr. Dangerfield," Craig said. "Our business is to gather data on this planet. Next to nothing is known about ecological conditions here; the planet has never been properly surveyed. We are naturally keen to secure your help; you should be a treasury of information—"

"I can't answer any questions! I never answer questions. You'll have to find out anything you want to know for yourselves. I'm a sick man—I'm in pain. I need a doctor, drugs .... Are you a doctor?"

"I can administer an analgesic," Craig said. "And if you will let me examine you, I will try to find out what you are suffering from."

Dangerfield waved a hand angrily in the air.

"I don't need telling what's wrong with me," he snapped. "I know every disease that's going on this cursed planet. I've got fiffins, that's my trouble, and all I'm asking you for is something to relieve the pain. If you haven't come to be helpful, you'd best get out altogether!"

"Just what is or are fiffins?" Barney asked.

"They're not infectious, if that's what's worrying you. If you have come only to ask questions, clear out. The pygmies will look after me, just as I've always looked after them."

As he turned to go, Dangerfield staggered and would have fallen, had not Tim caught his arm. The old fellow shook off the support and hurried back across the clearing in a shuffle that sent the captive animals squeaking to the far end of their tethers.

Catching him up, Tim laid a hand on his arm.

"Please be reasonable," he said pleadingly. "You look as if you need medical treatment, which we can give you."

"I never had help, and I don't need it now. And what's more, I've made it a rule never to be reasonable."

Full of conflicting emotion, Tim turned back. He caught sight of Craig's impassive face.

"We should help him," he said.

"He doesn't want help from you or anyone," Craig replied, not moving. "He is his own self, with his own ways."

"He may be dying," Tim said. "You've no right to be so damned indifferent." He looked defiantly at Craig, who returned his gaze, then walked rapidly away. Dangerfield, on the other side of the clearing, glanced back once and then disappeared into his hut. Barney made to follow Tim, but Craig stopped him.

"Leave him," he said quietly. "Let him have his temper out."

Barney looked straight at his friend. "Don't force the boy," he said, "He hasn't got your outlook on life."

"We all have to learn, and it isn't easy to learn fast," Craig observed. Then, changing his tone, he said, "Dangerfield seems unbalanced, which means he may soon swing the other way and offer us help: that we should wait for; I'd be interested to get a straight record of his nineteen years here. It would make a useful psychological document, if nothing else."

"He's a stubborn old guy, to my way of thinking," Barney said, shaking his head.

"Which is the sign of a weak man. That's why Tim was unwise to coax him; it would merely make him more stubborn. He will come to us when he feels like it. Meanwhile, let's make the usual ground sample survey and establish the intelligence status of these cayman-heads."

Now that it was quieter, they could hear a river flowing nearby. The pygmies had dispersed; some lay motionless in their crude shelters, only their snouts showing, the blue light lying like a mist along their scales.

"I'd hazard they have evolved as far as they're ever going to get," Barney remarked, picking from his beard an insect which had tumbled out of the thatched trees above. "They have restricted cranial development, no opposed thumb, and no form of clothing—which means the lack of any sexual inhibition, such as one would expect to find in this Y-type culture. I should rate them as Y gamma status, Craig."

Craig nodded, smiling, as if with a secret pleasure.

"Which implies you feel as I do about the cliff temple," he said, indicating the wealth of carving visible through the trees.

"You mean—the pygmies couldn't have built it?" Barney said. Craig agreed.

"These cayman-heads are far below the cultural level implicit in the architecture. They are its caretakers not its creators. This means, of course, that there is—or *was*—another species, a superior species, on Kakakakaxo, which may prove more elusive than the pygmies."

Craig was stolid; he spoke unemphatically. But Barney, who knew something of what went on inside that head, knew that Craig's habit of throwing away an important point revealed that he was chewing something over.

Understanding enough not to probe on the subject, Barney filed it away and switched to another topic.

"I'm just going to look at these furry pets the cayman-heads keep tied up outside their shelters," he said; "they're intriguing little creatures."

"Go carefully," Craig cautioned. "Those pets may not be pets at all; the pygmies don't look like a race of animal lovers."

"Well, if they aren't pets, they certainly aren't livestock. Judging by the smell, the cayman-heads eat nothing but fish."

Outside most of the shelters, two different animals were tethered. One was a grey, furry creature with a pushed-in face like a Pekingese dog, standing almost as high as the pygmies. The other was a little creature with brown fur and a gay, yellow crest; half the size of the "peke," it resembled a miniature bear. Both pekes and bears had little black monkey-like paws, which, as the ecologists approached, were now raised as if in supplication.

"They're a deal more cuddlesome than their owners," Craig said. Stooping, he extended a hand to one of the little bears. It leaped forward and clutched it, chattering.

"Do you suppose the two species, the pekes and the bears, fight together?" Barney asked. "You notice they are kept tied just far enough apart so that they can't touch each other. We may have found the local variation on cockfighting."

"These beasts are about as dangerous as bunny rabbits! Even their incisors are blunt. They have no natural weapons at all."

"Talking of teeth, they exist on the same diet as their masters—though whether from choice or necessity we'll have to discover."

Barney pointed to decaying piles of fish bones, fish heads, and scales on which the little animals were sitting disconsolately. Iridescent beetles scuttled among the debris.

"I'm going to take one of these pekes back to the overlander and examine it," he announced.

He could see a cayman snout sticking out of its shelter not three yards away; keeping it under observation, he bent over one of the pekes and tried to loosen the tightly drawn thong that kept it captive.

The cayman-head's speed was astonishing. One second, it was scarcely visible in its shelter; the next, it confronted Barney with its claws resting over his hand, its ferocious teeth bared. Small through the reptile was, it could have undoubtedly snapped his neck through.

"Don't fire, or you'll have the lot on us!" Craig said, for Barney's free hand dropped immediately for his blaster.

They were surrounded by pygmies, all scuttling up and clacking. The reptiles made their typical noises, waggling their tongues without moving their jaws. Though they crowded in, they made no attempt to attack Craig and Barney. One of them thrust himself forward and commenced to harangue them, waving his small upper arms.

"Some traces of a primitive speech pattern," Craig observed coolly. "Let's barter for your pet, Barney, while we have their attention."

Dipping into one of the pouches of his duty equipment, he produced a necklace in whose marble-sized stones spirals of colour danced, delicate internal springs ensuring that their hues changed continually as long as their wearer moved. It was the sort of trinket to be picked up for a few minicredits on almost any planet in Starswarm. Craig held it out to the pygmy who had delivered the speech.

The pygmy leader scrutinized it briefly, then resumed his harangue. The necklace meant nothing to him. With signs, Craig indicated that he would exchange it for one of the little bears. The leader showed no interest. Pocketing the necklace, Craig produced a mirror.

Mirrors unfailingly excite the interest of primitive tribes—yet the pygmies remained unmoved. Many of them began to disappear now the crisis was over, speeding off with their nervous, lizard movements. Putting the mirror away, Craig brought out a whistle.

It was like a silver fish with an open mouth. The pygmy leader snatched it from Craig's hand, leaving the red track of its claws across his open palm. It popped the whistle into its mouth.

"Here, that's not edible!" Craig said, instinctively stepping forward with his hand out. Perhaps the pygmy misinterpreted Craig's gesture and acted defensively. Snapping its jaws, it lunged at Craig's leg. As the ecologist fell, a blue shaft flashed from Barney's blaster. The noise of the thermonuclear blast rattled around the clearing, and the pygmy toppled and dropped dead, its hide smoking.

Into the ensuing silence broke the clatter of a thousand weaver birds, winging from their homes and circling high above the treetops. Barney bent down, seized Craig around the shoulders, and raised him with one arm, keeping the blaster levelled in his free hand. Over Craig's thigh, soaking through his torn trousers, grew a ragged patch of blood.

"Thanks, Barney," he said. "Trade seems to be bad today. Let's get back to the overlander."

The pygmies made no attempt to attack. It was impossible to determine whether they were frightened by the show of force or had decided that the brief quarrel was no affair of theirs. At last they bent over their dead comrade, seized him by his hind feet, and dragged him off briskly in the direction of the river.

When Barney got Craig onto his bunk, he stripped his trousers off, cleansed the wound, and dressed it with a restorative culture. Although Craig had lost blood, no damage was done; his leg would be entirely healed by morning.

"You got off lightly," Barney said, straightening up. "That baby could have chewed your knees off if he had been trying."

"One thing about the incident particularly interested me," Craig said. "The cayman-heads wanted the whistle because they mistook it for food; fish, as we gather from the stink outside, is a main item in their diet. The mirror and the necklace meant nothing to them; I have never met a backward tribe so lacking in simple, elementary vanity. Does it connect with the absence of sexual inhibitions you mentioned?"

"What have they to be vain about?" Barney asked, stripping off and heading for the shower. "After five minutes out there, I feel as if the stench of fish has been painted on me with a brush."

It was not long before they realized Tim Anderson was nowhere in the overlander.

"Go and see if you can find him, Barney," Craig said. "He isn't safe wandering about on his own. He'll have to learn to enjoy freedom of thought without freedom of action."

The afternoon was stretching its blue shadows across the ground. In the quiet, you could almost hear the planet turn on its cold, hard axis.

Barney set out towards the distant murmur of water, thinking that a river would hold as much attraction for Tim as for himself. He turned down a narrow track among the trees, then stopped, unsure which way to go. He called Tim's name.

An answer came almost at once, unexpectedly. Tim emerged from the bushes ahead and waved to Barney.

"You had me worried," Barney confessed, catching up with him. "It's wiser not to stroll off without telling us."

"I'm quite capable of looking after myself, you

know," Tim said. "There's a river just beyond these bushes, wide and deep and fast-flowing. I suppose these cayman-heads are cold-blooded?"

"They are," Barney confirmed. "I should know. I had one of them holding hands with me a while back."

"There's a bunch of them in the water now, and it's ice cold. It must flow straight down off the glaciers. The pygmies are superb swimmers, very fast, very sure; I watched them diving and coming up with fish the size of big salmon in their jaws."

Barney told him about the incident with the fish-whistle.

"I'm sorry about Craig's leg," Tim said, "but while we're on the subject, perhaps you can tell me why he's on my back, why he jumped down my throat when I went after Dangerfield."

"He isn't on your back, and he didn't jump down your throat. At present he's worried because he smells a mystery, but is undecided where to turn a key to it. He probably regards Dangerfield as that key; certainly he respects the knowledge the man must have, yet I think that inwardly he would prefer to tackle the whole problem alone, leaving Dangerfield out of it altogether."

"Why should Craig feel like that? PES HQ instructed us to contact Dangerfield."

"True. And HQ being a tidy few light-years away is often out of touch with realities. But Craig probably thinks that old Dangerfield might be—well, misleading, ill-informed ... Craig's a man who likes to work things out for himself."

They turned and began to make their way back to the settlement, walking slowly, enjoying the mild air uncontaminated by fish.

"Surely that wasn't why Craig was so ragged about helping Daddy Dangerfield?" Tim asked.

"No, that was something else," Barney said. "PES teams are the precursors of change, remember. Before we arrive, the planets are in their natural state—unspoiled or undeveloped, whichever way you care to phrase it. After we leave, they are going to be taken over and altered, on our recommendation. However cheery you feel about man's position in the galaxy, somehow you can't help regretting that this mutilation is necessary."

"It's not our business to care," Tim said impatiently.

"But Craig cares, Tim. The more planets we survey, the more he feels that some mysterious—divine—balance is being overthrown. You can't avoid the idea that you are confronting an individual entity—and your sworn duty is to destroy it, and the enigma behind it, and turn out yet another assembly-line world for assembly-line man.

"That's how Craig feels about planets and people. For him, a man's character is sacrosanct; anything that has *accumulated* has his respect. It may be simpler to work with people who are mere ciphers, but an individual is of greater ultimate value."

"That's what he meant when he said Dangerfield was still his own self?"

"Sound sceptical if you like. It'll hit you one day. Imagine this place in fifty years, if we give it a clean bill of health. Do you think this river will run as it does now? It may be dammed to provide hydroelectric power, it may be widened and made navigable, it may be even a sewer. These birds overhead'll be extinct, or force-bred in cages, or roosting on factory roofs. Everything'll be changed—and we take much of the credit and blame for it."

"I won't miss the stink of fish," Tim said.

"Even a stink of fish has—" Barney began, and broke off. The silence was torn right down the middle by screams. The two ecologists ran down the trail, bursting full tilt into the clearing.

A peke creature was being killed. A rabble of pygmies milled everywhere, converging on a large decayed tree stump, upon which two of their kind stood with the screaming peke held between them.

To its cries were added those of all the others tethered nearby. The cries stopped abruptly as cruel talons ripped its stomach open. Its entrails were then scooped, steaming, into a crudely shaped clay bowl, after which the ravaged body was tossed to the crowd. The pygmies scrambled for it.

Before the hubbub had died down, another captive was handed up to the two executioners, kicking and crying as it went. The crowd paused to watch the fun. This time, the victim was one of the bearlike animals. Its body was gouged open, its insides turned into a second bowl. It, too, was tossed to the cayman-head throng.

"Good old Mother Nature!" Barney said angrily. "How many more of the little creatures do they intend to slaughter?"

But the killing was over. The two executioner pygmies, bearing the bowls of entrails in their paws, climbed from the tree stump and made their way through the crowd. The vessels were carried towards the rear of the village.

"It looks like some sort of religious ceremony," Craig said. Barney and Tim turned to find him standing behind them. The screaming had drawn him from his bed, and he had limped over to them unobserved. "Or parody of same."

"How's the leg?" Tim asked him.

"It'll be better by morning, Tim."

"The creature that bit you—the one Barney killed—was thrown into the river," Tim said. "I was there watching when the others turned up and slung him in."

"They're taking those bowls of guts into Dangerfield's hut," Barney said, pointing across the clearing. The two cayman-headed bearers disappeared through the hut doorway; a minute later they emerged empty-handed and mingled with the throng.

"I wonder what he wants guts for," Tim said. "Don't say he eats them!"

"That's smoke!" Craig exclaimed. "His hut's caught fire! Tim, quick, fetch a foam extinguisher from the overlander. Run!"

Smoke, followed by licking flame, showed through Dangerfield's window. It died, then sprang up again. Craig and Barney ran forward as Tim dashed for the overlander. The pygmies, some of whom were still quarrelling over the pelts of the dead peke and bear, took no notice of them or the fire.

The interior of the hut was full of smoke. Flame crawled among the dry rushes on the floor. An oil lamp had been upset; it lay on its side among the flames. Only a few feet beyond it, Dangerfield sprawled on his bed, eyes closed.

Craig pulled a rug from the other side of the room, flung it onto the fire, and stamped on it. When Tim arrived with the extinguisher, it was hardly needed, but they doused the smouldering ashes with chemicals to make doubly sure.

"There might be an opportunity to talk to the old boy when he pulls out of his faint," Craig said. "Leave me here, will you, and I'll see what I can do."

As Tim and Barney left, Craig noticed the two bowls of entrails standing on a side table. They were still gently steaming.

On the bed, Dangerfield stirred. His eyelids flickered, and one frail hand went up to his throat.

"No mercy from me," he muttered, "you'll get no mercy from me, you scum."

He lay looking up at the ecologist. Shadows crept like faded inkstains over his face.

"I must have passed out," he said tonelessly. "Felt so weak."

"You knocked over your oil lamp as you collapsed," Craig said. "I was just in time to save a bad blaze."

The old man made no comment, unless the closing of his eyes was to be interpreted as an indifference to death.

"Every afternoon they bring me the bowls of entrails," he muttered. "It's a ... rite. They're touchy about it. I wouldn't like to disappoint them. But this afternoon it was such an effort to stand. You people coming here exhausted me. If you aren't making a film, you'd better get—"

Craig fetched him a mug of water. He drank without raising his head, allowing half the liquid to trickle across his withered cheeks. Craig produced a hypodermic from his emergency pack and filled it from a plastic vial.

"You're in pain," he said. "This will stop the pain but leave your head clear. Let's have a look at your arm, can I?"

Dangerfield's eyes rested on the syringe as if fascinated. He began to shake slowly, until the rickety bed creaked.

"I don't need your help, mister," he said, his face crinkling.

"We need yours," replied Craig indifferently, swabbing the thin, palsied arm. He nodded his head towards the bowls of entrails. "What are these unappetizing offerings? Some sort of religious tribute?"

Unexpectedly, the old man began to laugh, his eyes filling with tears.

"Perhaps it's to placate me," he said. "Every day for years, for longer than I can remember, they've been bringing me these guts. The pygmies must think I swallow them, and I don't like to disillusion them, in case—well, in case I lost my power over them."

He hid his gaunt, beaky face in his hands; the paper-thin skin on his forehead was suddenly showered with sweat. Craig steadied his arm, injected the needle deftly, and massaged the stringy flesh.

Standing away from the bed, he said deliberately, "It's strange that you stay here on Kakaka-kaxo when you fear these pygmies so much."

Dangerfield looked sharply up, a scarecrow of a man with a shock of hair and sucked-in mouth. Staring at Craig, his eyes became very clear. He made no attempt to evade Craig's statement.

"Everyone who goes into space has a good reason driving him," he said. "You don't only need escape velocity, you need a private dream—or a private nightmare." As always he spoke in Galingua, using it stiffly and unemphatically. "Me, I could never deal with people; you never know where you stand with them. I'd rather face death with the pygmies than life with humanity. There's a confession for you, Hughes, coming from Far-flung Father Dangerfield. Maybe all heroes are just escapists, if you could see into them."

"Hodges. You have it wrong. Though it may be that all escapists pose as heroes," Craig said, but the old man continued to mutter to himself.

". . . so I stay on here, God of the Guts," he said. "That's what I am, God of the Guts." His laugh wrecked itself on a shoal of wheezes.

He hunched himself up in the foetal position, breathing heavily. In a moment he was asleep. Craig sat still, integrating all he had learned or guessed about Dangerfield. At last he slipped the PES harness from his shoulders; unzipping a pouch, he extracted two specimen jars. He poured the bloody contents of the clay bowls into separate jars. Then he set down the bowls, covered the jars, and returned them to his pack.

"And now, I think, a little helminthology," Craig said aloud.

As he returned through the village, he noticed that several pygmies lay, glaring unwinkingly at each other over the lacerated remains of the recent sacrifice. Circling them, he entered the overlander. It was unexpectedly good to breathe air free from the taint of fish and corruption.

"Dangerfield's sleeping now," he announced to Barney and Tim. "I'll go back in a couple of hours to treat his 'fiffin' and get him in a talkative frame of mind. Let's eat."

"How about exploring the temple in the cliff, Craig?" Tim asked.

"We'll let it go till the morning. We don't want to upset the locals more than necessary—they might take offence at our barging in there. By morning I'm hoping Dangerfield will have given us more to go on."

Over the meal, Barney told Craig of two weaver birds that he had snared while Craig was with Dangerfield.

"The younger one had an unusually large number of lice on it," he said. "Not strange when you realize it's a bird living in a colony, and a youngster at that, not yet expert at preening. It goes to show that the usual complex ecological echelons are in full swing on Kakakakaxo."

With their meal, they drank some of Barney's excellent Aldebaran wine—only the wine of heavy-gravity planets will travel happily through space. As they lingered over coffee, Tim volunteered to go over and sit with Dangerfield.

"Excellent idea," Craig agreed. "I'll be over to relieve you. And be careful—night's coming down fast."

Collecting his kit and a flashlight, Tim went out. Barney returned to his birds. Craig shut himself up in the tiny lab with his jars of entrails.

Cassivelaunus was sinking below the western horizon. Beneath the sheltering trees, darkness was already dominant; a fish scale gleamed here and there like a knife. In the treetops, where the weavers were settling to roost, an entanglement of light and shade moved. Kept apart by their tethers, peke and bear lay staring at each other in disconsolate pairs, indifferent to day and night. Hardly a cayman-head moved; joylessly they sprawled beneath their crude shelters, not sleeping, not watching.

Five of them lay in the open. These were the ones Craig had noticed earlier. They waited with their heads raised. In the gloom, only their yellowwhite throats, where a pulse beat like a slow drum, were clearly distinguishable. As he made his way across the clearing, Tim saw that they were waiting around the bodies of the two creatures that had been sacrificed. They crouched tensely about the masses of battered fur, glaring at one another.

In Dangerfield's hut Tim found the oil lamp and a jar of fish oil with which to refill it. He trimmed the wick and lit it. Though it gave off a reek of fish, he preferred it to the glare of his solar flashlight.

Dangerfield slept peacefully. Tim covered the old man with a blanket. In the chill air moving through the hut, Tim thought he caught a breath of the glaciers only a few hundred miles away, north or south.

Over him moved a feeling of wonder. He felt nothing of Craig's dislike of altering the nature of a planet, and was suddenly impatient for the morning, when they would integrate and interpret the riddles they glimpsed around them.

A succession of leathery blows sounded outside. The three cayman-heads that crouched over one of the pelts were fighting. Though they were small, they battled like giants. Their main weapons were their long jaws, thrusting, slashing, biting. When their jaws became wedged together in temporary deadlock, they used their claws as well. Each one fought against the other two.

After some minutes of this murderous activity, the three fell apart. Collapsing with their jaws along the ground, they eyed each other once more over the remains of the bear.

Later, the two pygmies crouching over the dead peke rose and did battle, their ferocious duel ending again with a sudden reversion into immobil-

ity. The deep, sullen evening light made the battles
more terrible. However much the five pygmies suffered from wounds they received, they gave no
sign of pain.

"They are fighting over the gutted bodies of their
slaves. It's a point of honour with them," Tim
thought.

He turned from the window. Dangerfield had
roused, awakened by the thumping outside. He
spoke tiredly, without opening his eyes.

"What are they fighting for?" Tim asked, lowering his voice.

"Every sunset they fight in the same way."

"What does it all mean?" Tim asked, but Dangerfield had drifted back into sleep.

After an hour, the old man became restless,
throwing off his blanket and tearing open his shirt.
Tossing on the bed, he clawed repeatedly at his
chest, coughing and groaning.

Bending over him, Tim noticed a patch of discoloured skin under one of the sick man's ribs. A
red spot grew rapidly, lapping at the surrounding
grey flesh. He made to touch it and then thought
better of it.

Dangerfield groaned. Tim caught his wrist,
steadying him against a crisis he did not understand. The patch on the chest formed a dark centre
like a storm cloud. It oozed, then erupted thick
blood, which trailed around the cage of the ribs to
soak into the blanket below. In the middle of the
bloody crater, something moved.

A flat, armoured head appeared. A brown insect—it resembled a caterpillar larva—heaved itself into sight, to lie exhausted on the discoloured
flesh. Overcoming his disgust, Tim pulled a specimen jar from his pack and imprisoned the larva in
it.

"I don't doubt that that's what Dangerfield calls
a fiffin," he said. He forced himself to disinfect
and dress the hermit's wound. He was bending

over the bed when Craig came in to relieve him, carrying a tape recorder. Tim explained what had happened and staggered out into the open air.

Outside, in the darkness, the five cayman-heads still fought their intermittent battle. On every plane, Tim thought, endless, meaningless strife was continuing; strife and life—synonymous. He wanted to stop trembling.

The dead hour before the dawn; the time, on any planet in the universe, when the pulse of life falters before quickening. Craig entered the overlander with his tape recorder under one arm. Setting it down, he put coffee on the hot-point, rinsed his face with cold water, and roused the two sleepers.

"We shall be busy today," he said, patting the recorder. "We now have plenty of data on Kakakakaxo to work on—very dubious material, I might add. I recorded a long talk with Dangerfield, which I want you both to hear."

"How is he?" Tim asked as he slipped on his tunic.

"Physically, not in bad shape. Mentally, pretty sick. Suddenly he is chummy and communicative, then he silent and hostile. An odd creature . . . . Not that you'd expect other than oddity after twenty years in this stagnation."

"And the fiffin?"

"Dangerfield thinks it is the larval stage of a dung beetle, and says they bore through anything. He has had them in his legs before, but this one only just missed his lungs. The pain must have been intense, poor fellow. I gave him a light hypalgesic and questioned him before its effect wore off."

Barney brought the boiling coffee off the stove and filled three beakers.

"All set to hear the playback," he said.

Craig switched the recorder on. The reels turned slowly, re-creating his voice and Dangerfield's.

"Now that you are feeling better," Craig-on-tape said, "perhaps you could give me a few details about life on Kakakakaxo. How efficiently can these so-called pygmies communicate with each other?"

A silence followed before Dangerfield replied.

"They're an old race, the pygmies," he said at length. "Their language has gradually worn down, like an old coin. I've picked up all I can in twenty-odd years, but you can take it from me that most of the time they're just making noises. Their language only expresses a few basic attitudes. Hostility. Fear. Hunger."

"What about love?" Craig prompted.

"They're very secretive about sex; I've never seen 'em mate, and you can't tell male from female. They just lay their eggs in the mud . . . what was I saying? . . . oh yes, about their manner of speech. You've got to remember, Hodges, that I'm the only human—the *only* one—ever to master this clicking they do."

"Have you been able to explain to them where you came from?"

"That's a bit difficult for them to grasp. They've settled for 'beyond the ice.' "

"Meaning the glaciers to the north and south of the equatorial belt?"

"Yes; that's why they think I'm a god, because only gods can live beyond the ice. The pygmies know all about the glaciers. I've been able to construct a bit of their history from similar little items—"

"That was one of the next things I was going to ask you about," Craig-on-tape said, as Barney-in-the-flesh handed around more coffee.

"The pygmies are an ancient race," old Dangerfield said. "They've no written history, of course, but you can tell they're old by their knowing about the glaciers. How would equatorial creatures know about glaciers, unless their race survived the last Ice Age? Then this ornamented cliff in which many of them live—they could build nothing like that now. They haven't the skill. I had to help them put this hut up. Their ancestors must have been really clever; these contemporary generations are just decadent."

Craig's voice came sceptically from the loudspeaker: "We had an idea that the temple might have been built by another, vanished race. Any opinions on that?"

"You're on the wrong track, Hodges. The pygmies look on this temple as sacred; somewhere in the middle of it is what they refer to as 'The Tomb of the Old Kings,' and even *I* have never been allowed in there. They wouldn't behave like that if the place didn't have a special significance for them."

"Do they still have kings?"

"No. They don't have any sort of rule now, except each man for himself. The five pygmies fighting outside the hut, for instance; there's nobody to stop them, so they'll go on until they are all dead."

"Why should they fight over the pelts?"

"It's a custom, that's all. They do it every night; sometimes one of them wins quickly, and then it's all over. They sacrifice their slaves in the day and squabble over their bodies at night."

"Can you tell me why they attach such importance to these little animals—their slaves, as you call them?"

"Oh, they don't attach much importance to the slaves. It's just that they make a habit of catching them in the forest, since they regard the pekes and bears as a menace to them; their numbers have increased since I've been here."

"Then why don't the pygmies kill them outright? And why do they always keep the two groups separate? Anything significant in that?"

"Why should there be? The pekes and bears are supposed to fight together if they are allowed to intermingle, but whether or not that's true I can't say. You mustn't expect reasons for everything these pygmies do. They're not rational the way a man is."

"As an ecologist, I find there is generally a reason for everything, however obscure."

"You do, do you?" The hermit's tone was belligerent. "In nineteen years here, I haven't found one. Look, it's no good staring at me with one eyebrow cocked. I don't like your superior ways, whether you're a good doctor or not."

"You were saying the pygmies were not rational."

"True. They're living automatically on past glory. You can't do anything with 'em. I've tried. At least they acknowledge my authority . . . . It's a terrible thing to grow old. Look at my hands."

Craig reached forward and switched the recorder off. Outside, the first light pencilled in the outlines of trees.

"That's about all that's relevant," he said. "The rest of Dangerfield's remarks were mainly autobiographical."

"What do you make of it, Craig?" Barney Brangwyn asked.

They heard the first weaver birds wake and cry in the trees as Craig replied.

"Before Dangerfield crashed on Kakakakaxo, he was a salesman, hopping from one frontier planet to another. He was untrained as an observer."

"I think you feel as I do," Barney said. "Dangerfield has misinterpreted just about everything he has seen. It's easy enough to do on a strange planet, even if you are emotionally balanced. Nothing in his statement can be trusted; it's useless, except perhaps as case history."

"I wouldn't go so far as to say that," Craig remarked, with his usual caution. "It's untrustworthy, yes, but not useless."

"Sorry, but I'm adrift," Tim Anderson said, getting up and pacing behind his chair. "Why should Dangerfield be so wrong? Most of what he said sounded logical enough to me. Even if he had no anthropological or ecological training to begin with, he's had plenty of time to learn."

"True, Tim, true," Craig agreed. "Plenty of time to learn correctly or learn wrongly. I'm not trying to pass judgement on Dangerfield, but there is hardly a fact in the universe not open to two or more interpretations. Dangerfield's attitude to the pygmies is highly ambivalent, a classical love-hate relationship. He wants to think of them as mere animals, because that would make them less formidable for him; at the same time, he wants to think of them as intelligent beings with a great past, because that makes their acceptance of him as their god more impressive."

"And which are the pygmies, animals or intelligent beings?" Tim asked.

"That is where our powers of observation and deduction come in," Craig said.

Tim was irritated. His companions could be very uninformative. He wanted to get away from them and think things over for himself. As he left, he remembered the jar he had put the fiffin larva into; he had forgotten to place it in the overlander's lab.

Two jars were already clipped in the rack above the lab bench. They contained two dead tapeworms; by the labels on the jars, he saw that Craig had extracted them from the entrails of the animals sacrificed the afternoon before. The cestodes, one of which came from the peke, one from the little bear, were identical; white tapes some twenty-four inches long, with suckers and hooks at the head end. Tim stared at them with interest before leaving the overlander.

Outside, dawn was seeping through the trees. He drew the cold air into his lungs; it was still flavoured with fish. The weaver birds were beginning to call overhead. A few pygmies were about, moving sluggishly in the direction of the river.

Tim stood there, shivering slightly in the cold, thinking of the oddity of two diverse species harbouring the same sort of tapeworm.

The nightlong fight over the dead animals was ended. Of the five pygmies involved, only one remained alive; it lay with the gutted bear in its jaws, unable to move away. Three of its four legs had been bitten off. Tim's horror dissolved as he saw the whole situation *sub specie aeternitatis*, with pain and death an inevitable concomitant of life; perhaps he was acquiring something of Craig's outlook.

He picked up three of the dead pygmies, shouldered them, and, staggering slightly under their combined weight, carried them back to the overlander. He met Craig taking breakfast over to Dangerfield.

"Hello," Craig exclaimed cordially. "What are you going to do with them?"

"I thought I'd do a little dissection," Tim said guardedly.

Once in the lab, he donned rubber gloves and slit open the pygmies' stomachs one by one, attending to nothing else. Removing the three intestinal sacs, he found that two of them were badly damaged by worms. Soon he had uncovered half a dozen roundworms, pink in coloration and still alive; they made vigorous attempts with their vestigial legs to climb from the crucible in which he placed them.

He went excitedly in to Barney Brangwyn to report his findings. Barney was sitting at the table, manipulating metal rods.

"This contradicts most of the laws of phylogeny," Tim said, peeling off his gloves. "According to Dangerfield, the pekes and bears are both recent arrivals on the evolutionary scene; yet their endoparasites, which Craig has preserved in the lab, are well adapted to their environment inside the creatures; in most respects they resemble the ancient order of tapeworm parasitic in man. The roundworms from the cayman-heads, on the other hand, bear all the marks of being recent arrivals. They are still something more than virtual egg factories; they retain traces of a previous, more independent existence—and they cause unnecessary damage to their host, always a sign that a suitable status quo has yet to be reached between host and parasite."

Barney raised his bushy eyebrows and smiled at the eagerness on Tim's face.

"Very interesting indeed," he said. "What now, Doctor Anderson?"

Tim grinned, struck a pose, and said, in a creditable imitation of Craig's voice, "Always meditate upon all the evidence, and especially upon those things you do not realize are evidence."

"Fair enough," Barney agreed, smiling. "And while you're meditating, come and give me a hand on the roof with this patent fishing rod I've made."

"Another of your crazy ideas, Barney?"

"We're going hunting. Come on, your worms will keep!"

Getting up, he produced a long, telescopic rod Tim recognized as one of their spare aerials. The last and smallest section was extended; to it Barney finished tying a sharp knife.

"I'm still hankering to catch myself one of the local pets without getting eaten at the same time," Barney said.

Climbing up the stepped pole that led into the tiny radio room, he removed the circular observation dome that gave an all-around view of their surroundings. He swung himself up and onto the roof of the overlander. He crawled forward on hands and knees. Tim followed.

"Keep down," he muttered. "If possible, I'd like this act of folly to go unobserved."

A gigantic tree spread its boughs over them. They were well concealed. Cassivelaunus was breaking through a low cloud, and the clearing below was still fairly silent. Lying flat on his stomach, Barney pulled out the sections of aerial until he had a rod several yards long. Steadying this weapon with Tim's aid, he pushed it forward.

The end of it reached to the nearest pygmy shelter. Outside that shelter, two captive animals sat up, scratched, and watched with interest as the knife descended. Its blade hovered over the bear, shifted, and began rubbing gently back and forth across the thong that secured the animal.

The thong fell away. The bear was free. It scratched its yellow head in a parody of bewilderment. The neighbouring peke clucked encouragingly at it. A procession of pygmies appeared among the trees. Hearing them, the bear was spurred into action.

Grasping the aerial in its black hands, the bear swarmed nimbly up. It jumped onto the overlander roof and faced the men, without showing fear.

Barney retracted the aerial. This manoeuvre was glimpsed by the returning pygmies. They began to clack and growl. Other pygmies emerged from their shelters, scuttling towards the overlander and staring up.

The cayman-heads emerging from the forest wore the look of tired hunters, returning with the dawn. Over their shoulders, roughly tied, lay freshly captured bears or pekes. These pygmies unceremoniously dropped their burdens and scuttled at a ferocious pace to the PES vehicle.

Alarmed by the commotion, the weavers poured from their treetop homes, screeching.

"Let's get in," Barney said.

Picking up the bear, which offered no resistance, he jumped down inside the overlander.

At first, the creature was overcome by its surroundings. It stood on the table and rocked piteously from side to side. Recovering, it accepted milk and chattered to the two men. Seen close, it bore little resemblance to a bear, except for its fur covering. It stood upright as the cayman-heads did, attempting to smooth its bedraggled fur with its fingers. When Tim proffered his pocket comb, it used that gratefully, wrenching diligently at the knots in its long coat, which was still wet with dew.

"Well, it's male, it's intelligent, and it's more fetching than its overlords," commented Tim. "You have what you wanted, but the wolves are at the door, howling for our blood."

Through the window, Barney saw that the pygmies surrounded the overlander in ever-growing numbers, waving their claws, snapping their jaws. In the blue light they looked at once repulsive, comic, and malign.

"Evidently we have offended against a local law of property. Until they cool down, Craig's return is blocked; he'll have to tolerate Daddy Dangerfield for a while."

Tim did not reply; before Craig returned, there was something else he wished to do. But first he had to get away from the overlander.

He stood uncertainly, and then Barney turned his attention again to his new pet. Tim quickly climbed up into the radio nest unobserved, opened the dome, and stood once more on the roof of the overlander. Catching hold of an overhanging bough of the big tree, he pulled himself into it. Working his way along, screened from the clacking mob below, he got well away from them before dropping down from a lower branch onto clear ground. Then he walked briskly in the direction of the cliff temple.

Dangerfield switched the projector off. As the colours died, he turned eagerly to Craig Hodges.

"There!" he exclaimed, with pride. "What do you think of that?"

Though his chest was still bandaged, the hermit

moved easily. Modern healing treatments had speeded his recovery; he looked ten years younger than the old man who had yesterday suffered from fiffins. The excitement of the film he had just been showing had brought a flush to his cheeks.

"Well, what do you think of it?" he repeated, impatiently.

"I'm wondering what *you* think of it," Craig said.

Some of the animation left Dangerfield. He looked around the stuffy confines of his hut, as if seeking a weapon.

"You've no respect," he said. "I took you for a civilized man, Hodges. But you persist in trying to insult me in underhanded ways. Even the Droxy film men recognized me for what I am."

"You mean for what you like to think you are," Craig said. Dangerfield swung a heavy stick. Craig brought up his arm, and the blow landed close to his elbow. He seized the stick, wrenching it from Dangerfield's grasp and tossing it out of the door.

The two men stood confronting each other. Dangerfield's gaze wavered, and he turned away. Craig left the hut.

He walked briskly across the clearing towards the cayman-heads. As he drew nearer, part of the rabble detached itself from the overlander and moved towards him, jaws creaking open. Without slackening his stride, he pushed between their scaly green bodies. The cayman-heads merely croaked excitedly as Craig passed. Jostling, shuffling their paws in the dirt, they let him get by. He mounted the step of the overlander and entered unmolested.

Craig read something of the relief and admiration on Barney's face.

"They must have guessed how stringy I'd taste," he remarked. That was all that was said.

He turned his attention to Barney's bear-creature, already christened Fido. The animal chattered perkily as Barney explained how he got it.

"I'll swear Fido has some sort of embryo language," Barney said. "In exchange for a good rubdown with insecticide, he has let me examine his mouth and throat. He's well enough equipped for speech."

"Show him how to use a pencil and paper, and see what he makes of it," Craig suggested, stroking the creature's yellow crest.

As Barney did so, he asked Craig what had kept him so long with Dangerfield.

"I was beginning to think the lost race of Kakakakaxo had got you," he said, grinning.

"No. He has been showing me a film intended to impress me with the greatness of Dangerfield."

"A documentary?"

"Anything but! A squalid film made by Melmoth Studios on Droxy, supposedly based on the old boy's life. They presented him with a copy of it and a projector as a souvenir. It's called 'Curse of the Crocodile Men.' "

"Ye Gods!" Barney exclaimed. "I mustn't miss that when it's on circuit again! I'll bet you found it instructive."

"In many ways. The script writers and director spent two days—just two days!—here on Kakakakaxo, talking to Dangerfield and 'soaking up atmosphere,' before returning to Droxy to cook up their own ideas on the subject. No other research was done."

Barney laughed briefly. "Who gets the girl?"

"There is a girl, of course, and Dangerfield gets her. She's a coy blonde stowaway on his spaceship. You know."

"*I* know. Now tell me why you found it instructive."

"It was all oddly familiar. After the usual preliminaries—a spectacular spaceship crash on a plastic mountainside, et cetera—a Tarzanlike Dangerfield is shown being captured by the bear-race, who stand six feet high and wear tin helmets, so help me. Dangerfield could not escape because the blonde twisted her ankle in the crash. You know how blondes are in films.

"The pekes, for simplicity's sake, never appear. The bears are torturing our hero and heroine to death when the crocodile men raid the place and rescue him. The crododile men are Melmoth's idea of our cayman-headed pals outside."

"Stop giving me the trailer," Barney said, feigning suspense. "Get on with the plot. I want to know how the blonde makes out."

"The crocodile men arrive in time to save her from a fate worse than a sprained ankle. And here's an interesting point—these crocodile men, according to the film, are a proud and ancient warrior race, come down in the world through the encroachment of the jungle. When they get Dangerfield back to their village by the river, they don't like him. They, too, are about to put him to death and ravage the blonde when he saves the leader's son from foot-rot or something. From then on the tribe treats him like a god, builds him a palace, and all the rest of it."

"To think I missed it! It sounds like a real classic!" Barney cried. "Perhaps we can get Dangerfield to give a matinee tomorrow. I can see how such a bit of personal aggrandizement would be dear to his heart."

"It was very sad stuff," Craig said. "Nothing rang true. False dialogue, fake settings. Even the blonde wasn't very attractive."

Barney sat silent for a minute, looking rather puzzledly into space, tweaking his beard. "It's odd that, considering his hokum was cooked up on Droxy, it tallies surprisingly well in outline with what Dangerfield told you last night about the great past of the cayman-heads, their decline, and so on."

"Exactly!" Craig agreed with satisfaction. "Don't you see what that means, Barney? Nearly everything Dangerfield knows, or believes he knows, comes from a hack film shot in a Droxy studio, rather than vice versa."

They stared at one another with growing amusement. Into both their minds came the reflection that all human behaviour is ultimately inexplicable; even the explicable is a mystery.

"Now you see why he shied away from us so violently at our first meeting," Craig said. "He's got almost no firsthand information on conditions here. He's been afraid to go out looking for it. Knowing that, he was prepared to face Droxy film people—who would only be after a good story—but not scientists, who would want hard facts. Once I had him cornered, of course, he had to come out with what little he'd got, presumably hoping we would swallow it as the truth and go."

Barney made clucking noises. "He's probably no longer fit to remember what is truth, what lies. After nineteen years, the old boy must be quietly crazy."

"Fear has worked steadily on Dangerfield all this time. He's afraid of people, afraid of the cayman-heads, the crocodile men. He takes refuge from his terrors in fantasy. He's become a film god. And you couldn't budge him off the planet because he realizes, subconsciously of course, that reality would then catch up with him. He has no choice but to remain here, in a place he loathes."

"Okay, doctor," he said. "Diagnosis accepted. Brilliant field work—my congratulations. But, all we have collected so far are phantoms. Tell me where PES work stands after you've proved the uselessness of our main witness—presumably, at a standstill?"

"By no means," Craig said. He pointed to Fido. The little bear was sitting on the table cuddling the pencil.

He had drawn a crude picture on paper. It depicted a room in which a bear and a peke were locked in each other's arms, as if fighting.

A few minutes later, when Craig had gone into the laboratory with an assortment of coleoptera and anoplura culled from Dangerfield's hut, Barney saw the old hermit himself coming across to them, hobbling rapidly among the pygmy shelters with the aid of a stick. Barney called to Craig.

Craig emerged from the lab looking at once pleased and secretive.

"Those three pygmy carcasses Tim brought into the lab," he said. "I presume Tim cut them up—it doesn't look like your work. Did he say anything to you about them?"

Barney explained the point Tim had made about the roundworms.

"Is there anything wrong?" he inquired.

"No, nothing, nothing," Craig said, shaking his head. "And that's all Tim said .... Where is he now, by the way?"

"I've no idea! The boy's getting as secretive as you. He must have gone outside for a breath of fish. Shall I give him a call?"

"Let's tackle Dangerfield first," Craig said.

They opened the door. Most of the cayman-heads had dispersed. The old man refused to come into the overlander, his nose standing out from his head like a parrot's beak as he shook his head. He wagged a finger angrily at them.

"I always knew no good would come of your prying," he said. "Now that young fellow of yours is being killed by the pygmies—serves him right, too. But goodness knows what they'll do when they've tasted human flesh—tear us all apart, I shouldn't wonder. I doubt if I'll be able to stop them."

He had not finished talking before Craig and Barney had leapt from the overlander.

"Where's Tim? What's happened to him?" Craig asked.

"I expect it'll be too late by now," said Dangerfield. "I saw him slip into the cliff temple, the young fool. Now perhaps—"

But the PES men were already running across the clearing, scattering brilliant birds about their heads. They jumped the shelters in their path. As they neared the temple, they heard the clacking of the cayman-head pack. When they reached the heavily ornamented doorway, they saw a tight crowd of creatures, all fighting to get into the cliff.

"Tim!" bawled Barney. "Tim! Are you there?"

No answer came. The pack continued struggling to get into the temple.

"We can't massacre this lot," Craig said, glaring at the cayman-heads before them. "How're we going to get in there to Tim?"

"We can use the cry gas in the overlander!" Barney said. "That will shift them." He doubled back to their vehicle and in a minute brought it bumping across the clearing. The roof of the overlander snagged several branches, breaking the weavers' carefully constructed roof and sending angry birds flying in all directions. As the vehicle lumbered up, Craig unstrapped an outside container and pulled out a hose; the other end of it was already connected to internal gas tanks. Barney threw down two respirators and put one on himself.

Donning his mask, Craig slung the spare over his arm and charged forward with the hose. The gas poured over the nearest cayman-heads, who fell back like magic, coughing and pawing at their goat-yellow eyes. The two men entered the temple; they moved down the corridor past bodies fighting to get out of their way. The croaking was deafening; in the dark and mist, Craig and Barney could hardly see ahead.

The corridor changed into a pygmy-sized tunnel,

running upward through the mountain. The two ecologists had to struggle every foot of the way, and then . . .

The supply of cry gas gave out. Craig and Barney stopped, peering at each other in shock.

"I thought the gas tanks were full?" Craig asked.

"They were. Maybe one of the cayman-heads bit through the hose."

Their retreat was cut off: the cayman-heads at the mouth of the temple would have recovered by now, and be waiting for them. So they moved ahead, throwing off their respirators and pulling out blasters.

They turned a corner and stopped. This was the end of the passageway. The tunnel broadened into a sort of anteroom on the far side of which stood a wide wooden door. A group of cayman-heads were scratching at it; they turned and confronted the men. Tears stood in their eyes: a whiff of the gas had reached them, and served only to anger them. Six of them were there. They charged.

"Get 'em!" Barney yelled.

The dim chamber twitched with blinding blue-white light. But the best hand weapon has its limitations, and the cayman-heads had speed on their side.

Barney scarcely had time to dispatch one of them, and then another landed squarely on him. For a small creature, it was unbelievably powerful. He fell backward, bellowing as the jaws gaped up to his face. He tried to writhe away as he fired the blaster against the leathery stomach. The creature fell from him, and in a dying kick knocked the weapon from his hand.

Before Barney could retrieve his blaster, two more cayman-heads landed on him, sending him sprawling. He was defenceless against their claws.

Blue light leaped and crackled over him. An intolerable heat breathed above his cheek. The two cayman-heads rolled over beside him, their bodies black and charred. Shakily, Barney stood up.

The wooden door had been flung open. Tim stood there, holstering the blaster that had saved Barney's life.

Craig had settled his attackers. They lay smouldering on the floor in front of him. He stood now, breathing deeply, his tunic sleeve torn. The three men looked at each other, grimy and dishevelled. Craig was the first to speak.

"Close . . . too close," he muttered.

"I thought we'd had it then; thanks for the helping hand, Tim," Barney said.

His beard had been singed, its edges turned a dusty brown. He felt his cheek tenderly where a blister was already forming. Sweat poured from him; the heat from the thermonuclear blasts had sent the temperature in the anteroom soaring.

"I'm sorry you came in after me," Tim said. "I was safe enough behind this door. I've been doing a little research on my own, Craig—you'd better come in and see this place for yourself, now that you're here. I have discovered the Tomb of the Old Kings that Dangerfield told us about! You'll find it explains quite a lot we did not know."

"How did you manage to get as far as this without the cayman-heads stopping you?" Craig asked.

"Most of them were clustered around the overlander calling for Barney's blood when I entered. They only started creeping up on me when I was actually inside."

They entered the inner room. Tim barred the door before shining his flashlight down the long room. Its builders had known what they were doing. Decoration was kept to a minimum, except for the elaborate door arch and the restrained fan vaulting of the ceiling. Attention was focused on a large catafalque, upon which lay a row of sarcophagi. Everything was deep in dust, and the air was musty.

Tim pointed to the line of little coffins, which were embellished with carvings.

"Here are the remains of the Old Kings of Kakakakaxo," he said. "And although I may have made myself a nuisance, I think I can claim that with their aid I have solved the mystery of the lost race of this planet. It's like a jigsaw puzzle. We already had most of the pieces. Dangerfield supplied nearly all of them—but the old boy had fitted them together upside down. You see, to start with, there is not one lost race, but two."

"A nice buildup, Tim. Now let's have some facts," Craig said.

"You can have facts. I'm showing them to you. This temple—and doubtless others like it all over the planet—was hewn out of the rock by two races who have engraved their own likenesses on these sarcophagi. Take a look at them! Far from being lost, the races have been under our noses all the time: they are the beings we call the pekes and bears. Their portraits are on the sarcophagi, and their remains lie inside. Their resemblance to Droxian animals has blinded us to what they really are—the ancient top dogs of Kakakakaxo!"

"I'm not surprised," Barney said, turning from an inspection of the stone coffins. "The bear people are brighter than the cayman-heads. As I see it, the caymans are pretty stodgy reptiles whom nature has endowed with armour but precious little else. I had already decided that that was another thing Great God Dangerfield had garbled; far from being an ancient race, the caymans are neoteric, upstart usurpers who have only recently appeared to oust the peke and bear people.

"Dangerfield said they know about the glaciers. They probably drifted down from the cold regions until the river brought them to these equatorial lands. As for the bear people—and I suspect the same goes for the pekes—their chatter, far from being the beginning of a language, is the decadent tail end of one. They were the ancient races, already in decline when the parvenu pygmies descended on them and completed their disintegration."

"The helminthological evidence supports this theory," Tim said eagerly. He turned to Craig. "The cayman-heads are too recent to have developed their own peculiar cestodes; they were almost as much harmed by interior parasites, the roundworms, as was Daddy by his fiffin. In a long-established host-parasite relationship, the amount of internal damage is minimal."

"As was the case with the peke and bear cestodes I uncovered," Craig agreed.

"As soon as I saw these roundworms, I realized that Dangerfield's claim that the pygmies were the ancient species and their 'pets' the new might be the very reverse of the truth. I came over here hoping to find proof; and here it is."

"It was a good idea, Tim," Barney said heartily, "but you shouldn't have done it alone—far too risky."

"The habit of secretiveness is catching," Tim said.

He looked at Craig, but the chief ecologist seemed not to have heard the remark. He marched to the door and put an ear to it. Barney and Tim listened, too. The noise was faint at first, then became unmistakable—a chorus of guttural grunts and croaks. The cry gas had dispersed. The pygmies were pressing back into the temple.

The noise took on weight and volume. It rose to a climax as claws struck the outside of the door. Craig stood back. The door shook.

"This is not a very healthy place," Craig said, turning back to the others. "Is there another way out?"

They moved down the long room. Its walls were blank. Behind them, the door rattled and groaned. At the far end of the chamber stood a screen; there

was a narrow door behind it. Barney pushed the
screen away and with one thrust of his great shoulders sent the door shattering back. Rusted hinges
and lock left a bitter, red powder floating in the
air. Climbing over the door, they found themselves
in a steep and narrow tunnel, where they were
forced to go in single file.

"I should hate to be caught in here," Tim said.
"Do you think the cayman-heads will dare enter
the tomb room? They seem to regard it as sacred."

"Their blood's up. A superstition may not bother
them," said Barney.

"What I still don't understand," Tim said, "is
why the cayman-heads care so much for the temple if it has nothing to do with them."

"You probably never will," Craig said. "The temple may be for them a symbol of their new domi-
nance, and one man's symbol is another man's
enigma. I can hear that door splintering; let's get
up this tunnel. It must lead somewhere."

One behind the other, they literally crawled along
the shaft. It bore steadily upward at an angle of
forty-five degrees. On all sides, the mountain made
its presence felt, dwarfing them, threatening to
engulf them.

They had climbed some distance when Barney
stopped.

"The way's blocked!" he exclaimed.

The tunnel was neatly stoppered with a solid
substance. "Rock fall!" he cried.

"We can't use a blaster on it in this space," Tim
said, "or we'll cook ourselves."

Craig passed a knife forward.

"Try the blockage with this," he said, "and see
what it's made of."

The substance flaked reluctantly as Barney
scraped. They examined the flakes; Tim recognized
them first.

"This is guano—probably from bats!" he exclaimed. "We must be very near the surface. Thank goodness for that!"

"It's certainly guano," Craig agreed, "but it's almost as hard as stone with age. You can see that a limestone shell has formed over the bottom of it: it may be hundreds of years old. There may be many feet of guano between us and the surface."

"Then we'll have to dig through it," Barney said.

There was no alternative. The ill-smelling guano became softer as they dug upward, until it reached the consistency of moist cake. They rolled lumps of it back between their knees, sending it bouncing back, down into the mountain. It clung stickily to them, like paste.

Twenty-five feet of solid guano had to be tunnelled through before they struck air. Barney's head and shoulders emerged into a small cave. A six-legged, doglike creature backed growling into the open and fled. It had taken over the cave for a lair long after the bats had deserted it.

The others followed Barney out, to stand blinking in the intense blue light. They were plastered with filth. Without speaking, they left the cave and drew in lungfuls of fresh air.

Trees and bushes surrounded them. The ground sloped steeply down to the left. When they had recovered, they began to descend in that direction. They were high up the mountainside; Cassivelaunus gleamed through the leaves above them.

"There's nothing else to keep us on Kakakakaxo," Barney said. "Dangerfield will be glad to see the back of us. I wonder how he'll like the colonists? They'll come flocking in once HQ gets our clearance. They'll find some opposition, but there's nothing here the biggest fool can't handle."

"Except Dangerfield," Craig interjected.

"The man with the permanent wrong end of the stick!" Tim added, laughing. "He will see out his days selling signed picture postcards of himself to colonists and tourists."

They emerged from the trees. Before them was a cliff, steep and bush-studded. The ecologists went to its edge and looked down.

A fine panorama stretched out before them. In the distance, a range of snow-covered mountains seemed to hang suspended in the blue air. Nearer, winding between stretches of jungle, ran the cold river. On its banks, the ecologists could see cayman-heads basking in the sun; in the water, others swam and dived.

"Look at them!" Craig exclaimed. "They are really aquatic creatures. They've hardly had time to adapt to land life. The dominating factor of their lives remains—fish!"

"They've already forgotten us," Barney said.

They could see that the crude settlement was deserted. The overlander was discernible through trees, but it took them an hour of scrambling down hazardous paths before they reached it.

Craig went around to look at the severed cry gas hose. It had been neatly chopped, as if by a knife. This was Dangerfield's work—he had expected to trap them in the temple! There was no sign of the old man anywhere. Except for the melancholy captives, sitting at the end of their tethers, the clearing was deserted.

"Before we go, I'm setting these creatures free," Barney said.

He ran among the shelters, slashing at the thongs with a knife, liberating pekes and bears. As they found themselves free, they banded together and trotted off into the jungle without further ado.

"Two more generations," Barney said regretfully, "and there probably won't be a bear or a peke on Kakakakaxo alive outside a zoo; the colonists will make shorter work of them than the cayman-heads have. As for the cayman-heads, I don't doubt they'll only survive by taking to the rivers again."

"There's another contradiction," Tim remarked thoughtfully, as they climbed into the overlander and Barney backed her through the trees. "Danger-field said the peke and bear fought with each other if they had the chance, yet they went off peacefully enough together—and they ruled together once, as the tomb proves. Where does the fighting come in?"

"As you say, Dangerfield always managed to grab the wrong end of the stick," Craig answered. "If you take the opposite of what he told us, that's likely to be the truth. He has always been too afraid of his subjects to go out and look for the facts."

Barney laughed. "Here it comes," he said. "I warn you, Tim, the oracle is about to speak! In some ways you're very transparent, Craig; I've known ever since we left the tomb of the old kings that you had something up your sleeve and were waiting for an appropriate moment before you produced it."

"What is it, Craig?" Tim asked curiously.

Barney let Fido out of the overlander; the little creature ran off across the clearing without a backward glance.

"You were careless when you cut open those three pygmies in the lab, Tim," Craig said. "I know that you were looking for something else, but if you had been less excited, you would have observed that the cayman-heads are parthenogenic. They have only one sex, reproducing by means of self-fertilized eggs."

"I see. Does this make any difference to the situation?" Tim asked.

Barney smote his forehead in savage surprise.

"Ah, I should have seen it myself! Parthenogenic, of course! Self-fertilizing! It explains the lack of vanity or sexual inhibition we noticed. I swear I would have hit on the answer myself, if I hadn't been so occupied with Fido."

He climbed heavily into the driver's seat, slam-

ming the door. The air conditioning sucked away
the invading smell of fish at once.

"Yes, you have an interesting situation on Kakakakaxo," Craig continued. "Try and think how difficult it would be for such a parthenogenic species
to visualize a bisexual species like man. Nevertheless, the cayman-heads grasped one weakness in-
herent in the bisexual system: if you keep the two
sexes apart, the race cannot breed and dies out.

"And that is just what they were doing—separat-
ing male and female. That is how they managed to
hold this place. Of course, no scheme is perfect,
and quite a few of both sexes escaped into the
forest to breed."

Barney revved the engine, moving the overlander
forward and leaving Tim to ask the obvious question.

"Yes," Craig said. "As Fido tried to explain to us
with his drawing, the 'bears' are the males and the
'pekes' the females of one species.

"It just happens to be a dimorphous species, the
sexes varying in size and configuration, or we would
have guessed the truth at once. The cayman-heads,
in their dim way, knew. They tackled the whole
business of conquest in a way only a parthenogenic
race would—they segregated the sexes."

Tim whistled.

"So when Dangerfield thought the pekes and
bears were fighting," he said, "they were really
copulating! And of course the similar cestodes you
found in their entrails would have put you on the
right track; I ought to have guessed it myself!"

"It must be odd to play god in a world about
which you really know or care so little," Barney
commented, swinging the vehicle down the track
in the direction of their space ship. "I wonder if
the Creator is as indifferent to us?"

The old man hid behind a tree, watching the
overlander leave. He shook his head, braced him-

self, hobbled back to his hut. His servants would have to hunt in the jungles before he got today's offering of entrails. He shivered as he thought of those two symbolic and steaming bowls. He shivered for a long time. He was old; from the sky he had come; to the sky he would one day return. But before that, he was going to tell everyone what he really thought of them.

How he despised them.

How he needed them.

Sector Green

Kakakakaxo is presently being colonized by ten thousand men, women and children from the depressed worlds of the Rift.

Craig Hodges has every reason for being concerned about these populations and their depredations on "new" planets. Fortunately, Starswarm Birthstrike has the matter very much under control. This galaxy-wide organization educates the planets of the federation in new methods of mental contraception.

Although this operation is costly, it proves less expensive—and exacts less toll on human sensibilities—than the business of establishing colonists on virgin planets.

Birthstrike is undoubtedly the chief factor causing a slowdown in the rate of galactic expansion. With its enlightened use practised on some eleven and a half thousand worlds, overcrowding is not the problem it was even two eras ago.

We are apt to forget that the methods of mental contraception were formulated on the watery world of Banya Ban, in Sector Green, over fifty eras ago. That they have taken so long to spread is hardly surprising to anyone familiar with the Theory of Multigrade Superannuation, which has some sensible things to say about ideas being acceptable only to the group in which they emerge.

Banya Ban has changed almost as much as Droxy

*and Dansson in the last fifty eras. It is a world of
immense inventiveness coupled with little drive. These
characteristics are evident as much in Banya Ban's
literature as its life, as the following brief chronicle
shows.*

I

The way of telling time in Mudland was ingenious.
Double A had a row of sticks stuck in the mud in
the blackness before his eyes. With his great spongy
hands that sometimes would have nothing to do
with him, he gripped the sticks one by one, counting as he went, sometimes in numbers, sometimes
in such abstractions as lyre birds, rusty screws,
pokers, or seaweed.

He would go on grimly, hand over fist against
time, until the beastly old comfort of degradation
fogged his brain and he would forget what he was
trying to do. The long liverish gouts of mental
indigestion that were his thought processes would
take over from his counting. And when later he
came to think back to the moment when the take-
over occurred, he would know that that had been
the moment when it had been the present. Then he
could guess how far ahead or behind the present
he was, and could give this factor a suitable name—
though lately he had decided that all factors could
be classified under the generic term Standard, and
accordingly he named the present time Standard
O'Clock.

Standard O'Clock he pictured as a big red soldier with moustaches sweeping around the roseate
blankness of his face. Every so often, say on pay-
day, it would chime, with pretty little cuckoos
popping out of all orifices. As an additional touch
of humour, Double A would make O'Clock's pen-
dulum wag.

By this genial ruse, he was slowly abolishing

time, turning himself into the first professor of a
benighted quantum. As yet the experiments were
not entirely successful for ever and anon his grop-
ing would communicate itself to his hands, and
back they'd come to him, slithering through the
mud, tame as you please. Sometimes he bit them;
they tasted unpleasant; nor did they respond.

"You are intellect," he thought they said. "But
we are the tools of intellect. Treat us well, and
without salt."

II

Another experiment concerned the darkness.

Even sprawling in the mud with his legs ampu-
tated unfortunately represented a compromise. Double A had to admit there was nothing final in his
degradation, since he had begun to—no, nobody
could force him to use the term "enjoy the mud,"
but on the other hand nobody could stop him using
the term "ambivelling the finny claws (clause?)"
with the understanding that in certain contexts it
might be interpreted as approximately synonymous
with "enjoying the mud."

Anyhow, heretofore it remained to be continued
that everywhere was compromise. The darkness
compromised with itself and with him. The darkness was sweet and warm and wet.

When Double A realized that the darkness was
not utter, that the abstraction utterness was beyond
it, he became furious, drumming imaginary heels
in the mud, urinating into it with some force and
splendour, and calling loudly for dark optics.

The optics were a failure, for they became covered in mud, so that he could not see through
them to observe whether or not the darkness increased. So they came and fitted him with a pair
of ebony contacts, and with this game condescen-

sion on their part, Double A hoped he had at last
reached a point of noncompromise.

Not so! He had eyelids that pressed on the lenses,
drawing merry patterns on the night side of his
eyeballs. Pattern and darkness cannot exist together,
so again he was defeated by myopic little Lord
Compromise, knee-high to a pin and stale as rats'
whiskers, but still Big Reeking Lord of Creation.
Well, he was not defeated yet. He had filled in
Application Number Six Oh Five Bark Oomph Eight
Eight Tate Potato Ten in sticks and sandbars and
the old presumption factor for the privilege of Person Double A, sir, late of the Standard O'Clock
Regiment, sir, to undergo total, partial and complete Amputation of Two Vermicularform Appendages in the possession of the aforesaid Double A
and known henceforth as his Eyelids.

Meanwhile, until the application was accepted
and the scalpels served, he tried his cruel experiments on the darkness.

He shouted, whispered, spoke, gave voice, uttered, named names, broke wind, cracked jokes,
split infinitives, passed participles, and in short
and *in toto* interminabley talked, orated, chattered,
chatted, and generally performed vocal gymnas-
tics against the darkness. Soon he had it cowering
in a corner. It was less well-equipped orally than
Double A, and he let it know with a rollicking
"Fathom five thy liar fathers, all his crones have
quarrels made, Rifle, rifle, fiddle-faddle, hey," and
other such decompositions of a literary-religio-
medico-philosophico-nature.

So the powers of darkness had no powers against
the powers of screech.

"Loot there be light!" boomed Double A: and
there was blight. Through the thundering murk,
packed tight with syllables and salty with syllo-
gisms, he could see the dim, mudbound form of
Gasm.

"Let there be night!" boomed Double A. But he

was too late, had lost his chance, had carried his experiment beyond the pale. For in the pallor and squalor, Gasm remained revoltingly *there*, whether invisible or visible. And his bareness in the thereness made a whereness tight as harness.

III

So began the true history of Mudland. It was now possible to have not only experiments, which belonged to the old intellect arpeggio, but character conflict, which pings right out of the middle register of the jolly old emotion chasuble, not to mention the corking old horseplay archipelago. Amoebas, editors and lovers are elements in that vast orchestra of classifiable objects to whom or for whom character conflict is ambrosia.

Double A went carefully into the business of having a C.C. with Gasm. To begin with, of course, he did not know whether he himself had a C.: or, of course squared, since we are thinking scientifically, whether Gasm had a C. Without the first C., could there be the second? Could one have a C.–less C.?

Alas for scientific inquiry. During the o'clock sticks that passed while Double was beating his way patiently through this thicket of thorny questions, jealousy crept up on him unawares.

Despite the shouting and the ebony contacts, with which the twin polarities of his counternegotiations with the pseudo-dark were almost kept at near-maximum in the fairly brave semistruggle against compromise, Gasm remained ingloriously visible, lolling in the muck no more than a measurable distance away.

Gasm's amputations were identical with Double A's: to wit, the surgical removal under local anaesthetic, and with two aspirin, of that assemblage of ganglions, flesh, blood, bone, toenail, hair and knee-

cap referred to hereafter as Legs. In this, no cause
for jealousy existed. Indeed, they had been scrupu-
lously democratic: one vote, one head; one head,
two legs; two heads, four legs. Their surgeons were
paragons of the old equality regiment. No cause
for Double A's jealousy.

But. It was within his power to *imagine* that
Gasm's amputations were other than they were.
He could quite easily (and with practise he could
perfectly easily) visualize Gasm as having had not
two legs but one leg and one arm removed. And
that amputation was more interesting than Double A's own amputation, or the fact that he had
fins.

So the serpent came even to the muddy paradise
of Mudland, writhing between the two bellowing
bodies. C.C. became reality.

IV

Double A abandoned all the other experiments to
concentrate on beating and catechizing Gasm. Gradually Mudland lost its identity and was transformed
into Beating and Catechizing, or B & C. The new
regime was tiring for Double A, physically and
especially mentally, since during the entire proce-
dure he was compelled to ask himself why he should
be doing what he was, and indeed *if* he was doing
what he was, rather than resting contentedly in
the mud with his hands.

The catechism was stylized, ranging over several topics and octaves as Double A yelled the
questions and Gasm screamed the answers.

"What is your name?"

"My name is Gasm."

"Name some of the other names you might have
been called instead."

"I might have been called Plus or Shob or Droo
or Harm or Finney or Cusp."

"And by what strange inheritance does it come about that you house your consciousness among the interstices of lungs, aorta, blood, corpuscles, follicles, sacro-iliac, ribs and prebendary skull?"

"Because I would walk erect if I could walk erect among the glorious company of the higher vertebrates, who have grown from mere swamps, dinosaurs and dodos. Those that came before were dirty brates or shirty brates; but we are the vertebrates."

"How many are pervertebrates?"

"Why, sir, thirtebrates."

"What comes after us?"

"After us the deluge."

"How big is the deluge."

"Huge."

"How deluge is the deluge?"

"Deluge, deluger, delugest."

"Conjugate and decline."

"I decline to conjuge."

"And what comes after the vertebrates?"

"Nothing comes after the vertebrates, because we are the highest form of civilization."

"Name the signs whereby the height of our civilization may be determined."

"The heights whereby the determination of our sign may be civilized are seven in number. The subjugation of the body. The resurrection of the skyscraper. The perpetuation of the speeches. The annihilation of the species. The glorification of the nates. The somnivolence of the conscience. The omnivorousness of sex. The conclusion of the Thousand Years War. The condensation of milk. The conversation of idiots. The confiscation of monks—"

"Stop, stop! Name next the basic concept upon which this civilization is based."

"The interests of producer and consumer are identical."

"What is the justification of war?"

"War is its own justification."

"Let us sing a sesquipedalian love-song in octo-genarian voices."

At this point they humped themselves in the mud and sang the following tuneless ditty:

"No constant factor in beauty is discernible.
Although the road that evolution treads is not returnable,
It has some curious twists in it, as every shape and size
And shade of female breast attestifies.
Pendulous or cumulus, pear-shaped, oval, tumu-lus.
Each one displays its beauty of depravity
In syncline, incline, outcropping or cavity.
Yet from Droxy to Feroxi
The bosom's lines are only signs
Of all the pectoral muscles' tussles
With a fairly constant factor, namely gravity."

They fell back into the mud, each lambasting his mate's nates.

V

Of course, for a time it was difficult to be certain of everything or anything. The uncertainties became almost infinite, but among the most noteworthy were: the uncertainty as to whether the catechiz-ings actually took place in any wider arena of reality than Double A's mind; the uncertainty as to whether the beatings took place in any wider arena of reality than Double A's mind; the uncer-tainty as to whether, if the beatings actually took place, they took place with sticks.

For it became increasingly obvious that neither Double A nor Gasm had hands with which to wield sticks. Yet on the other appendage, evidence ex-isted tending to show that some sort of punish-ment had been undergone. Gasm no longer resembled a human. He had grown positively torpedo-shaped. He possessed fins.

The idea of fins, Double A found to his surprise, was not a surprise to him. Fins had been uppermost in his mind for some time. Fins, indeed, induced in him a whole watery way of thinking; he was flooded with new surmises, while some of the old ones proved themselves a washout. The idea, for example, that he had ever worn dark glass optics or ebony contacts—absurd!

He groped for an explanation. Yes, he had suffered hallucinations. Yes, the whole progression of thought was unravelling and clarifying itself now. He had suffered from hallucinations. Something has been wrong in his mind. His optic centres had been off-centre. With something like clarity, he became able to map the area of disturbance.

It occurred to him that he might some time investigate this cell or tank in which he and Gasm found themselves. Doors and windows had it none. Perhaps, like him, it had undergone some vast sea change.

Emitting a long liquid sigh, Double A ascended slowly off the floor. As he rose, he glanced upward. Two men floated on the ceiling, gazing down at him.

VI

Double A floated back to his former patch of mud only to find his hands gone. Nothing could have compensated him for the loss except the growth of a long, strong tail.

His long, strong tail induced him to make another experiment—no more nor less than the attempt to foster the illusion that the tail was real by pretending there was a portion of his brain capable of activating the tail. More easily done than thought. With no more than an imaginary flick of the imaginary appendage, he was sailing above Gasm on a controlled course, ducking under but on the whole successfully ignoring the two men floating above.

From then on, he called himself Doublay and had no more truck with time or hands, or ghosts of hands and time. Though the mud was good, being above it was better, especially when Gasm could follow. They grew new talents—or did they find them?

Now the questions were no sooner asked than forgotten, for by a mutual miracle of understanding, Doublay and Gasm began to believe themselves to be fish.

And then they began to dream about hunting down the alien invaders.

VII

The main item in the laboratory was the great tank. It was sixty feet square and twenty feet high; it was half full of sea water. A metal catwalk with rails around it ran along the top edge of the tank; the balcony was reached by a metal stair. Both stair and catwalk were covered with deep rubber, and the men that walked there wore rubber shoes, to ensure maximum quiet.

The whole place was dimly lit.

Two men, whose names were Rabents and Coblison, stood on the catwalk, looking through infrared goggles down into the tank. Though they spoke almost in whispers, their voices nevertheless held a note of triumph.

"This time I think we have succeeded, Dr. Coblison," the younger man was saying. "In the last forty-eight hours, both specimens have shown less lethargy and more awareness of their form and purpose."

Coblison nodded.

"Their recovery has been remarkably fast, all things considered. The surgical techniques have been so many and so varied. Though I played a major part in the operations myself, I am still overcome by wonder to think that it has been possible to transfer at least half of a human brain into such a vastly different metabolic environment."

He gazed down at the two shadowy forms swimming around the tank.

Compassion moving him, he said, "Who knows what terrible traumata those brave souls have had to undergo? What fantasies of amputation, of life, birth and death, or not knowing what species they were."

Sensing his mood, and disliking it, Rabents said briskly, "They're over it now. They can communicate with each other—the underwater mikes pick up their language. They've adjusted well. Now they're raring to go."

"Maybe, maybe. I still wonder if we had the right—"

Rabents gestured impatiently, guessing Coblison spoke only to be reassured. He knew how proud the old man secretly was and answered him in the perfunctory way he might have answered one of the newspapermen who would be around later.

"The security of Banya Ban demanded this drastic experiment. It's a year since that alien Flaran ship 'landed' in our Western Ocean. Our submarines have investigated its remains on the ocean bed and found proof that the ship landed where it did *under control*, and was only destroyed when the aliens left it.

"You know these Flarans, Dr. Coblison—they're fish people, aquatics. The ocean is their element, and undoubtedly they have been responsible for the floods extending along our seacoast and inundating the pleasure islands of Indura. The popular press is right to demand that we fight back."

"My dear Rabents, I don't doubt they're right, but—"

"How can there be any 'buts?' We've failed to make contact with the aliens. They have eluded the most careful probes. Nor is there any 'but' about their hostile intent. Before they upset our entire oceanic ecology, we must find them out and gain the information about them without which they cannot be fought. Here are our spies, here in this tank. They have post-hypnotic training. Soon, when they're fit, they can be released into the sea to go and get that information and return with it to us. There are no 'buts,' only imperatives, in this equation."

Slowly the two men descended the metal stairway, the giant tank on their left glistening with condensation.

"Yes, it's as you say," the other agreed wearily. "I would so much like to know, though, the sensations passing through the shards of human brain embedded in fish bodies."

"It doesn't really matter—so long as they're successful," the first said firmly.

In the tank, in the twilight, the two giant sea creatures swam restlessly back and forth, readying themselves for their mission.

Sector Yellow

In a short time, Banya Ban will not have to fight alone. They have agreed to accept help from Iron Arm, the force that most nearly represents an interstellar police.

Assistance sent over such large distances has a habit of arriving years or even generations late. Unfortunately the most speedy means of transportation cannot operate over large distances. The matter transmitters that convey us so easily from one point on a globe to another are ineffective between widely spaced stars.

The reason for this is, of course, that the image at the receiving end has to be an exact replica of the article transmitted. Interstellar interference is such that the signal, even when masered, is not reliable over a distance greater than eighty light years.

During the early days of mattermitters, before this factor was fully understood, there were many accidents; a man sent across a hundred light years where cosmic activity is high can emerge from the receiver as so many kilos of shredded protein. In Starswarm, where we are accustomed to thinking in terms of thousands of light years, this factor has imposed severe limitations.

In certain sectors where the suns are set closely and the enormous expense of the mattermitters can thus be justified, they are used. One such region lies *in the thickly swarming worlds of Sector Yellow bordering the Rift. Sector Yellow lies at the hinge between the two main arms of Starswarm, sectors Diamond and Green.*

Although it is on an important trade route, Sector Yellow has a poor reputation and is avoided by the general run of humanity, though the outcasts of many societies have found a home there. It is in Sector Yellow that we find the greatest concentration of nonhuman phyla. Not only are they often unreliable, but no great dependency can be placed on the physical laws of the worlds on which they live.

All this is particularly true of Smith's Burst, the most notable intragalactic nebula of the region. So it is appropriate, if regrettable, that the narrative that follows should also be unreliable.

Before man became homo interstellar, travellers' tales were notoriously filled with exaggeration. This narrative appears to be in the tradition.

We include it because it gives a vivid glimpse of a chaotic part of our universe. The text has been somewhat abridged and some indecencies removed. It is a firsthand account of the adventures of one Jami Lancelo Lowther on the Planet Glumpalt in the Hybrid Cluster of Smith's Burst.

Internal evidence forces us to question some of the incidents related. This much, however, we know: a financier called Lowther made an illegal mattermitter journey, and a planet called Glumpalt exists, on which the Black Sun still rises.

I

A man must suffer many moments of indignity in his life, but see to it that you are never put up for sale as I was.

There I stood, propped up by two shapeless roughs, on an auction platform. I had barely recovered consciousness when I saw below me a crowd yelling prices. It was a nightmare, for the freaks around me could only have issued from a troubled sleep.

The auctioneer had the biggest head of them all. Supported less by his puny body than by four stalks, which had the power of movement like thin legs, the head itself was covered with hair, through bald patches of which glittered eyes and orifices. He was at once ludicrous and frightening.

All the people gathered around this creature were as ugly or as fantastic. None of them had the decency to own one normal head or one ordinary pair of hands. No two were alike, though many were similar. Each one had something fantastic about him: jaws or claws or maws or paws, eyes or antennae or tails.

Surveying this repellent multitude, I knew I was far from sanity and civilization and the law of Starswarm. I guessed at once that I was on one of the benighted planets in Smith's Burst.

If the crowd did not confirm this supposition, my surroundings did. The town, which I shall describe more fully later, was a ramshackle series of fortresses and villages set on little islands about which lapped a filthy lake. The name of this town, I discovered, was Ongustura, although the superstitious rabble was reluctant to name names.

The lake was circled by mountains, featureless and unwelcoming. Cloud obscured most of the sky, but the part that was clear glittered with many points of light. I knew I was somewhere where the stars lay thickly.

All this I took in before being sold.

"Let's have a rope around you, creature, and neither of us will come to harm," my purchaser said to me, leading me from the platform. In my bewilderment I noticed little, but I thought that he seemed more comely than his fellows, until later observation showed that what I thought was his head was his posterior; his face was set in what I took to be his belly.

For all that, it was a joy to hear him speak Galingua. The rest of the speech had been in some local tongue that meant nothing to me.

"Heaven be praised that you are civilized, sir—"

"Silence, you freak," he growled, interrupting me, "or I'll have your tongue tied around your wrist."

The confusion in my mind and about me was such that it took a while to realize that I was in a market square. Among the ugly mob were many who rode and many who were ridden upon, yet between one and the other there was little to choose. My master—I must call him such—climbed onto a thing like a porpoise, which talked; I was dragged up behind him, he jerked the rein, and we were off.

"Mind to right! Mind to the left!" my master called, as we jostled along. We took a street that sloped down into the water of the lake. The porpoise-thing nosed into it and bore us to another island, getting us rather wet in the process. Heaving us along another street, it stopped before a tall, dirty building.

We dismounted. My master and the porpoise argued in the local tongue until the former produced some coins as big as a saucer, which the creature slipped into a pocket in his saddle before moving off. I was led into the building.

Gloom and squalor surrounded us. May I be preserved from describing *any* structure on that foul globe! Its owner had once built a single room, covering it with a sloping roof to fend off the rains. When he needed more space, he built another room nearby, connecting them with a covered way. Over the years he had required more and more rooms as he turned his abode into a lodging house. Since no more space was available for him horizontally, he had been forced to build upward—in the most casual manner possible, for the cell (it was no more) to which my master and I ascended was made of sloping tile underfoot. It had once been the roof of the second-storey room below; no one had seen fit to alter it.

There we squatted uncomfortably, my master on a pile of rags I avoided for their smell's sake.

"Sleep, you execrable example of protoplasm!" he cried to me, tugging at the rope around my neck. "Sleep, for in only two dervs you and I set out for Anthropophagi Land. Rest while you can."

A *derv* was a fifth part of a day, a day being an *awderv* (*aw* meaning five)—but the local day was as uncertain as much else there, and an *awderv* was simply an arbitrary period of about twenty hours.

It seemed sensible to win the confidence of this creature. Were he foolish enough to trust me, my chances of escape would be increased.

"I cannot sleep for looking at you," I said. "How beautiful you are, with thost massive pincers at the end of your four arms, and that exquisite fringe of green hair—or is it moss?—down the front of your legs."

"No two are born alike," he said complacently, as if repeating an ancient saying.

"Some are more beautiful than others."

"That talk's punishable as heresy here in Ongustura," my master said, lowering his voice. "The law states each fellow is as beautiful as his neighbor."

"Then you demonstrate the stupidity of the law."

He was pleased, and by such touches I won him around to a better mood. He soon told me what I had suspected from his mastery of Galingua, that he was a traveller, a trader, moving from one part of the planet to another. The planet was called Glumpalt; he knew it to be in the intragalactic nebula called Smith's Burst; beyond that he was totally ignorant. He had never heard of matter-mitters, nor had he ever left this accursed world—nor did he ever wish to.

His name was Thrash Pondo-Pons. He was superstitious like all Glumpaltians and as vain as most of them. He looked and smelled bizarre. He had no manners, education or friends, except such as he acquired by accident—a fine representative of his entire heterogeneous race. He had many good points, although these took me longer to discover. He was brave, industrious, resolute, and had a peculiarly sweet resigned attitude towards the blows of fate, which fell as liberally on Glumpalt as elsewhere in the cosmos.

Thrash Pondo-Pons was not even remotely human. Many of his characteristics were not human. Yet I got on with him as well as I could have with a human under similar circumstances.

I did not sleep out the two dervs, nor did he. Towards the end of that time we rose and made a meal. My first food on Glumpalt! Realizing I was hungry, I set out to eat as much as I could from the communal trough set before us. Part of the dish was cooked, part raw, part still alive.

Thrash then got his cart ready. It stood behind the lodging house, a complex structure with an iron chassis and a superstructure of wood and canvas. To this, two "horses" were harnessed; one looked something like a caterpillar, one something like an elephant. I was pulled aboard and secured in the back of the cart, and off we started on what was to be a fantastic journey.

When we came to water, we embarked onto a sort of barge and, as we moved among the islands, I had time to observe Ongustura from the back of the cart. With its crazy buildings, it was most like a series of rubbish dumps, for the debris piled up to make houses covered every bit of land. How many people and things lived there could not be computed—but the place swarmed with multi-formed life.

Imagine, then, the leap my heart took when I sighted, amid one rubble pile, a great clean snout of polished metal pointing up to the clouds! There stood a spaceship, its bulk indicating that it was some kind of star freighter.

My immediate predicament had not blinded me to the possibility that I might be stranded forever on this godforsaken globe. It was so primitive that I had not dared to hope it would be on any space lane.

"Whose is the ship?" I called to Thrash.

"TransBurst Traders," he replied. "I came here to sell them skins and carcasses. They'll be off for Acrostic in ten awdervs, the day after the Black Sun sets. It'll be rising in about a week now."

Acrostic! That was the name of a planet I knew. It lay towards the edge of Smith's Burst, beyond the Hybrid Cluster in which Glumpalt belonged. Once on Acrostic, it would be comparatively easy to work back to civilization. I knew now that all my efforts must be bent on escaping from Thrash and getting onto that ship. It was my only hope.

Yet I stayed quiet, for one of Thrash's five eyes was upon me.

II

We finally reached the edge of the lake. The cart was trundled ashore, and we began to climb a twisting track that led over the mountains.

A leather halter around my neck, a rope around my waist, I walked beside Thrash as we creaked along.

"Let's hope Chance will be with us once we cross the pass," Thrash muttered. "The country is riddled with demons at this time of year. What's more, we shall pass through the realm of the Ungulph of Quilch. He's without mercy to those who come from Ongustura, for he and it are traditional enemies. Fortunately, you should be some protection to me."

"How so?"

"You have the same peculiar outward form—only

one head and four main limbs—as the Ungulph's youngest daughter."

On this remark he would not elaborate, growing more withdrawn as we climbed higher. As I stared at him, he grew two shadows.

I found I also had two shadows. Looking up, I saw the clouds had partly cleared. A pair of suns shone there, one a monstrous pink thing, like a blob of Instant Whip, the other a more powerful yellow globe. I have been on planets of binary stars before, and always curse the complications they make in the calendar.

Under their heat, we were sweating profusely by the time we reached the pass. Behind us, like a series of grimy sand castles in a pool, lay Ongustura. I could still make out the nose of the TransBurst ship.

Checking to see that I was securely tied, Thrash released his steeds from the shafts of the cart. The three of them went into some sort of magical routine to appease the anger of any local spirits who might be about. They burned reeking fat, danced, sprinkled powder over themselves, and declared that danger lay ahead.

While this mumbo jumbo went on, I had time to observe what never ceased to interest me. On Glumpalt, no distinction is made, or can be made, between homo, animal, fish, reptile or insect. There is only one great miscellaneous class, the individuals of which may have at one and the same time some of the characteristics of man, horse, crab, toad and grasshopper. Most individuals could produce by chirps, barks, twitters or twangs one of the many Glumpaltian dialects. The only valid difference between Thrash and his steeds was that the steeds had no sort of manual appendages like hands or claws, whereas he had; they were thus condemned to the life of beasts of burden—but in his conversations with them he ignored this distinction.

They finished their magic. We proceeded.

Few landmarks existed on the way ahead. Steadily we covered the miles. The custard sun set behind a wall of cloud, but the day remained bright.

"Tell us your history," Thrash said. "And make it amusing so that I and my friends may laugh aloud to scare the demons who beset our route."

So I told him my history. He translated it as I spoke, into a Glumpaltian tongue, for his friends' enjoyment.

"I am a financier," I said. "Rather, I am an entrepreneur for a loan company that is not recognized by any Starswarm government. There is a great deal of risk in all our transactions, and consequently our rates are high. I myself am frequently involved with the law in trying to save my company from loss.

"Last week I pulled off a considerable deal with the rebel government of Rolf III. I earned a vacation on New Droxy and planned to travel there by mattermitter. Being at some disagreement with the authorities, I arranged to be broadcast by an illegal beam.

"Obviously that beam was not powerful enough. Having to pass through a disturbed region of space like Smith's Burst, it must have been momentarily broken. And in consequence I materialized here!"

They failed to laugh. But from then on I was watched more closely than ever. Thrash took to wearing a great bow over his shoulder; a quiver of brass-tipped arrows hung at his side. This did not encourage me to make a sudden run for freedom. They never let me from their sight even when I fulfilled my natural functions.

Our progress was not rapid. Stopping at villages meant much delay, for an elaborate ritual had to be undergone each time before we entered the ramshackle walls. This was to exorcize wayside demons: we had to be purged of their company before those within the villages allowed us to enter. The ceremonies sometimes took a whole derv, or four hours. I was liberally daubed with a stinking white substance made from powdered shell Thrash kept in a silver casket.

In the villages, conditions were miasmic. I soon lost track of the road back to Ongustura, for there were many trails leading everywhere. To keep account of time was also impossible. Glumpalt evidently had an erratic orbit. Though I heard no more about the Black Sun for a while, the pink and yellow suns rose and sank in a manner to me quite unpredictable.

Thrash had some trouble about the route through the lands of the Ungulph of Quilch; he grew increasingly anxious about the road ahead.

On one occasion, the caterpillar-horse was pulling the cart while Thrash rode on the elephant-horse with me behind him. We came to a many-branched tree by the wayside. Raising his claw, Thrash halted us.

"Climb up that tree and say if you see anything in the way of landmarks ahead, shoe-shaped one," he ordered, turning to me.

"Unbind my hands and I will," I said.

"Don't try to escape or I spit you through on an arrow," he warned, untying my wrists.

I climbed the tree until I came to the highest branch that would bear me. Then I stared ahead and began calling loudly and anxiously.

"Oh Lord Thrash!" I bellowed. "Come back! Don't ride away from me so fast and leave me in this desolate place! I shall be lost without you! Come back!"

In puzzlement and anger Thrash called out to me from where he stood below.

"Are you out of your senses, monster-man? I am standing here. I have not moved. Come down at once!"

Taking no notice, I still cried out to him not to ride away and leave me, and so I descended the tree. When I got down and faced him, I shook my head and rubbed my eyes, feigning disbelief.

"But I saw you gallop away on your elephant-horse friend!" I exclaimed bewilderedly. "You disappeared over that hill, I'll swear!"

"Rubbish!" he said. "We never moved from this spot. Climb up again and deliver truly of what you see ahead."

Obediently I climbed the tree a second time. A second time I cried out.

"Come back, my master! You gallop away so fast! What have I done to deserve such treatment? Oh, come back, come back!"

Ignoring his shouts from below, I slid down the trunk and stood before him on the ground.

"I never moved," he said. "What's this foolishness?"

Then I burst into laughter, seizing one of his claws to show my relief.

"There's a glorious illusion, Lord Thrash. You stayed here, yet from the top of this tree I had a perfect picture of you galloping off at full speed over the nearest hill. How wonderfully comic! I beg you, climb up, climb up and see if you can't see something similar. This is a magic tree, set here for the edification of travellers by benevolent spirits. Climb up and laugh your fill!"

The face on his belly broke into a reluctant smile. Obediently he began to climb the tree. Once he was well in the tree, I jumped onto his elephant-horse.

"I am a great enchanter," I snarled into the thing's ear. "Gallop your hardest for the nearest hill or I turn you into a flaming faggot on the instant."

He set off with a start that nearly threw me and went as if pursued by devils. Turning, I saw Thrash Pondo-Pons in the top of the tree. He was pointing at me.

"This is in truth a magic tree!" he roared. "I

swear it looks as if you are galloping off for the nearest hill on my steed. The illusion is complete! Wonderful! Marvellous!"

He shook with laughter, and the tree shook with him. Soon we were over the brow of the hill.

III

I had got away, but was by no means out of my predicament. In which direction lay Ongustura I knew not. All the food I had would not nourish a cockroach; of the local language I could pronounce only a few simple words, mostly obscenities, which I had picked up from Thrash on the journey. And as if all this were not enough, both the suns were obviously determined to set at once.

My problems were soon complicated further. The elephant-horse put on the burst of speed one might expect from a creature ridden by a great enchanter. Unfortunately I was never a great horseman, and an especially fierce jolt flung me from the saddle.

Falling in short grass, I sat up in time to see my charger disappear. His flanks had been loaded with paraphernalia; the jolt that dislodged me had also shaken loose a casket of worked silver. It represented my only possession. On opening it, I found it was half-filled with the nauseous crushed-shell powder, which was worth having, since without it I could not enter any village.

An evening wind blew chill. I stood up and was aware of a curious sensation. One of my legs was lighter than the other. The ground here was broken, as if by a minor earth fault. Walking to and fro, I discovered that my whole body felt lighter when over this fault line. No doubt this unaccountable shift in weight was responsible for my fall.

Dusk was coming on. Unable to solve the mystery, I took the casket under my arm and stepped forward. After a while I saw a light ahead, and came to a hamlet inside a wooden compound.

Now this was the time to call to those within that a stranger sought shelter, and to begin the absurd magical ritual that would render me fit to enter. But the place was oddly silent. I was cold, in no mood to loiter about. The pink sun had been swallowed by the dark hills. Boldly, I pushed through the wooden gate and entered the compound.

The dwellings were the usual motley collection, made of stones or boulders, wood or mud. They huddled about me like so many old cows under blankets. The light I had seen from a distance came from a sort of beacon set in the middle of a "street" to furnish illumination for the hovels nearby.

Nobody stirred. Taking my courage into my hands, for it was growing too cold to be cowardly outdoors, I entered the dwelling into which the most light was cast. Huddled in the room were several Glumpaltians in their usual variety of shapes and sizes. They crouched motionless under rugs or skins, some snoring gently.

I crept into a rear room to seek food. There I found a barrel containing something very like salted water snails. I was debating with my stomach whether I could ever bring myself to eat them when there came the sound of footsteps in the street. Shrinking into one corner, I saw a fellow enter the house by the door I had used. I say "fellow," but he was in truth more like a crab, with eyes on stalks and several legs to walk on.

Without hesitation he came through to where I hid, seized the barrel of snails and some other food, and tucked them into the pockets of his mighty coat. It was vexing to see burgled what I had been about to steal, but I made no outcry. If this fellow was one of society's outcasts, I reasoned that he might be of more use to me than the others; and if he was off to a safe refuge with plenty of food, then I could not do better than to follow him.

This I did. The crabman went from hovel to hovel with no care for silence, adding to his load at each stop. Frost crunched beneath his feet. Desperate with cold, I snatched a thick skin off one of the sleepers; he did not stir; probably he was hibernating.

Completing his rounds, the crabman left the hamlet and set off across country at a good pace. I followed discreetly. The risk of discovery was greater now; a bright moon had risen and was racing across the sky, flooding the country with radiance.

We entered a valley, then climbed again. Around a sharp cliff, an extraordinary sight greeted me. A rainbow curtain hung across the path, reaching from the ground to about ten feet high. I was in time to see the crabman scurry through it.

The rainbow was mainly violet, red and blue, the colours subdued but perfectly clear. As I approached, the feeling of lightness again assailed me. It became more and more difficult to plant my feet on the ground or to move forward.

Now I could see that the rainbow sprang from a precipice about ten feet wide. I took a good run and cleared it easily. Landing gently, I was in time to see the crabman vanish into a little house carved in the rock.

"Stay and have a word with me!" I cried in Galingua. I did not expect him to understand; I merely wanted to see how he would react. I had a stout stick ready, reckoning I could tip him into the precipice with it if it came to a tussle.

"I have words for everyone," he replied. It was incredible to believe that this misshapen crab could speak the galaxy's tongue. Forgetting my caution, I went to his door, through which a light shone.

"Where did you learn Galingua?" I asked.

He was rummaging about in an antiquated cupboard, and answered without looking at me, as far as I could see.

"I am the Interpreter. I speak all languages. There is not a tongue talked on Glumpalt I do not know."

If this were true, I had indeed followed the right fellow.

"We could be useful to each other," I said.

"I am useful to no one, unless they can teach me a new language," he said. Now he turned to survey me. He was massive, but his shell looked fragile enough. I mustered as much confidence as possible and closed the door behind me.

"How many languages are there on Glumpalt?" I asked him.

"Two thousand and thirty-two, and I speak them all."

"Wrong! There are two thousand and thirty-three!" And I began to address him in the language of Rolf III. He was amazed. Finally he said, "We will eat and discuss this. Come sit down, Flat-eyes; we are friends."

We sat on either side of an upturned tub, on top of which he piled edibles. The more he talked, the madder I thought him, particularly as he interrupted his talk often to circle the table and me. He told me that learning languages was about all he could do. He had a freak brain; he could learn a whole new language in a week. On Glumpalt there were many languages, each province speaking a different one. So he had been taken on as interpreter at the court of the Ungulph of Quilch.

Eventually he had fallen out with the Ungulph, who had stolen his name and sent him packing. Now he lived a hermit's life without a name, known only as the Interpreter.

At the end of this farrago of facts, when I had eaten as much of the beastly food as I could, I rose.

I was trapped! Sticky threads bound me. When I grasped them, they adhered to my hands. I could not break them.

"You are my prisoner," he said. "Sit down again. You will remain here for a week, teaching me this dialect you call Rolfial. Then I will let you free again."

From what he then said, I gathered that he was less crab than spider. The threads were spun from his own entrails. When he had circled the table, he had been secretly imprisoning me.

I did not despair. The thought of the TransBurst Traders ship gave impetus to my racing brain.

"We are within seven awdervs of Ongustura," I said. "I will happily teach you Rolfial if you will take me there."

"I can learn in comfort here."

"I cannot teach you here. Your name is taken from you; I have had all my prepositions taken from me. I was on my way to collect them from a magician in Ongustura. If you will take me there, I will teach you everything but the prepositions on the journey, and those you shall willingly have when we arrive."

"Who is this magician?" he asked suspiciously.

"His name is Bywithanfrom."

"Hm. I will think on it."

So saying, he hauled himself up by a self-made thread to the rafters and dropped into a coma. Despite my discomfort, I fell asleep over the tub.

IV

When I woke, a pallid morning had dawned, and the Interpreter was up and about. He released me from my bonds, leaving only one long rope around my waist.

"We start soon," he said. "I accept your suggestion. We shall go to Ongustura, there to collect your prepositions and complete my mastery of Rolfial."

While he was preparing, I ventured outside. The

rope around my middle allowed me to go as far as the precipice. Again a feeling of lightness came over me.

Floating rather than jumping, I launched myself into the gulf. The bottom, muddy and full of stones, offered no explanation for the sensation of weightlessness it gave off. Prodding with a sharp stone, however, I dug into something solid. When I pulled at it, a fragment broke off. It looked like natural chalk.

I dropped it. At once it soared up into the air and headed towards the clouds.

Beside myself with excitement, I filled my pockets with the crumbling stuff. Soon I was so light that I would have taken off myself had I not filled other pockets with ordinary heavy stones.

I ran back into the tawdry hut, in my enthusiasm treating the Interpreter as if he were human. Releasing a chunk of the light stuff, I showed him how it shot up to the ceiling.

"It's antigravity material, occurring naturally," I exclaimed. "You have a fortune at your doorstep; don't you realize it?"

He shook his eyestalks at me in a dreadful way.

"This material occurs all over Glumpalt in small veins," he said. "But it is not touched because it is bad magic. You will die if you persist in keeping it."

I did persist. When we set out on our journey to Ongustura, my pockets were loaded with the stuff. Only a sack full of stones on my back enabled me to walk in the usual way.

Thinking back over that trek, I can laugh now, for we can make as merry over our own past hardships as over our friends' present ones. It was a mad journey! The way lay along stony tracks and barren hills; we were forever slipping down or climbing up the sides of ravines. The Interpreter on his eight legs had an easy journey; I was often dropping from fatigue.

Yet one or the other of us was talking all the time. The Interpreter imbibed his languages by a Gestalt principle obscure to me; all I had to do was chatter of this and that in Rolfial and he took it in. I cannot tell you how vexing it is, while ascending a steep slope, to have to discourse on, say, the origins of the Starswarm federation, remembering at the same time to omit all prepositions from one's sentences. My cleverness imposed a sore talk on me.

After his fashion, the Interpreter was no bad companion. Often I said something that touched off a train of thought he pursued vocally for hours. When on the subject of the creation of Glumpalt, he told me many things I wanted to know.

"The nebula you call Smith's Burst," he said, "was formed by the collision of two clouds of cosmic gas, one of them composed of antimatter. This little planet condensed out of the resultant mixture. What you call antigrav materials, that chalky stuff, is decayed AM which, when freed from its surroundings, is violently repelled by the material around it."

"Now you offer me a scientific explanation for what you previously called magic."

"Magic covers the entire cosmic system of functions," he replied. "Science covers only the small patch of that system we can rationalize." He told me how the strange composition of Glumpalt had affected the life developing upon it. The customary subdivisions of animal life never occurred. AM genes made it possible for a fish-man to produce bird-man progeny. Uncertainties of day and climate did nothing to regularize matters.

This mention of bird-men was the first I had heard of them. A derv later I saw one with my own eyes. It had begun to snow with a tranquil determination that took the heart out of me. I looked hopelessly up at the thick sky.

Poised a few feet above me was a skinny thing

with flapping wings. I saw the wings were of skin, mottled now with gooseflesh and with dangling raw pink fingers at their outer edges. The eyes of this creature, like holes scooped in mud, were fixed upon me.

I flung a stone at it.

The flying creature, rattling its obscene pinions, swerved higher through the snow.

The Interpreter tilted up his rump and shot from it a line of that sticky strand I knew so well. It sailed up and curled about the flying thing's ankle. Of all that I saw on Glumpalt, this incident stands out most vividly in my mind. The birdman lost his equilibrium, toppling backward with hoarse cries.

The poor creature made a bad landing and sat a few yards from us in the snow, shivering. When we approached, he clucked for mercy in a bizarre tongue.

He was naked except for a helmet strapped to his skull. Untidy fur covered his body from the waist down. He was pigeon-chested. His face resembled a mole's, with bristles sticking from his snout. His skin, including those disgusting wings that hung from his shoulders like two empty sacs, was blue or yellow. He looked near to death with cold and fright.

The Interpreter questioned him ferociously in the clucking tongue. He knocked the pathetic creature over into the snow before swivelling an eyeball at me.

"This is bad, friend biped," he said. "The Ungulph of Quilch is now engaged in another season of looting. If he finds me, my gravestone is made. His men are hereabouts—this creature is one of them. We must take to the nearest village and hide."

From what I had heard of the Ungulph from Thrash Pondo-Pons, I knew he would be unpleasant. I pressed on with the Interpreter, the birdman dragging along behind us, tethered by his ankle and uttering chirps of woe.

The village we arrived at was the most disgusting I had come upon. Its inhabitants took their dominant characteristic from the rabbit; they had long ears and lived underground. We underwent the usual purification rites; fortunately I still had with me the silver casket containing the purification powder that had belonged to Thrash. When we had performed the ritual in the snow, we were allowed to go with stooped shoulders down a passage into the earth.

On either side of our way ran tunnels, some only cul-de-sacs that were filled with squalling families.

"This place stinks!" I gasped. Underfoot was like a refuse heap.

"It *is* warm," replied the Interpreter. I wondered if a sense of smell existed on this forsaken planet.

The tunnel we were in seemed to be a main road. It ended in a broad cavern through which ran a river. Along the waterfront were hovels hanging onto the very edge of the water. To one of these we were led by a rabbit-man the Interpreter accosted.

We were shown a foul-smelling cupboard they called a room. Here the rabbit-man left us, taking the bird-man with him. The latter chirped in protest as he was dragged away.

"What will happen to the bird-man?" I inquired when we were alone.

"I have sold him for our night's board," said the Interpreter. "Proceed with my Rolfial lesson. We were on the subject of religions, but you will have to explain to me again what the Assumption was."

So I talked. I pictured my Rolfial words being imprisoned by that incredible brain within which two thousand other languages already lay captive. I saw them lined up like bottles gathering dust in an attic.

When we were called to feed, we descended to a room full of long-eared and variegated creatures, who paid less attention to us than to the meal. The meal tasted better than anything I had eaten on Glumpalt. It was a yellowy stew, bony and greasy perhaps, but with a savour.

"Excellent!" I said at last to my companion. "I am grateful to you for so excellent a feed."

"Direct your gratitude to the bird-man. He has provided."

"How's that?"

"Only the wings are not edible. And they can be tanned and will make someone an excellent cloak."

V

To overcome my nausea, I forced the Interpreter to take me outside. We walked up and down. Several local inhabitants were listening to a fellow with long ears and whiskers who stood on a stool to address them. His gestures were violent and excited. I asked the Interpreter what was happening.

"The talkative fellow is a politician. He says that if everyone supports him, he will banish short ears from the warren forever."

My companion, yawning furiously, dragged me back to our cupboard. Everyone else was going home. Lights were winking out, doors were closing. The underground town was preparing for hibernation.

For some while, I slept. Waking with a headache, I lay motionless. A red light filtered through the window. A noise like a pistol shot roused me.

The Interpreter lay close by me. The great shell covering most of his body had split clean across. This was the noise I had heard. As I looked, peering through the red glow, I saw his shell gape wider. Frightened now, I called to him; he did not move.

The edges of shell were wide apart and still slowly opening. I became belatedly aware of a chorus of shrieks outside. For the first time it occurred to me to wonder what the red glow was.

Thrusting my head out of the window, I saw an alarming spectacle. Sailing down the river were a number of fire rafts loaded high with burning wood. Some of them drifted to the edge of the river, where they set fire to the closely-packed houses. The screaming increased as the people ran from the flames.

Again I turned to the Interpreter; we were in danger. Shaking did not rouse him. His carapace fell off with a clatter. Beneath it I saw a new, soft shell and realized he was shedding the old one, remaining in a trance during the process.

Seizing the sticky rope that secured me, I cut it easily on the sharp edge of the old carapace. But why should I run away, when this poor bag of crab flesh was taking me to Ongustura and the Trans-Burst Traders' rocket as swiftly as possible? Alone I should be at a loss.

Smoke billowed in through the window.

Glancing out, I saw a fire raft jammed against the river bank only a few yards away, setting light to the next house. I took hold of my companion by two legs, slung him over my shoulder, and hurried from the house.

A mob seethed around the waterfront, dashing that way and this in their alarm. Through the din of their voices one oft-repeated word came to me: "Ungulph!"

Now the Ungulph's soldiers appeared. They had chosen the village for one of their raids. After the fire rafts, rafts loaded with warriors drifted down the underground river. The rabbit people fled, shrieking. I followed.

The tunnels were full of people, all rushing to escape. One could only press forward and hope to be ejected into the night. I had the Interpreter on my back and panic in my heart. At last the darkness seemed to thin. The crowds fell away ahead. The next moment I was out into the open.

At once, a crushing blow caught me over the shoulders. I fell to my knees. Looking up under the carapace I bore, I saw silhouetted against the night sky two giant soldiers of the Ungulph. Posted at the entrance to the warren-village, they each bore a mighty axe with which they cleft in two all who emerged into the open. I had escaped death only because the Interpreter lay over me and took the blow. I found he was almost cut in half; his new shell had done nothing to protect him.

I was grabbed and flung to one side, onto a pile of bodies being searched for valuables. Beyond the pile, sitting in an open tent, was a swinish fellow in robes. He sat gazing at the trinkets laid before him.

I had no doubt this was the Ungulph of Quilch. His four tusks were capped with gold, and from them hung four little bells that tinkled when he turned his great head. Bristles covered his face. His lower jaw was an immense scoop; he had a yard of underlip. Long, dark robes covered his shaggy body.

Behind him, in the tent, stood a slighter figure. It was human! It was, indeed, a beautiful girl with dark, short-cropped hair. If this was the Ungulph's daughter, I had heard of her from Thrash.

I lay where I was, shocked by the Interpreter's death as much as anything. When my wits returned, dawn was breaking. The sky along one stretch of the horizon grew suddenly pale; a blazing white sun appeared.

Jumping up, I plunged down the mound of bodies. I ran past the Ungulph's tent and towards open country. The Ungulph's men instantly gave chase. Several bird-men took off and flew after me.

I would have escaped but for the abyss!

I pulled up on its very edge. There I stood shuddering, for I had almost plunged in. Before me lay a great gorge thousands of feet deep, its sides so sheer as to be unclimbable. I turned, but my pursuers were upon me, and I was hauled struggling before the Ungulph, who came striding up to inspect me.

Knowing it to be useless to ask such a swine for mercy, I took the opposite tack.

"So, Ungulph, you come before me to ask for mercy!" I cried in Galingua, though my voice shook. "I planned to lead your men into this great abyss of mine, but repented at the last moment. Let me go free or I will cause my abyss to open still further and swallow you all."

The Ungulph's savage face regarded me. Then he turned around and bellowed so that his four bells shook. His daughter timidly answered him. He barked at her; she replied and turned to me.

"My father, the Ungulph, does not speak Galingua; he asks you to speak in the local court tongue."

"I am the great magician Bywithanfrom," I declared. "I speak in what language I prefer. Who else speaks Galingua here?"

"Only I, sir."

"What is your name, fair one?"

"I am dark, sir, and my name is Chebarbar."

"Tell your father my abyss will devour him unless he lets me go."

When this was translated, the Ungulph gave a bellow of rage. His four hooves pawed the ground. Then he rushed forward and seized me by the waist. For a second I hung upside down—then he flung me forward into the abyss.

A dying man sees and knows many things. Among all the terrible details that stood out in my mind, one in particular was clear: as I plunged down, some stones fell too.

My descent slowed. I began to float up again. The AM materials and the ballast had lain forgotten in my pockets; as I fell, some of the ballast dropped free, saving my life. Buoyed by the AM material, I rose again, righting myself as I went.

My head appeared over the lip of the drop. A groan came from the ragged crowd. As one man, they fell to the ground, the Ungulph and Chebarbar with them, and grovelled with superstitious awe. This gave me a chance to scramble to safety and weigh my pockets with fresh stones. Then I went to Cherbarbar, helped her to her feet, and motioned to her father to stand.

"Tell you father the Ungulph," I said, "that despite his wickedness I bear him no malice, for he can do me no harm. If he will provide me with a steed, I will leave him in peace."

She repeated this in her own tongue. I was nervous and uneasy. Still, I had to get away and find a guide and interpreter to lead me to Ongustura. While I worried, the Ungulph grunted.

"My father the Ungulph says he regrets trying to harm so great a magician. He will furnish you with a steed. He will do anything you desire for the benefit of your great magic. He needs protection from his enemies."

"He is a wise man," I said. I thought rapidly. Chebarbar was hardly as pretty as I had believed at first. She had a snub nose, freckles, and uneven teeth—but I was fortunate that she had a normal face at all. She seemed intelligent and not too disagreeable; her figure was good. I spoke again, producing from my pack the silver powder casket I had taken from Thrash.

"Tell your father the Ungulph that this casket is powerful magic. The thing it contains is what the most contented man on Glumpalt needs. It is something mightier than the whole universe. It is what will save the Ungulph even if he is faced with inevitable death. Tell him that he may have this casket and all it contains if I may have you, Chebarbar, in exchange."

Her voice faltered as she translated this.

By now we had about us a jostling multitude of
half-men in all varied shapes and sizes that made
up the Ungulph's legions. I hated them for the cruel
way they had destroyed the warren-village. They
made me more determined than ever to get to
Ongustura quickly.

Chebarbar turned back and addressed me. She
was very pale.

"My father the Ungulph says that since I am a
woman I am of little value to him. He will happily
exchange me for the magic casket, if it holds what
you say."

"It contains just what I say. Tell him to open it
only in emergency."

Already a steed was being brought forward. It
was striped like a tiger, though it had the horn of a
rhinoceros and six legs. A ladder was set at its
flank. I mounted, pulling up Chebarbar and setting her before me.

When I whacked the creature's behind with a
sort of paddle affixed to the saddle for that purpose, it burst immediately into a gallop—much to
my relief. The soldiery fell back to let it through.
Bearing away from the abyss, we headed for a
track leading towards wooded country. I kept glancing back to see if we were pursued.

"Why do you look back so often?" Chebarbar
protested. "My father the Ungulph will not follow
unless you tricked him."

"I am afraid he may open the casket. It is empty,
Chebarbar."

"Then what does it contain that the most contented man on Glumpalt needs?"

"A contented man needs nothing."

"What is in it mightier than the universe?"

"Nothing is mightier than the universe."

"What is in it that will save my father from
inevitable death?"

"Nothing can save a man from inevitable death. And that is what the casket contains—nothing!"

I saw that her shoulders were heaving. I regretted having played a trick on her father; then I realized that she was not crying, but laughing. It was the first pleasing laughter I had heard since materializing in Smith's Burst.

VI

When we had put some distance between us and the Ungulph, I let the tiger-rhino rest. We stopped by a brook amid a clump of trees and climbed down.

"I must have a drink," I said, dropping to the ground beside the brook. One of the trees lifted its root from the brook and squirted me with a jet of water. Chebarbar laughed. She explained that these trees were semi-sentient, capable of moving at will along a moisture supply. They had used a typical way of defending that supply.

I moved to a free section of the brook; there we drank and held a council of war. We had no food; my time was running out, making it imperative to reach Ongustura without further delay. Chebarbar told me she thought we could be no more than three days from the city, but confessed that she did not know the way. Her father had an old rivalry with the place, never visiting it except to attack its outskirts.

This news, just when success was almost within my reach, flung me into great depression. I buried my face in my hands and groaned. To my surprise, Chebarbar put an arm around my shoulders.

"Don't be unhappy," she said. "I cannot bear to see a brave man despair. I think I have something that may comfort you."

Releasing me, she began to untie the cord that confined her breast to her tunic.

"This is most womanly—" I began, but she was fishing out a small, dagger-shaped talisman that hung by a chain around her neck. She dangled the bauble before me.

"With this we can summon Squexie Oxin. It will surely help us when it sees this talisman."

I asked the obvious question, and she told me that her father the Ungulph had long ago saved the Squexie Oxin from death. Recognizing it as a useful ally, he had given it a castle in his lands; there it lived in isolation, although it would come forth to aid the Ungulph when summoned by talisman.

"Squexie Castle is only a short way from here," Chebarbar explained. "I will take you there, and then the Squexie will take us to Ongustura, protecting us all the way."

I jumped up, ready to be moving. The Ungulph's daughter added, "There are two hindrances to the plan. In the first place, the Squexie must not discover who I am, or it would deliver me forcibly back to my father. But it is hardly likely to find out, since it has never seen me."

"And the other snag?"

"The Squexie only becomes available when the Black Sun rises. Fortunately, by the look of the sky, that will not be long now."

I squinted upward. The dazzling white sun had already passed its zenith, though I judged it to be some hours from setting. The yellow and the pink-custard suns had risen again without my knowing. Between them, the three suns had driven every cloud from the sky; it was uncomfortably hot. The nearby tree-things ambled along by the brook, squirting water over themselves.

Recalling what Thrash Pondo-Pons had said about the TransBurst ship lifting off the day after the Black Sun set, I asked Chebarbar, "How long will the Black Sun remain above the horizon? We have to be in Ongustura when it sets, or very shortly after."

"It depends," she said. "The Black Sun's orbits are so irregular that my father's astronomers cannot compute them, for they are controlled by a magician in a far country."

"Tell your father's astronomers to buy themselves a telescope," I growled, climbing up into the saddle.

Chebarbar snuggled up in front of me and we were off, the girl pointing out the way. The landscape became almost pretty. We passed through great plantations of holly, with berries the size and colour of oranges. Indeed, they tasted quite like oranges, except for an unpleasant tang about them that Chebarbar said was neon, an inert gas tapped from the air by the plants' sharp leaves.

As we ate, we heard people approaching. Entering painfully into the holly thicket, we persuaded our steed to lie down, and lay beside him ourselves. Some of the Ungulph's men appeared; Chebarbar learned from what they were saying that they searched for her; she clung tightly to me. . . .

At last we picked ourselves up and went on.

Beyond the plantation the ground rose. Mounting the incline, we found at the top of the lip of a shallow crater perhaps a mile in diameter.

I gazed at it in awe, for it was an impressive, though dreary, sight. An island stood in the middle of the crater, and on this island stood a castle built, as it seemed, of a random pile of flaking slate. It had no regular shape, no windows, no towers. Its plane surfaces were as dull as death.

"The castle of the Squexie Oxin," Chebarbar said, clinging to my arm.

There was no way of getting to the ghastly castle. The island on which it stood was surrounded with a sort of oily water that filled the crater to its lip. There was no bridge.

Everything about us was absolutely still, the holly plantation behind, the great, bright landscape ahead. It might all have been a weird, meaningless painting, quite without life, but for the waters of the crater. They bubbled and moved like a mindless creature heaving in its sleep. In one place in particular, in a line stretching from rim to island, the liquid milled and tumbled.

Diving in and out of this stuff, flying, then diving again, were strange birds like plucked pelicans. From the eminence on which we stood we heard their desolate cries.

We stood there in a kind of trance—and so were easily surrounded by the Ungulph's men, who burst from the holly bushes. Ten of them, miscellaneous-shaped brutes, stood there, waving tentacles, claws or swords at us. This time I knew I would need more than cunning to save us from death.

I was seized before I could move. My hands were pulled behind my back by a sort of ox-head insect who stank of fish. Chebarbar was also seized, and a rough paw clapped across her mouth to stop her screams.

Yet the screams went on. The creature who held me drew a great sword and pointed it at my chest. Then he, too, as the others were doing, paused to see who screamed. It was one of the Ungulph's men. His shaking claw went to the horizon beyond the Squexie's castle.

Into the bright sky there was growing a great fan of blackness. At its edges it was a pallid grey, in the centre it was as dark as midnight. Though the three suns still burned in the sky, they had no effect on that segment of night.

The impression this produced on the Ungulph's men was immediate. They let go of us and turned to run for shelter in the plantation. Chebarbar and I were miraculously free again.

"The Black Sun's rising!" Chebarbar cried, and

she too would have run away in panic had I not grasped her tightly.

"Now we can call on the Squexie," I said.

In their haste to get away the soldiers had dropped a sword, a bundle of disgusting food, a primitive lantern and a cloak of skins. Picking up the cloak, I put it around Chebarbar, who shivered though it was still hot. I thrust the sword through my belt, hung the lantern over my shoulder, and kicked the food away.

The birds in the crater had fallen silent. All was quiet everywhere. That great black fan was spilling over the horizon into the sky.

Over the crater's oily contents a thick mist was forming. Colour whirled in it, so that I was reminded of the rainbow curtain that stood before the Interpreter's house; this made me think that if there were AM material in the crater, it would probably cause the curious disturbance of the waters. Proof of this theory seemed to be that the mist was especially dense over the turbulent strip. As the sky grew darker, the mist became thicker and brighter.

Now more than half the sky had turned ashy grey or else completely black. The three suns still shone, but their power had left them. They were as useless as balloons against the encroaching dark.

Then the Black Sun rose over the horizon!

Just for a moment I saw it clearly by the light of the other suns. It was a great sooty ball, crammed with darkness, radiating blackness. A chilly wind swept the land. Though the other three suns still burned in the sky, they were fast disappearing. Everything turned to night.

Never tell me you have seen a fearful sight until you have stood on Glumpalt and watched the Black Sun rise!

It absorbs all light like blotting paper, and an intense cold prevails. The explanation of this unique phenomenon soon occurred to me. Bearing in mind the origins of Smith's Burst, it became obvious that this monstrous, impossible sun was a ball of antimatter of such strength that even its visible emissions were of reverse polarity.

The darkness that embraced us was complete. Shivering, I pulled the primitive lantern from my shoulder and attempted to light it.

It gave forth no light. Only the fact that I burned my finger on it assured me that it was functioning. The AM radiations of the Black Sun had blanketed it entirely. Though I held it before my eyes until my eyebrows singed, I could see nothing.

Yet a light was visible ahead of us.

Seizing Chebarbar's hand and the bridle of the tiger-rhino, I ventured cautiously to the lip of the dark crater.

The thick mist that spanned the water had frozen solid. Glowing with many hues, it illuminated its own way over the waters. No doubt a certain AM content explained its luminosity.

"A way to Squexie Oxin," Chebarbar murmured. "I told you it was available only when the Black Sun rose. Come, I am not afraid."

For myself, I could not say as much. At any time I would have been loath to visit that frowning castle; at this forbidding midnight, doubly so. Moreover, I hated to trust myself to that fragile bridge. As we stepped onto it, it groaned in protest.

Leaving our steed on the bank with instructions to remain, we ventured forward. Once we were onto the bridge, it was steady enough, being of the consistency of firm snow. We sank up to our ankles in it but no more.

Thus we came to the island and to the castle of the Squexie. As we reached it, a slab of it fell inward. A piping voice uttered words that Chebarbar translated to me as "welcome." We passed in, Chebarbar swinging her talisman, and found a fire, giving forth warmth and light. The flames came from a sort of trough, beneath which a pipe ran down through the floor. I guessed that some sort of oil was being burned—an oil possibly from the crater, containing AM matter, or else it would have been powerless to pierce the Black Sun's darkness. Before this fire stood the Squexie Oxin.

"We greet you!" Chebarbar said, or words to that effect.

She was greeting what I first mistook for a giant Christmas tree. The castle seemed to have only one room, and this tree seemed to be the only thing in the room. Regarding it more closely, I saw that its shaggy texture resembled a cactus covered with spikes. Even as I looked, it fell apart.

It disintegrated into hundreds of identical logs, each the size of a rolled hearth rug, each covered with the spikes. Most of these logs contented themselves with milling about our feet; one stood on end and sprouted a sort of flower that assumed lips and ears. It conversed with Chebarbar.

While they talked, one of the logs inspected me, rubbing my leg with its spikes. These were fleshy and not particularly sharp. The feeling nauseated me so much that I gave the log a kick. Every log twitched in sympathy; the ones nearest me blossomed forth with mouths and squealed in protest.

So I learned that the Squexie was a sort of Gestalt entity, all its parts serving a greater whole. This did not surprise me. Nothing surprised me. I began again feverishly thinking of the comfort of a bunk on a TransBurst ship.

At last Chebarbar finished talking.

"Well, does this thing help us?" I demanded.

"For the sake of the Ungulph of Quilch, the Squexie will take us to Ongustura. It seems to have very little regard for you; you would be advised not to molest it again."

The Squexie informed us it was ready to go, and shortly we were being bundled out of the castle.

We crossed the frozen bridge, the logs bounding along all around us.

To my surprise and delight, we found the tiger-rhino still waiting in the crater rim. Chebarbar and I climbed onto it with cries of affection; it was like meeting an old friend again! Also, it solved a severe problem. In this unnatural blackness, the Squexie—obviously composed in part of AM material—could see as easily as we see in a normal day. It needed no light. But we did, and we had none. The way to Ongustura would have been hell had it not been for the tiger-rhino, which seemed to pick its way through the impenetrable black by divine instinct.

Almost at once, another quarrel developed—or rather the Squexie developed it. His high-pitched voice sounded from lips ranged all around us.

"What's it raving about now? Let's get moving!" I snapped.

"The Squexie says it only offered to take two of us to Ongustura—not three. Accordingly, it will not take us at all."

"My godly galaxy! Tell him we are not three, nor two, but one. Together we make a creature called a Syllabub, a Gestalt beast with magical properties."

This rubbish was translated to the Squexie, who mercifully swallowed it. We moved on. It seemed a terrible pity to me that such a marvellous creature as the Squexie should in all its multitude of parts be unable to muster the intelligence of a monkey.

Nevertheless, on our cold and tedious journey, I did manage to extract some information from it. In particular I was interested to learn more about the behaviour of antimatter. Hitherto I had thought that a violent explosion resulted when it came into contact with ordinary matter. Although the Squexie knew little and cared less about the origins of Smith's Burst, it too accepted that this was what had happened originally. But it said there was a third force present on Glumpalt called "noggox."

"Tell it that all matter must have either a positive or negative charge," I instructed Chebarbar.

She translated its reply.

"The Squexie says that between plus numbers and minus numbers lies a point of neutrality called 'nought' or 'zero.' This point exists also in matter, though it is rare, and it is called 'noggox.' It can act as a binding agent between anti and ordinary matter."

I fell silent. Chunks of the AM stuff were still in my pocket. I knew I had only to get them and my knowledge back to civilization and I could become rich enough to buy Glumpalt many times over. But what would you do with a hell like Glumpalt?!

Such speculations, and two breaks for sleep, when Chebarbar and I huddled close, were almost our only distractions on that journey. An AM moon spun across the sky, giving some welcome light, and was too quickly gone. Apart from the stray moon we had one other source of light, though it was only occasional and weak. We journeyed past several plantations of the orange-bearing hollies. The neon they contained had evidently an anti-matter element that made them shine with a faint, ghostly glow.

As we rode on, I became rather tired, and called a brief halt. Just a short distance away from our resting place ran a tiny stream. On its nearer bank stood one tall and ancient tree. Hoping it was not a tree-being, such as I had encountered earlier, I ran to the stream for a drink of water. Sure enough, the tree lifted a taproot from the water and squirted me. The liquid was freezing; it stopped me dead in my stride. I panicked for the moment and thought that my only escape was to climb swiftly into its branches.

I was frozen from the wetting I had got. A cool breeze stirred, making me shiver uncontrollably.

Hoping to warm my hands at least, I unhitched the primitive lantern from my shoulder and lit it. Its glow was so gratifying that only after some while did I observe the light to be not only warming but illuminating me!

VII

Amazed, I stared up. Many stars, the luridly complex constellations of Smith's Burst, shone down on me. Ghostly forms of the distant Glumpaltian landscape were again visible. The Black Sun had set! The relief of being rid of that stygian gloom was great—and rudely shattered. Angry shouts below made me look down. I was discovered. Too late, I doused my wick; I had already given myself away.

My tree was besieged. Nor was that all. Squexie and the Ungulph's soldiers stood peaceably side by side, all their belligerence directed at me. A great fire was being kindled near the plantation. By it I saw the demon king figure of the Ungulph of Quilch himself; the caps of his four tusks sparkled.

Cupping my hands, I shouted down to Chebarbar and asked her what had happened.

"Alas, we are lost!" she cried. "My father the Ungulph has just arrived on the scene. He has shown the Squexie *his* talisman and told that treacherous creature who I am. He says I must be killed for what he calls my desertion. The Squexie has turned against us."

Though my thoughts raced, I could think of nothing to say—I, who had always hoped my last words would be memorable.

"Do something!" she called. "In a minute they will have you down from there, and kill us both."

"Don't worry," I said. "Tell your father that I will come down and spin my sword in the air. If it lands with its point in the earth, he shall kill me personally; if it lands flat, his gallant soldiers shall have the honour of tearing me into little pieces."

When this was translated, a roar of excitement rose from the watchers. They obviously regarded this fancy with delight. Almost with love, the Ungulph beckoned me to descend. My offer was accepted.

Trembling with cold and tension, I climbed down the tree and landed among the motley rabble. They moved aside for me with some show of respect. When I drew my sword, the mutter swelled in volume, and they pressed closer. I cleared myself a circle, taking care that Chebarbar, who was held firmly on her mount, should be near its circumference.

I waved my sword.

"Here it goes!" I cried. "Watch it!"

Though they did not understand, the exhortation was unnecessary. Every eye followed that glittering blade as it rose, turning over and over; every face was upturned to follow its course. Since I had taken the precaution, before descending the tree, of tying a small chunk of AM material to the weapon, I reckoned the sword would continue to climb for ten seconds and take twice as long to come down. I could use those ten seconds.

As the eyes turned upward, glued to that fateful weapon, I ran for it.

The wretch holding the tiger-rhino's bridle scarcely noticed as I snatched it from him. Leaping into the saddle, I applied the paddle hard. Our brave beast shot forward so rapidly that Chebarbar and I were almost thrown off. A moment later we had broken through the crowd and were away.

In another moment the whole mob was screaming after us.

VIII

Chebarbar and I could only hang on tightly and hope that our steed would increase the lead he had over the rest of the field. We had no idea of direction. We could but hope.

We were lucky. The flat terrain soon turned into an incline up which the six-footed tiger-rhino moved easily. Small rocky hills loomed around us; the way grew so narrow that our pursuers were forced to proceed in single file, to their great confusion.

We trotted through a pass and began to descend. From then on our followers gave up the chase. They camped there, on the heights; during part of our descent we saw their fires burning above us. The Ungulph's men and the Squexie together made a formidable body of creatures; gradually more and more points of fire, diminished by distance, sprang up, until a half-circle glittered like a tiara over our heads.

Although we were safe from pursuit, trouble, my constant companion on Glumpalt, had not forsaken us. Dawn was on its way, and ahead of us through the paling light I discerned a considerable town filling the valley. Chebarbar and I—and the tiger-rhino, for that matter—needed nourishment and rest. Since we had no magical powder with which to perform the usual absolution ceremony, we had to get into the town unobserved.

The town—like every other town on Glumpalt—was a rubbish dump. The only difference here was that the rubbish-houses were separated into islands of rubbish by the typically wide dust tracks. In the tired light of dawn, we had no trouble entering and finding safety.

Chebarbar sold her talisman to a foul old woman at an old stall. With the proceeds we hired ourselves an unsanitary cupboard of a room and bought ourselves food.

Eating ravenously—nothing could turn my stomach now—we stared out of our tiny windows. Hills ringed the town; on their heights we could just make out fires and the figures of men. The Ungulph and the Squexie were still there; it looked as if they had the place surrounded and were intending to attack it as they had attacked the warren-village.

Above the hills rose the yellow sun, striking brightly onto the muddle about us. Any hope I might have drawn from it was dashed by my knowledge that this was the day the TransBurst Traders' ship would be leaving for Acrostic and other civilized ports. How long before the next one would call, or how far away Ongustura was, I knew not.

"Don't be so gloomy!" Chebarbar cried, taking my hand. "Here we are both safe and together."

Absently, I stroked her hair. I had never told her I came from a distant planet and intended to return there unaccompanied as soon as possible.

"We are the same shape and colour," she said. "Why don't you kiss me?" We clung passionately.

The floor moved, the whole building shook. For a moment, I thought these were illusions produced by emotional strain. Then we ran to the window, in time to see a nearby collection of houses collapse into a column of dust. Over the distant heights a puff of smoke hung.

"My father is bombarding the city!" Chebarbar cried.

"With artillery?"

"Yes, indeed. He has half a dozen good cannons imported from a distant world."

"I never knew there would be any such weapons on Glumpalt. Why didn't you tell me before?"

She looked furious. Her mouth tightened at each corner. "I didn't tell you because you never asked me! You ask me nothing about anything but immediate necessities. Though I have followed you and helped you, you have taken absolutely no interest in me. How do you think I feel, eh?"

By a happy turn of fate I was spared having to

reply, for the building collapsed beneath our feet. Though we had suffered nothing like a direct hit, the house was so haphazardly constructed that the distant shock tumbled it. Chebarbar and I were on the first floor; three upper storeys descended upon us.

It was alarming, but little more dangerous than being bombarded by a pack of cards. The worst part was being half-stifled by dust.

Dizzily, I sat up, stood up, and then pulled Chebarbar up after me. We climbed from the debris. Another building on our left fell slowly as we passed. Glancing back, I spotted the enemy close behind. In my bones I felt the end was near.

Pounding through the dust, we rounded another corner.

Bright, light, trebly blessed, the sweet slender snout of an interplanetary freighter pierced the sky ahead. My heart leaped in joy and astonishment.

"Come on!" I cried.

The ship stood behind a wall eight feet high. Double gates bearing the legend TRANSBURST TRADERS were firmly closed. Over them glared a red notice: BLAST OFF IMMINENT.

The Glumpaltian horde swept around the corner behind us. Wildly emptying all my pockets of stones, I found I had only two sizable chunks of AM matter left. Tucking them under my armpits, I seized Chebarbar again, and with an enormous jump, cleared the wall.

Officials—wonderful, symmetrical officials—came up at once. I explained who I was; I gave them my galactic Credit Card, which stood high enough to make them welcome me as an unexpected passenger.

"Well, you'd better get aboard, sir," the bursar said. "Everything's ready for countdown. We've had clearance."

"I thought your Glumpaltian-routed freighter only called at Ongustura," I remarked.

He stared at me curiously. "This *is* Ongustura," he said.

I was flabbergasted. "But the islands ... the lake ..."

"Oh, didn't you recognize the place with the tide out? For about a fortnight after the rising of the Black Sun, Ongustura is left high and dry, as you see it at present. Now you'd better get aboard with your lady."

Chebarbar was sobbing. She clung to my dusty shirt, talking almost incoherently.

"I cannot come with you, my dearest. The magic of this ship is too powerful for me. If I entered it, I should die! You know I love you—yet I cannot, cannot come!"

There was nothing I could say. This was as well, since I had been about to explain tactfully that I was unable to take her. Mutely, I pressed one of the two chunks of AM into her palm; it would help the quick-witted girl to buy her way out of future trouble.

"Weep not, Chebarbar," I said, kissing her nose. "Time heals all things."

Smarting under the cliché, I climbed the freighter's ramp. The smell of canned air ahead was like perfume. Just before entering the air lock I turned to look back at the weeping Chebarbar.

Without surprise I noticed that her tears were falling upward towards the tatterdemalion clouds.

Sector Azure

Even in a survey of contemporary Starswarm so brief as this, it would be absurd not to look at the most used form of galactic transportation.

The mattermitters of Sector Yellow and the Burst, or the leisurely light-pushers that are popular in remote regions like sectors Grey or Violet, carry between them only fifteen per cent of the galaxy's traffic. Small ferry ships and freighters such as those operated by TransBurst Traders account for another eighteen per cent. The rest of the tonnage, goods or passenger, plunges through phase space in FTL (faster-than-light) ships.

The history of the starships is too well known for us to need to go into it here. Many civilizations go through phases in their development when their most typical transport is the oxcart, the stagecoach, or some kind of train. Particularly in their obsolescent stages, these forms of transport excite much affection.

But the FTL ships are most loved of all. They have taken many forms. Always they are just developing or becoming obsolete in some parts of Starswarm. We know that Dansson and the Fire Planets of Sector Diamond cut themselves off from the rest of the galaxy during Eras 83, 84 and 85, and forbade all movement by FTL to or from their planets.

Such post-technological epochs are common. They pass—indeed, under the Theory of Multigrade Super-

*annuation, they must pass. Then the FTL ships roar
back.*

*The following narrative deals with an incident in
Sector Azure, where they are developing new (for
them) braking systems for their ships. The story,
however, does not concern technicalities. It shows
what can happen to human character when influ-
enced by new technologies.*

*If you will, you can regard it as a study in a new
(for Azure) perversion. Or you may prefer to think of
it as an example of the old (for Azure) problem of
where a man should direct his love.*

Murrag lay on the ground to await consummation.
It was less than five minutes away, and it would
fall from the air.

The alarms had sounded near and distant. Their
echoes had died from the high hills of Region Six.
Stretched full length on the edge of a grassy cliff,
Murrag Harri adjusted the plugs in his ears and
laid his fume mask ready by his side.

Everything was calm and silent now, the whole
world silent. And in him there was a growing tension, as strange and ever delightful as the tensions
of love.

He raised oculars to his eyes and peered into the
valley, where lay the Flange, that wide and forbidden highway down which the starships blazed.
Even from his elevation, he could hardly discern
the other side of the Flange; it ran east-west right
round the equator of Tandy Two, unbroken and
unalterable, an undeviating—he'd forgotten the
figure—ten, was it, or twelve, or fifteen miles wide.
In the sunlight, the innumerable facets of the Flange
glittered and moved.

His glasses picked out the mountains on the
south side of the Flange. Black and white they
were, gnawed as clean as a dead man's ribs under
the abrasion of total vacuum.

*   *   *

"I must bring Fay here before she goes back to Earth," he said aloud. "Wonderful, wonderful." Assuming a different tone, he said, "There is terror here on Tandy's equator, terror and sublimity. The most awesome place in Starswarm. Where vacuum and atmosphere kiss: and the kiss is a kiss of death! Yes. Remember that: 'The kiss is a kiss of death.'"

In his little leisure time, Murrag was writing—he had been ever since I first met him—a book about Tandy Two as he experienced it. Yet he knew, he told me, that the sentences he formed there on the hill were too highly coloured, too big, too false. Under his excitement, more truthful images struggled to be born.

While they struggled, while he lay and wished he had brought Fay with him, the starship came in.

This! This was the moment, the fearsome apocalyptic moment! Unthinking, he dropped his oculars and ducked his head to the earth, clinging to it in desperate excitement with all his bones from his toes to his skull.

Tandy Two *lurched*.

The FTL ship burst into normal space on automatic control, invisible and unheard at first. Boring for the world like a metal fist swung at a defenceless heart, it was a gale of force. It was brutality . . . but it skimmed the Flange as gently as a kiss brushes a lover's cheek.

Yet so mighty was that gentleness that for an instant a loop of fire was spun completely around Tandy Two. Over the Flange, a mirage flickered: a curious elongated blur that only an educated retina could take for the after-image of a faster-than-light ship chasing to catch up with its object. Then a haze arose, obscuring the Flange. Cerenkov radiations flickered outward, distorting vision.

The transgravitic screens to the north of the Flange—on Murrag's side of it, and ranged along the valley beneath his perch—buckled but held, as they always held. The towering BGL pylons were bathed in amber. Atmosphere and vacuum roared at each other from either side of the invisible screens. But as ever, the wafer-thin geogravitics held them apart, held order and chaos separate.

A gale swept up the mountainsides.

The sun jerked wildly across the sky.

All this happened in one instant.

And in the next moment it was deepest night.

Murrag dug his hands out of the soft earth and stood up. His chest was soaked with sweat, his trousers were damp. Trembling, he clamped his fume mask over his face, guarding himself against the gases generated by the FTL's passage.

Tears still ran down his face as he limply turned to make his way back to the highland farm.

" 'Kiss of death, embrace of flame . . . ' " he muttered to himself as he climbed aboard his tractor; but still the elusive image he wanted did not come.

In a fold of hills facing north lay the farmhouse, burrowed deeply into the granite just in case of accidents. Murrag's lights washed over it. Its outhouses were terraced below it, covered pen after covered pen, all full of Farmer Dourt's sheep, locked in as always during entry time; not a single animal could be allowed outside when an FTL came down.

Everything lay still as Murrag drove up in his tractor. Even the sheep were silent, crouching mutely under the jack-in-a-box dark. Not a bird flew, not an insect sparked into the lights; such life had almost died out during the hundred years the Flange had been in operation. The toxic gases hardly encouraged fecundity in nature.

Soon Tandy itself might rise to shine down on its earthlike second moon. The planet Tandy was a gas giant, a beautiful object when it rose into Tandy Two's skies, but uninhabitable and unapproachable. Tandy One, equally, was not a place for human beings. But the second satellite, Tandy Two, was a gentle world with mild seasons and an oxygen-nitrogen atmosphere. People lived on Tandy Two, loved, hated, struggled, aspired there as on any of the multitudinous civilized planets in Sector Azure, but with this difference: that because there was something individual about Tandy Two, there was something individual about its problems.

The southern hemisphere of Tandy Two lay life-less under vacuum; the northern existed mainly for the vast terminal towns of Blerion, Touchdown and Ma-Gee-Neh. Apart from the cities, there was nothing but grassland—grass and lakes and sili-cone desert stretching to the pole. And by courtesy an occasional sheep farm was allowed on the grasslands.

"What a satellite!" Murrag exclaimed, climbing from the tractor. Admiration sounded in his voice. He was a curious man, Murrag Harri—but I'll stick to fact and let you understand what you will.

He pushed through the spaced double doors that served the Dourt farmstead as a crude air lock when the gases were about. In the living-eating-cooking complex beyond, Col Dourt himself stood by the CV watching its colours absently. He looked up as Murrag removed his face mask.

"Good *evening*, Murrag," he said with heavy joc-ularity. "Great to see so nice a morning followed by so nice a night without so much as a sunset in between."

"You should be used to it by now," Murrag mur-mured, hanging his oculars with his jacket in the A–G cupboard. After being alone in the overwhelm-ing presence of Tandy, it always took him a mo-ment to adjust to people again.

"So I should, so I should. Fourteen earth years and I still see red to think how men have bollixed about with one of God's worlds. Thank heaven we'll be off this crazy moon in another three weeks! I can't wait to see Droxy, I'm telling you."

"You'll miss the grasslands and the open spaces."

"So you keep telling me. What do you think I am? One of my sheep! Just as soon—"

"But once you get away—"

"Just a minute, Murrag!" Dourt held up a brown hand as he cocked his eye at the CV. "Here comes Touchdown to tell us if it's bedtime yet."

Murrag halted on the way upstairs to his room. He came back to peer into the globe with the shepherd. Even Hoc the house dog glanced up momentarily at the assured face that appeared in the bright bowl.

"CVA Touchdown talking," the face said, smiling at its unseen audience. "The FTL ship *Droffoln* made a safe and successful entry on the Flange some three hundred and twenty miles outside Touchdown station. As you can see from this live shot, passengers are already being met by helicar and taken to the FTL port in Touchdown. The *Droffoln* comes from Ryvriss XIII in Sector Maroon. You are looking at a typical Ryvrissian now. He is, as you observe, octipedal.

"We will bring you news and interviews with passengers and crews when all the occupants of the FTL have undergone revival. At present they remain under light-freeze.

"We go now to Chronos-Touchdown for the revised time check."

The assured face gave way to a shaggy one. Behind it, the untidy computing room of this astronomical department greeted viewers. The shaggy face smiled. "As yet we have only a rough scheme for you. It will, as usual, take a little while to feed accurate figures into our pressors, and some reports have still to come in.

"Meanwhile, here is an approximate time check. The FTL ship entered Flange influence at roughly 1219 hours 47–66 seconds today, Seventeenday of Cowl Month. Impetus-absorption thrust Tandy through approximately 108–75 degrees axial revolution in approximately 200 milliseconds. So the time at the end of that very short period became roughly 1934 hours 47–66 seconds.

"Since that was about twenty-four and a half minutes ago, the time to which everyone in Touchdown zone should set their watches and clocks is ... coming up ... 1959 hours and 18 seconds ... Now! I repeat, the time is now 1959 hours, one minute to eight o'clock at night, plus 18 seconds.

"It is still, of course, Seventeenday of Cowl.

"We shall be back to bring you more accurate information on the time in another two hours."

Dourt snorted and switched the globe off. It slid obediently out of sight into the wall.

"Here I've just had my midday bite," he growled, "and there's Bes upstairs putting the kids to bed!"

"That's what happens on Tandy Two," Murrag replied, edging from the room. Without wishing to seem rude, he was bored with Dourt's complaints, which occurred with little variation once a fortnight—whenever, in fact, an FTL ship arrived. He almost scuttled up the stairs.

"It may happen on Tandy Two," Dourt said, not averse to having only Hoc to talk to, "but that don't mean to say Col Dourt has to like it." He squared his broad shoulders, thrust out his chest, and stuck his thumbs in his spunsteel jacket. "I was born on Droxy, where a man gets twenty-four hours to his day—every day."

Hoc thumped his tail idly as if in ironic applause.

As Murrag came upstairs, Tes marched past him on her way from the washing room. She was absolutely naked.

"High time the girl was taken to civilization and learned the common rules of decency," Murrag thought good-humouredly. The girl was several months past her thirteenth birthday. Perhaps it was as well the Dourt family were off back to Droxy in three weeks.

"Going to bed at this hour of the day!" Tes grunted, not deigning to look at her father's helper as she thudded past him.

"It's eight o'clock at night. The man on the CV has just said so," Murrag replied.

"Poof!"

With that she disappeared into her room. Murrag entered into his room. He took the time changes in his stride; on Tandy now the changes had to be considered natural, for use can almost change the stamp of nature. Life on the farm was rigorous. Murrag, Dourt and his wife rose early and went to sleep early. Murrag planned to lie and think for an hour, possibly to write a page more of his book, and then to take a somnulizer and sleep till four the next morning.

His thinking had no time to grow elaborate and deep. The door burst open and Fay rushed in, squealing with exuberance.

"Did you see it? Did you see it?" she asked.

He had no need to ask to what she referred.

"I sat on the top of a cliff and watched it," he said.

"You *are* lucky!" She did a pirouette, and pulled an ugly grimace at him. "That's what I call my life-begins-at-forty face, Murrag; did it scare you? Oh, to see one of those starships actually plunk down in the Flange. Tell me all about it!"

Fay wore only vest and knickers. A tangle of arms and legs flashed as she jumped onto the bed beside him and began tugging his ears. She was Tes's younger sister and, six years old, the storm centre of the household.

"You're supposed to be in bed. Your mother will be after you, girl."

"She's always after me. Tell me about the starships, and how they land, and—"

"When you've wrenched my ears off, I will."

He was not easy with her leaning on him. Rising, he pointed out of his little window with its double panes. Since his room was at the front of the farmhouse, he had this view out across the valley. The girls slept in a room considered more safe, at the back of the house, tucked into solid granite ("the living granite," Dourt always called it) and without windows.

"Outside there now, Fay," he said, as the little girl peered into the dark, "are vapours that would make you ill if you inhaled them. They are breathed off by the Flange under the stress of absorbing the speed of the FTL ships. The geogravitic screens on this side of the Flange undergo terrific pressures and do very peculiar things. But the beautiful part is that when we wake in the morning the odours will all have blown away; Tandy itself, this marvellous moon we live on, will absorb them and send us a fresh supply of clean mountain air to breathe."

"Do the mountains have air?"

"We call the air on the mountains 'mountain air.' That's all it means."

As he sat down beside her, she asked, "Do the vapours make it dark so quickly?"

"No, they don't, Fay, and you know they don't. I've explained that before. The faster-than-light ships do that."

"Are the vaster-than-light ships dark?"

"*Faster*-than-light. No, they're not dark. They come in from deep space so fast—at speeds above that of light, because those are the only speeds they can travel at—that they shoot right around Tandy one and a half times before the Flange can stop them, before its works can absorb the ship's momentum. And in so doing they twirl Tandy around a bit on its axis with them."

"Like turntables?"

"That's what I told you, didn't I? If you ran very fast onto a light wooden turntable that was not moving, you would stop, but your motion would make the turntable turn—transference of energy, in other words. And this twirling sometimes moves us around from sunshine into darkness."

"Like today. I bet you were scared out on the hillside when it suddenly got dark!"

He tickled her in the ribs.

"No I wasn't, because I was prepared for it. But that's why we have to get your Daddy's sheep all safely under cover before a ship comes—otherwise *they'd* all get scared and jump over precipices and things, and then your Daddy'd lose all his money and you wouldn't be able to go back to Droxy."

Fay looked meditatively at him.

"Those vaster-than-light ships are rather a nuisance to us, aren't they?" she said.

Murrag roared with laughter.

"If you put it like that—" he began, when Mrs. Dourt thrust her head around the door.

"There you are, Fay! I thought as much. Come and get into bed at once."

Bes Dourt was a solid woman in her early forties, plain, very clean. She of them all was least at home on Tandy Two, yet she seldom grumbled about it; among all her many faults one could not include grumbling. She marched into Murrag's room and seized her younger daughter by the wrists.

"You're killing me!" Fay yelled in feigned agony. "Murrag and I were discussing transparency of energy. Let me kiss him good night and then I'll come. He is a lovely man, and I wish he was coming to Droxy with us."

She gave Murrag an explosive buss that rocked him backward. Then she rushed from the room. Bes paused before following; she winked at Murrag.

"Pity you don't like anyone else to carry on a bit more in that style, Mr. Harri," she said, and shut the door after her as she left.

It was something of a relief to him that her advances were now replaced by nothing more trying than innuendo. Murrag put his feet up on the bed and lay back.

He looked around the room with its spare plastic furniture. This would be home for only three weeks more: then he would move on to work for Farmer Cay in Region Five. Nothing would he miss—except Fay, who alone among all the people he knew shared his curiosity and his love for Tandy Two.

A phrase of hers floated back to him—"the vaster-than-light ships." Oddly appropriate name for craft existing in "phase space," where their mass exceeded "normal" infinity! His mind began to play with the little girl's phrase; reverie overcame him, so that in sinking down into a nest of his own thought he found, even amid the complexity gathered around him, a comforting simplicity, a simplicity he had learned to look for because it told him that to see clearly into his own inner nature, he had merely to crystallize the attraction Tandy Two held for him and all would be clear eternally; he would be a man free of shackles, or free at least to unlock them when he wished. So again, as on the cliff and as many times before, he plunged through the deceptions of the imagination towards the wished-for truthful image.

Perhaps his search itself was a delusion; but it led him to sleep.

Murrag and Dourt were out early in the cool hour before dawn. The air, as Murrag had predicted, was sweet to breathe again, washed by a light rain.

Hoc and the other dog—Pedo, the yard dog—ran with them as they whistled out the autocollies. Ten of them came pogoing into the open, light machines unfailingly obedient to the instructions from Dourt's throat mike. Although they had their limitations, they could herd sheep twice as quickly as live dogs. Murrag unlocked the doors of the great covered pens. The autocollies went in to get the sheep as he climbed aboard his tractor. The sheep poured forth, bleating into the open, and he and Dourt revved their engines and followed behind, watching as the flock fanned out towards the grasslands. They bumped along, keeping the auto-collies constantly on course.

Dawn seeped through the eastern clouds, and the rain stopped. Filmy sun created miracles of chiaroscuro over valley and hill. By then they had the sheep split into four flocks, each established on a separate hillside. They returned to the farm in time to breakfast with the rest of the family.

"Do they get miserable wet days on Droxy like this?" Tes asked.

"Nothing wrong with today. Rain's holding off now," her father said. Breakfast was not his best meal.

"It depends on what part of Droxy you live in, just as it does here, you silly girl," said her mother.

"They haven't got any weather in the south half of Tandy," Fay volunteered, talking around a mouthful, " 'cuz it's had to be vacuumized so's the starships coming in at such a lick wouldn't hit any molecules of air and get wrecked, and without air you don't have weather—isn't that so, Murrag?"

Murrag agreed it was so.

"Shut up talking about the Flange. It's all you seem to think of these days, young lady," Dourt growled.

"I never mentioned the Flange, Daddy. You did."

"I'm not interested in arguing, Fay, so save your energy. You're getting too cheeky these days."

She put both elbows on the plastic table and said with deliberate devilment, "The Flange is just a huge device for absorbing FTL momentum, Daddy, as I suppose you know, don't you? Isn't it, Murrag?"

Her mother leaned forward and slapped her hard across the wrist.

"You like to sauce your Dad, don't you? Well,

take that! And it's no good coming crying to me about it. It's your fault for being so saucy."

But Fay had no intention of going crying to her mother. Bursting into tears, she flung down her spoon and fork and dashed upstairs, howling. A moment later her bedroom door slammed.

"Serves her *right*!" Tes muttered.

"You be quiet too," her mother said angrily.

"Never get a peaceful meal now," Dourt said.

Murrag Harri said nothing.

After the meal, as the two men went out to work again, Dourt said stiffly, "If you don't mind, Harri, I'd rather you left young Fay alone till we leave here."

"Oh? Why's that?"

The older man thrust him a suspicious glance, then looked away. "Because she's my daughter and I say so."

"Can't you give me a reason?"

A dying bird lay in the yard. Birds were as scarce as gold nuggets on Tandy Two. This one must have been overcome by the fumes generated in the previous day's entry. Its wings fluttered pitifully as the men approached. Dourt kicked it to one side.

"If you must know—because she's getting mad on the Flange. Flange, Flange, Flange, that's all we hear from the kid! She didn't know or care a thing about it till early this year, when you started telling her all about it. You're worse than Captain Roge when he calls, and he has an excuse because he works on the damn thing. So you keep quiet in the future. Bes and me will leave here with no regrets. Tes doesn't care either way. But we don't want Fay to keep thinking about this place and upsetting herself, thinking Droxy isn't her proper home, which it's going to be."

This was a long speech for Dourt. The reasons he gave were good enough, but irritation made Murrag ask, "Did Mrs. Dourt get you to speak to me about this?"

Dourt stopped by the garage. He swung around and looked Murrag up and down, anger in his eye.

"You've been with me in Region Six nigh on four years, Harri. I was the man who gave you work when you wanted it, though I had not much need of you, nor much to pay you with. You've worked hard, I don't deny—"

"I can't see—"

"I'm talking, aren't I? When you came here you said you were—what was it—'in revolt against ultra-urbanized planets,' you said you were a poet or something; you said—heck, you said a lot of stuff, dressed up in fine phrases. Remember you used to keep me and Bes up half the night listening sometimes, until we saw it was all just talk!"

"Look here, if you're—"

The farmer bunched his fists and stuck out his lower lip.

"You listen to me for a change. I've been wanting to say this for a long time. Poet indeed! We weren't taken in by your blather, you know. And luckily it had no effect on our Tes either. She's more like me than her sister—she's a quiet sensible girl. But Fay is a baby. She's silly as yet, and we reckon you're having a bad influence on her—"

"All right, you've had your say. Now I'll have mine. Leaving aside the question of whether you and your wife can understand any concept you weren't born with—"

"You be careful now, Harri, what you're saying about Bes. I'm on to you! I'm not so daft as you think. Let me tell you Bes has had about enough of you giving her the glad eye and making passes at her as if she was just some—"

"By God!" Murrag exploded in anger. "She tells you that? The boot's on the other foot by a long chalk, and you'd better get that clear right away. If you think I'd touch—if I'd lay a hand—"

The mere thought of it took the edge of Murrag's wrath. It had the opposite effect on Dourt. He swung his left fist hard at Murrag's jaw. Murrag blocked it with his right forearm and counterattacked with his left. He caught Dourt glancingly on the ear as the farmer kicked out at him. Unable to step back in time, Murrag grabbed the steel-studded boot and wrenched it upward.

Dourt staggered back and fell heavily to the ground.

Murrag stood over him, all fury gone.

"If I had known how much you resented me all these years," he said miserably, staring down at his employer's face, "I'd not have stayed here. Don't worry, I'll say no more to Fay. Now let's go and get the tractors out, unless you want to sack me on the spot—and that's entirely up to you."

As he helped the older man to his feet, Dourt muttered shamefacedly, "I've not resented you, man, you know that perfectly well."

Then they got the tractors out in silence.

The result of Dourt's fall was what he termed a "bad back." He was—and when he said it, he spoke with an air of surprise more appropriate to a discovery than cliché—not as young as he was. For a day or so he sat gloomily indoors by his CV, letting Murrag do the outside work, and brooding over his lot.

Tandy Two is a harder satellite to take than it seems at first—I know that after two five-year spells of duty on it. The density of its composition gives it a gravity of 1.35 Gs. And the fortnightly time hop when the FTLs enter takes a psychological toll. In the bit towns, like Touchdown and Blerion, civilization can compensate for these disadvantages. On the scattered sheep stations there are no compensations.

Moreover, Col Dourt had found his farming far less profitable than it had looked on paper from

Droxy fourteen years ago. Tandy Two offered good grazing in a stellar sector full of ready-made mutton markets—twenty hundred over-urbanized planets within twice twenty light years. But his costs had been stiff, the costs of transport above all, and now he counted himself lucky to be able to get away with enough credits saved to buy a small shop on his old home planet. As it was, margins were narrow: he was reckoning on the sale of farm and stock to buy passage home for himself and his family.

Much of this I heard on my periodic tours through Region Six, when I generally managed a visit to the Dourts. I heard it all again the next time I called, thirteen days after the scuffle between Dourt and Murrag.

I looked in to see Bes, and found Dourt himself, sitting by a fire, looking surly. He had returned to work and wrenched his back again, and was having to rest it.

"It's the first time I've ever known you to be off work. Cheer up, you've only got a week to go before you'll be making tracks for home," I said, removing my coat.

My truck was outside. Though only half a mile away by hill paths, the unit to which I was attached was at least ten miles off by the circuitous track around the mountains.

"Look how long the flaming journey back to Droxy takes when we do get off from Touchdown," he complained. "But with all my family I can't afford to travel FTL."

He spoke as if the FTL ships were my responsibility, which in a sense they were.

"Even STLs are fast enough to make the subjective time of the journey no more than three or four months."

"Don't start explaining," he said. He waved his hand, dismissing the subject. "You know I'm only a simple farmer. I don't grasp all the technical stuff about subjective time. I just want to get home."

The two girls Fay and Tes came in after finishing their CV lessons. Tes was preparing lunch; eyeing me warily—she was a mistrustful creature—she told me that her mother was out helping Murrag with the flocks. Both girls came over to the farmer to join in the discussion; I coaxed Fay up onto my knee.

She wanted the whole business of how they would get home explained to her. "You're a Flange maintenance officer, Captain Roge," she said. "Tell *me* all about it, and then I'll tell Daddy so's he can understand."

"You don't have to understand," her father said. "We just take a ship that'll get us there eventually. That's all there is to it, thank God. The likes of us don't need to bother our heads about the technicalities."

"I want to *know*," Fay replied.

"It's *good* for us to listen," Tes said, "though *I* understand it all already. A child could understand it."

"I'm a child and I don't understand it," her sister said.

"The universe is full of civilized planets, and in a week's time you're all going to hop from one such to another such," I began. And as I sought for simple words and vivid pictures to put my explanation across to them, the wonder of the universe overcame me as if for a moment I, too, was a child.

For the galaxy has grown up into a great and predominantly peaceful unit. Crime survives, but does not flourish. Evil lives, but knowledge keeps pace with it and fights it. Man prospers and grows kindlier rather than otherwise. Certainly our old vices are as green as ever, but we have devised sociological systems that contain them better than was the case in earlier eras.

Starships are our Starswarm's main connecting links.

Bridging all but the lesser distances are the FTL ships, travelling in super-universes at multiple-light velocities. Bridging the lesser distances go the STLs, the slower-than-light ships. The two sorts of travel are, like planetary economies, interdependent.

The FTL ship, that ultimate miracle of technology, has one disadvantage: it moves—as far as the "normal" universe is concerned—at only two speeds: faster than light and stationary.

An FTL ship has to stop the moment it comes out of phase space and enters the quantitative fields of the normal universe. Hence the need for bodies such as Tandy Two, spread throughout the galaxy; they are the braking planets, or satellites.

An FTL cannot "stop" in space. Instead, its velocities are absorbed by the braking planets, or, more accurately, by the impetus-absorbers of the Flanges that girdle such planets. The FTLs burst in and are reduced to zero velocity within a time limit of about 200 milliseconds—in which time they have circuited the Flange, gone completely around the planet, one and a half times.

STLs or mattermitters then disperse the passengers to local star systems much in the way that stratoliners land travellers who then disperse to nearby points by helicab.

Though STLs are slow, relativistic time contractions shorten the subjective journeys in them to tolerable limits of weeks or days.

So the universe ticks; not perfectly, but workably.

And this was what I told Dourt and his daughters.

"Well, I'd better go and finish getting your dinner, Daddy," Tes said, after a pause.

He patted her bottom and chuckled with approval. "That's it, girl," he said. "Food's more in our line than all this relativistic stuff. Give me a lamb cutlet any day."

I had no answer. Nor had Fay, though I saw by her face that she was still thinking over what I had said, as she slid off my knee to go and help Tes. How much did it mean to her? How much does it all mean to any of us? Though Dourt had little time for theory, I also relished the thought of the lamb cutlet.

Before the food was ready, I took a turn outside with the farmer, who used his stick as support.

"You'll miss this view," I said, gazing over the great mysterious body of Tandy whose contours were clad in green, freckled here and there with sheep. I must admit it, I am fonder of the beauties of women than of landscape; for all that, the prospect was fine. In the voluptuous downward curve between two hills, Tandy the primary was setting. Even by daylight the banded and beautiful reds swirling over its oblate surface were impressive.

Dourt looked about him, sniffing, admitting nothing. He appeared not to have heard what I said.

"Rain coming up from somewhere," he observed.

In my turn I ignored him.

"You'll miss this view back on Earth," I repeated.

"The view!" Dourt exclaimed and laughed. "I'm not a clever man like you and young Murrag, Captain; I get simple satisfaction out of simple things, like being in the place where I was born."

Although I happened to know he was born eight layers under the skyport in Burming, a Droxian manufacturing city, where they still metered your ration of fresh air, I made no answer. All he meant was that he valued his personal illusions, and there I was with him all the way. Convictions or illusions: what matter if all conviction is illusion, so long as we hang onto it? You would never shift Dourt from his, fool though he was in many ways.

I could never get under his skin as surely as I could with some people—Murrag, for instance, a more complicated creature altogether; but often the simplest person has a sort of characterless opacity about him. So it seemed with Dourt, and if I have drawn him flat and lumpy here, that was how I experienced him then.

To make talk between us, for his silence made me uneasy, I asked after Murrag.

Dourt had little to say. Instead he pointed with his stick to a tracked vehicle bumping towards us.

"That'll be Murrag with Bes now, coming home for a bit of grub," he said.

He was mistaken. When the tractor drew nearer, we saw that only Bes was inside it.

As we strolled forward, she drove around the covered pens and pulled up beside us. Her face was flushed, and, I thought, angry looking, but she smiled when she saw me.

"Hullo, Captain Roge!" She climbed down and clasped my hand briefly. "I was forgetting we'd be having your company today. Nice to see a strange face, though I'd hardly call yours that." She turned straight to her husband and said, "We got trouble on Pike's Brow. Two autocollies plunged straight down a crevasse. Murrag's up there with them now trying to get them out."

"What were you doing up on Pike's Brow?" he demanded. "I told you to keep number three flock over the other side while I was off work—you know it's tricky on Pike's with all that faulting, you silly woman. Why didn't you do as I told you?"

"It wouldn't have happened if my throat mike hadn't jammed. I couldn't call the autocollies off before they went down the hole."

"Don't make excuses. I can't take a day off without something going wrong. I—"

"You've had six days off already, Col Dourt, so shut your mouth—"

"How's Harri managing?" I asked, thinking an interruption was necessary.

Mrs. Dourt flashed me a look of gratitude. "He's trying to get down the crevasse after the autocollies. Trouble is, they're still going and won't answer to orders, so they're working themselves down deeper and deeper. That's why I came back here, to switch off the juice; they work on maserbeamed power, you know."

I heard Dourt's teeth grind. "Then buck up and switch off woman, before the creatures ruin themselves! You know they cost money. What're you waiting for?"

"What? For some old fool to stop arguing with me, of course. Let me by."

She marched past us, an aggressive woman, rather plain, and yet to my taste pleasing, as though the thickness of her body bore some direct if mysterious relationship to the adversities of life. Going into the control shed, she killed the power and then came back to where we stood.

"I'll come with you, Mrs. Dourt, and see what I can do to help," I said. "I don't need to get back to my outfit for another hour."

A look of understanding moved across her face, and I climbed onto the tractor with her after a brief nod to Dourt.

There was some justification for this. If the situation was as she said it was, then the matter was one of urgency—the next FTL ship was due in under four hours, and forty thousand sheep had to be herded under lock and key before that. *Had to be*: or darkness would be on them, they would stampede and kill or injure themselves on the rocky slopes, and Dourt's hard-earned savings would be wiped out . . . that is, if the situation was as Bes said it was.

When we were out of sight of old Dourt and the farm, Bes stopped the tractor. We looked at each other. My whole system changed gear as we saw the greed in each other's eyes.

"How much of this story is a lie to get me along and at your mercy?" I asked.

She put her hard broad hand over mine. "None of it, Vasko. We'll have to shift back to Murrag as soon as possible, if he hasn't already broken his neck down the crevasse. But with Col hanging about the house, I couldn't have seen you alone if this opportunity hadn't turned up—and this'll be our last meeting, won't it?"

"Unless you change your mind and don't go to Droxy with him next week."

"You know I can't do that, Vasko."

I did know. I was safe. Not to put too fine a point on it, she'd have been a nuisance if she had stayed for my sake. There were dozens of women like Bes Dourt—one on nearly every hill farm I visited, bored, lonely, willing, only too happy to indulge in an affair with a Flange maintenance official. It was not as if I loved her.

"Then we'll make it really good this last time," I said.

And there was the greed again, plain and undisguised and sweet. We almost fell out onto the grass. That's how these things should be: raw, unglamorized. That's the way it must be for me. Bes and I never made love. We coupled.

Afterwards, when we came to our senses, we were aware that we had been longer than we should have been. Scrambling back into the tractor, we headed fast and bumpy for Pike's Brow.

"I hope Murrag's all right," I muttered, glancing at my arm watch.

She neither liked nor understood my perpetual interest in Murrag Harri.

"He's queer!" she sneered.

I didn't ask her to elaborate. I had heard it before, and the pattern behind it was obvious enough: Murrag disliked her hungry advances—and why not? She was plain, solid, coarse . . . No, I do myself no justice saying all this, for Bes had a pure peasant honesty that in my eyes excused everything—or so I told myself.

At first when Murrag arrived at Dourt's farm, I

had been jealous, afraid that he would spoil my innocent little game. When it was clear he would do no such thing, I grew interested in him for his own involved sake. Sometimes this had caused trouble between Bes and me—but enough of this; I am trying to tell Murrag's tale, not my own. If I digress, well, one life is very much tangled with the next.

We must have created some sort of a speed record to the spot of Pike's Brow. Then the terrain became so steep that we had to halt, leave the tractor, and go the rest of the way on foot.

Bending our backs, we climbed. Sheep moved reluctantly out of our path, eyeing us with the asinine division of feature that marks a Tandy sheep's face—all rabbity and timid about the eyes and nose, as arrogant as a camel about the lower lip.

Rain came on us with the unexpectedness it reserves for Region Six, as if a giant over the hump of the mountains had suddenly emptied his largest bucket across our path. I remembered Dourt's forecast as I turned up my collar. Still we climbed, watching little rivulets form among the short blades under our boots. I began to wish I hadn't volunteered for this.

At last we reached the crevasse. We scrambled along by its side towards the point where Murrag had climbed over into it, a point marked by the two live dogs, Hoc and Pedo who sat patiently in the rain, barking at our approach.

The downpour was lessening. We stood, pulled our back bones painfully upright, and breathed the damp air deeply before bothering about Murrag.

He was some twenty feet down into the crack, where it was so narrow that he could rest with his back on one side and his feet on the other. He was drenched from the water pouring over the edge; it splashed past him and gurgled down into a ribbon of a stream about thirty feet beneath his boots.

One of the autocollies was wedged beside him, covered by mud. The other lay a short distance away and a little lower down, overturned but seemingly unharmed.

I noted the expression of Murrag's face. It was blank; he seemed to gaze into nothing, ignoring the rivulets that splashed around him.

"Murrag!" Bes called sharply. "Wake up. We're back."

He looked up at us. "Hello," he said. "Hello, Vasko! I was just communing with the great earth mother. She's really swallowed me ... It's funny, stuck down here in a fissure ... like climbing between the lips of a whale."

And there would have been more like that! Generally I had patience with his curious fancies, enjoyed them even, but not at such a moment, not with Bes standing there staring, and the water running down my back, and a stitch in my side, and the time against us.

"It's raining," I reminded him. "In case you didn't notice, we're all wet through. For God's sake, stir yourself."

He seemed to pull himself together, dashing wet hair back from his face. Peering upward rather stupidly, as if he were a fish, he said, "Fine day for mountaineering, isn't it? If we're not careful, the earth under this autocollie will crumble and the machine may get wedged or damaged. As it is, it is still in working order. Fling me the rope down, Bes. You and Vasko can haul it up while I steady it."

She stared blankly into my face. "Damn it, I left the rope back in the tractor," she said.

I remembered then. She unhooked it from her waist when we lay on the grass and in her haste had not bothered to tie it on again later, tossing it instead into the back of the vehicle.

"For God's sake go and get it then," Murrag shouted impatiently, suddenly realizing how long he had waited. "I can't stay down here much longer."

Again Bes looked at me. I gazed away down at the muddy boots.

"Go and get it for me, Vasko," she urged.

"I'm out of breath," I said, "I've got the stitch."

"Damn you!" she said. She started off down the hillside again without another word.

Murrag looked sharply at me; I did not return his stare.

It took her twenty-five minutes to return with the rope. In that time, the rain cleared entirely. I squatted by Pedo and Hoc, gazing over the dull and tumbled terrain. Murrag and I did not speak to each other.

The best part of another hour passed before we three bedraggled creatures managed to haul the autocollies up safely. We could have done the job in half the time, had we not been so careful to preserve them from harm; we all knew the balance of the Dourt finances, and the autocollie can cost anything from twenty percentages to five parapounds.

Panting, I looked at my arm watch.

In two hours less six minutes the next FTL was due for entry on Tandy Two. It was past the time I should have reported back to my unit for duty.

I told Murrag and Bes that I must be going— told them curtly, for after missing my lunch, getting a soaking, and nearly wrenching my arms off rescuing the dogs, I was none too sweet-humoured.

"You can't leave us *now*, Vasko," Murrag said. "The whole flock's in jeopardy, and not only his lot on the Brow. We've *got* to have every sheep under cover in two hours—and first of all someone must go back to the farm and switch the beam on again to get the dogs going. We need your body still."

His eyes were as appealing as Bes's.

God, I thought, the way some people need people! He has his emotional requirements just as she has her physical ones. Hers are crashingly simple, his I don't understand; once these autocollie dogs were running again, they would see the sheep home in no time, without help.

Right then, I could not think of two people I would less like to be stuck on a mountain with. But all I said was, "I'm a maintenance officer, Murrag, not a shepherd. I've made myself late for duty as it is. Since my truck's at the farm, I'll have to go back and collect it, so when I get there I'll tell Col to beam the juice to you—but from then on you're on your own."

As I turned to go, Bes put her hand on my wrist. When I swung around on her, I saw her flinch from my expression.

"You can't just ditch us like this, Vasko," she said.

"I'm ditching no one. I helped you drag the 'collies out, didn't I? I've got a job to do, and I'll be listed for reporting back late as it is. Now let me go."

She dropped my hand.

I made off down the slope at a slow trot, digging my heels as I went. Now and again I slipped, falling back on the wet grass. Before I got to the level, I saw another tractor approaching.

Dourt was in it. He yelled to me as he drew nearer. "I came to see what you lot were doing all this time. You've been taking so long I thought you'd all fallen down the hole with the 'collies."

Briefly I told him what was happening, while he climbed slowly out of the tractor, clutching his back.

"I'm borrowing Bes's tractor to go back and switch on the juice, so that the autos can start herding as soon as possible," I finished.

He fell to cursing, saying he was going to lose all his livestock, that they could never be driven under cover before the FTL arrived. I tried to reassure him before going over to the other vehicle.

As I climbed in he said, "When you get there, tell Tes to come back here with the tractor. She can drive well enough, and we'll need her help. The more hands here the better. And tell her to bring the signal pistols. They'll get the sheep moving."

"And Fay?"

"She'd only be in the way."

Giving him a wave, I stood on the acceleration and rattled back to the farm. By now the sun was bright and the sky free of cloud, which did not stop my boots from squelching or my clothes from clinging to me like wet wallpaper.

The moment I reached the farm buildings I marched into the control shed, crossed to the appropriate board, and pushed the rheostat over. Power began its ancient song, the hum of content that sounds perpetually as if it is ascending the scale. Up on the pastures, the electronic dogs would be leaping into activity.

Everything appeared in order, though Col Dourt was not a man to keep his equipment spotless—and I reflected, not for the first time that day, that if he had cared to lay out an extra twenty parapounds or so he could have had switchboard-to-flock communication, which would have saved him valuable time on a day like this.

Well, it was not my concern.

In the living complex, Tes was alone. She stood in her slip, cutting out a dress for Droxy wear, and I surveyed her; she was developing well.

As usual, she seemed displeased to see me— baffling creatures, adolescent girls; you never know whether they are acting or not. I gave her her father's orders and told her to get out to Pike's Brow as soon as she could.

"And where's Fay?" I asked.

"It's none of your business, Captain Roge."

As if she felt this was a bit too sharp, she added, "And anyhow I don't know. This is one of my great not-knowing days."

I sniffed. I was in a hurry, and it was, as she said, none of my business now, although I would have liked a farewell word with her younger sister. Nodding to Tes, I squelched out of the building, got into the maintenance truck, and began speeding back to my unit around the other side of the mountains. To perdition with all Dourts!

Murrag used to say that there wasn't a more interesting job than mine on all Tandy. Though he was prepared to talk for hours about his feelings— "my Tandian tenebrosities," he sometimes called them—he was equally prepared to listen for hours while I explained in minute detail the working of the Flange and the problems of repair it posed. He learned from me any facts he filtered on to Fay.

Maintaining the Flange is a costly and complicated business, and would be even more so had we not costly and complicated machines with which to operate. Between FTL arrivals, my unit works ceaselessly over the strip—testing, checking, replacing, making good.

The complex nature of the Flange necessitates this.

To start with, there is the BGL—the Bonfiglioli Geogravitic Layer—marked by tall pylons, along the north of the Flange, which maintains all of Tandy Two's atmosphere within its stress; were this to contract more than a minimum leakage, the lives of everyone on the planet would be in jeopardy.

Before the BGL comes the "fence," which prevents any creature from entering the Flange zone; after it come our equipment stores, bunkers, etc., before you get to the actual twelve-mile-wide Flange itself.

The Flange is a huge shock absorber, three storeys deep, girdling the planet. It has to absorb the biggest man-made shock of all time, though it is a delicate instrument with an upper surface of free-grooved pyr-glass needles. Its functioning depends first and foremost on the taubesi thermocouple, of which there is one to every square millimetre of surface; these detect an FTL ship before it re-enters normal space and activate the rest of the system immediately. The rest of the system is, briefly, an inertia vacuum. The FTL ship never actually makes contact with the Flange surface, of course, but its detectors mesh with the inertial and transfer velocities, stopping it in milliseconds—the figure varies according to planetary and ship's mass, but for Tandy Two it is generally in the order of 201.5 milliseconds.

The whole Flange is activated—switched on section by section of its entire twenty-five thousand miles length—two hours before an FTL ship arrives (only the computers beneath the strip know precisely when the starship will materialize from phase space.) At that time, the various maintenance units give the whole system a final check, and the needlelike surface of the Flange looks first one way and then another, like stroked fur, as it searches for the breakthrough point. I should have been back for that event.

I had come down to the valleys by now. Over to my left ran the graceful BGL pylons, with the Flange itself behind, already stretching itself like a self-activated rubber sheet; beyond it burned the dead half of Tandy, sealed off in vacuum, bleached dust-white in the sun. Less than a mile remained between me and the unit post. Then I saw Fay.

Her blue dress showed clearly against a tawny ground. She was several hundred yards ahead of me, not looking in my direction and running directly towards an electrified "fence" that guards the BGL and the Flange itself.

"Fay!" I yelled. "Come back!"

Instinctive stuff; I was enclosed in the truck;

had she heard my cry it would only have speeded her on her way.

This was her last chance to see an FTL ship enter before she went back to Droxy. The absence of her father and mother had given her the chance to slip out, so she had taken it.

"Fay!" I yelled as I drove, letting my lungs shout, because in my fear I could not stop them.

The fence was built of two components, an ordinary strand fence with a mild shock to keep sheep away, and then, some yards beyond, a trellis of high voltage designed simply and crudely to kill. Warning notices ran all the way between the two fences, one every three hundred and fifty yards— 125,714 of them right around the planet.

She dived through the strand fence without touching it.

Now I was level with her. Seeing me, she began running parallel between the two fences. Beyond her the eyes of the needles of the Flange turned first this way then that, restless and expectant.

I jumped from the truck before it stopped moving. "You'll get killed, Fay!" I bellowed.

She turned then, her face half mischievous, half scared. She was running off-course towards the second fence as she turned. She called something to me—I could not make out, still cannot make out, what.

As I ducked under the sheep strand after her, she hit the other fence.

Fay! Ah, my Fay, my own sweet freeborn daughter! She was outlined in bright light, she was black as a cinder, the universe screamed and yapped like a dying dog. My face hit the dust shrieking as I fell. Noise, death, heat, slapped me down.

Then there was mind-devouring silence.

Peace rolled down like a steamroller, flattening everything, the eternal hush of damnation into which I wept as if the universe were a pocket handkerchief for my grief.

Fay, oh Fay, my own child!

Beyond the BGL, safe in vacuum, the Flange peered towards the heavens, twisting its spiked eyes. I rolled in the blistered dust without comprehension.

How long I lay there I have no idea.

Eventually the alarms roused me. They washed around me and through me until they, too, were gone, and the silence came back. When my hearing returned, I heard a throbbing in the silence. At first I could not place it, had no wish to place it, but at last I sat up and realized that the motor of my truck was still patiently turning over. I stood up shakily. The ill-coordinated action brought a measure of intelligence back to my system.

All I knew was that I had to return to the farm and tell Bes what had happened. Everything else was forgotten, even that the FTL ship was due at any time.

I got back somehow under the sheep fence, and into the cab. Somehow I kicked in the gears, and we lurched into action. *Fay, Fay, Fay*, my blood kept saying.

As I steered away from the Flange, from the burned ground to grass again, a figure presented itself before me. Blankly, I stopped and climbed out to meet it, hardly knowing what I did.

It was Murrag, waving his arms like one possessed.

"Thanks to your aid we got the flocks under cover in time," he said. "So I came down here to see the FTL entry. You know, for me to see an entry—well, it's like watching creation."

He stopped, eyeing me, his face full of a private emotion.

"It's like the creation, is it?" I said dumbly. My mouth felt puffy. *Fay, Fay, Fay*.

"Vasko, we've always been friends, so I don't have to mind what I say to you. You know that this event once a fortnight—it's ultimate excitement for me. I mean . . . well, even something like sex palls beside watching an FTL entry."

In the state I was in I could not grasp what he was saying. It came back to me long after, like finding a private letter behind the wainscoting of an empty house.

"And I've got the image of Tandy Two I was after, Vasko." His eyes were alight, full of some inner fire. "Tandy's a woman—"

There was no warning.

The FTL ship entered.

Cerenkov radiations belched outward, distorting our vision. For a second Murrag and I were embedded in amber. Tandy was girdled in a noose of flame, most of which expanded south safely into vacuum. The giant fist of impetus reaction struck us.

The sun plunged across the sky like a frightened horse.

As we fell, day turned to night.

For one of those long minutes that seemed a small eternity, I lay on the ground with Murrag face-down nearby.

He moved before I did. When it penetrated my mind that he was slipping a fume mask on, I automatically did the same; without thinking, I had carried my mask from the vehicle with me.

He had switched on a flashlight. It lay on the ground as we sprouted bug-eyed jumbo faces, and splashed a great caricature of us up the mountainside. In the sky, the planet Tandy appeared, near full, and bright, a phantom. As ever, it was impossible to believe it was not our moon rather than vice versa; facts have no power against the imagination.

Sitting there stupidly, I heard the words of an old poet scatter through my head, half of his verse missing.

O, moon of my delight who know'st no wane,
Something something once again.
How oft hereafter rising shall she look
Through this same garden after me—in vain!

But I had no time to connect up the missing words; if I had thought of it, I preferred it that way, thus emphasizing my sense of loss. But no rational thought came.

All that came was the clash of two nightmares, Murrag's and mine. It seemed that I kept crying "Fay is dead!" and that he kept crying "Tandy Two's a woman!" We were fighting, struggling together while the ground steamed, I hating him because he did not care where I had expected him to care, he hating me because I had spoiled his vigil, ruined his climax.

My mind ran in shapes, not thoughts, until I realized that I had begun the fight. When I went limp, Murrag's fist caught me between the eyes.

I do not have to say what I felt then, slumped on the ground—the place I hated and Murrag loved—for this is supposed to be his story, not mine, although I have become entangled in it in the same directionless way I became entangled in Bes's life.

Murrag—you have to say it—could not feel like ordinary people. When I heard from him again, he did not even mention Fay; he had only used her to talk to about his obsession.

When, a week later, the STL ship *Monteith* departed for Droxy from Tandy, Col, Bes, and Tes Dourt travelled in it. So did I. I lay in the bunk in the medical bay, classified under some obscure technical label that meant I was dull of mind and unfit for further service.

The Dourts came to see me.

They were surprisingly cheerful. After all, they had made their money and were about to begin life anew. Even Bes never referred to Fay; I always said she was hard.

They brought me a letter from Murrag. It was elaborate, overwritten. Wrapped in his own discoveries, he clearly mourned as little for Fay as did the Dourts. His letter, in fact, displayed his usual sensitivity, and his blindness where other humans were concerned. I had no patience with it, though I later reread the final passages (which he has since used in his successful book, *To My Undeniable Tandy*).

"... Yilmoff's fifty-fourth era classic, *Theory of Images*, reveals how settings can hold deep psychic significances for men; we acquire early an Experience of place. When a planet exists with as distinct a personality—for the term in context is no exaggeration—as Tandy Two's, the significance is increased, the effect on the psyche deepened.

"I declare myself to be in love, in the true psychological sense of the word, with Tandy. She is my needful feminine, dwelling in my mind, filling it to the exclusion of others.

"So I give you my true portrait image of her: the planethead of a girl, all sweet, rich hair north, but the south face a skull, and bound round her brow a ribbon of flame. This the portrait of my terrible lover."

Make of this what you will. Crazy? I think not.

Only Murrag of all mankind has his mistress perpetually beneath him.

Sector Mauve

No voice is entirely lost. No action is without result. Time passes, yes, but the past is never dead. The human race carries the past in its bloodstream. And that bloodstream is the guarantee of the future as well.

Starswarm is not only a business of cosmic bodies, moving in the great void; it is also very much a matrix of genetic material, of biological signals carried from one generation to another. This is the case for human and non-human races alike. Messages from prehistory saturate the most advanced galactic centres of culture. We are ourselves sophisticated codes, ciphers of a continuity of which we can as yet see no end.

It is generally agreed that Credibility is a dull planet. Sector Mauve itself lies in a remote galactic arm. Nevertheless, within its star clusters, ceaseless interstellar traffic goes on; within its system-wide cities, which men weep to leave, life is lived with an intensity that only schizophrenes can endure. The schizophrenes of Mauve and elsewhere have multiple personalities. When one personality sleeps, another wakes. Each physical body is a nest, a council, a brothel, a charade.

Off the spaceways lies Credibility, only offspring of binary suns. It has no mineral wealth. Solar power is its main fuel. Other fuels and metals must be imported. Yet Credibility is a kind of utopia, knee deep in wheat, barley, rice, maize, and other crops. Its climate is innocuous. Its polar regions are used as skating rinks. Credibility is a kind of utopia—and, like all utopias, orderly, bland, dull. Not a dreaded schizophrene in sight.

A lot of wrinkled old men inhabit Credibility. So the humans see them. The wrinkled old men move around the planet, appearing and disappearing as they will. They never quit the planet, though there are no laws against their doing so. There are no laws against wrinkled old men; equally, there are no laws for them. They travel among small towns full of human beings who don't know they are bored, and cause no trouble—much.

These wrinkled old men are the autochthonous inhabitants of Credibility, a genus apart. They were there long before the planet acquired its name. They are male and female, young and old and middle-aged. Little girl babies are born smooth as foetal rats; but within a few weeks they also resemble wrinkled old men.

This pseudo-senility is a kind of protective device, a camouflage. A camouflage adopted long ago by a non-human species with an extremely long life-span. The past is never dead, even though time passes. No action is without result. No voice is entirely lost.

The second sun was setting, ripe, full of leisure and grandeur.

"Always seems to be eating time in this house," Mabel said, wiping her hands on her apron.

She dumped the ceramic salt- and pepper-pots down at Arthur's end of the table and hurried through to the kitchen to get the supper from the micro-wave. Arthur's gaze followed her admiringly. She was a fine figure of a young woman, his Mabel. None too easy to handle, but a good-looker. Arthur, on the other hand, looked like a young bull; none too bright a bull either. Strong. Prepared to take on whatever life offered.

"Drink it while it's hot," Mabel said, returning and placing a bowl of soup before him.

As Arthur picked up his spoon, he noticed a truck stopping outside in the road. Its hood went up. The driver stood with his head tucked under it, gazing dreamily at the engine.

Arthur looked at his steaming soup, at Mabel, back out of the window. He scratched his scalp.

"Feller's going to be stranded in the dark in another half-hour," he said, half to himself.

"Nearly time we were putting the light on," she said, half to herself. They burned sunflower-oil, outside of town.

"I could maybe earn a couple of palmers going to see what was wrong," he said, changing tack.

"This is food like money won't buy or time won't improve on, my mother used to say," Mabel murmured, stirring her bowl, evading his gaze.

Mabel and Art had been married only four local months, but it had not taken Arthur that long to notice the obliquity of their intentions. Even when they were apparently conversing together, their two thought-streams seemed never quite to converge, let alone touch. But he was a determined young man, not to be put off by irrelevancies. He stood up, hitching his jeans.

"I'll just go see what the trouble seems to be," he said. And as a sop to her culinary pride, he called, as he went through the screen door, "Keep that soup warm—I'll be right back!"

Their bungalow stood in its own untidy plot of ground. A kilometre along the highway, the outskirts of Hapsville began. Hapsville was okay—there was talk of it building a spaceport. Sunflowers grew on either side of the highway, all bright yellow-brown as far as eye could see. The stationary truck was a dusty grey. It looked threadbare, all patched and mended, as if it had been travelling the roads long before humans ventured on Credibility.

The overalled figure by the engine waited till Arthur was almost up to it before snapping down the hood and turning. He was a small wrinkled old man with spectacles and a long long face which must have measured all of eighteen inches from crown of skull to point of jaw. In among a mass of crinkles, an expression of melancholy played.

"Got trouble, stranger?" Arthur asked.

"Who hasn't?" His voice, too, sounded crinkled. "Trouble's like fleas to a dog—keeps you scratching."

"Anything I can fix?" Arthur enquired. "I'm a hand at the service station down the road in Hapsville. Well ..." he gave his bovine grin, "more'n just a hand ..."

"Well," the wrinkled old man said, "I come a long way. A long way. I daresay if pressed I could put a bowl of steaming soup between me and the night."

"Your timing sure is good!" Arthur said. "You better come on in and see what Mabel can fix you. Then I'll have a look-see at your engine. These old nuclear jobs fix easy."

He led the way back to the bungalow. The wrinkled old man scuffed his feet on the mat, rubbed his spectacles on his dirty overalls, and followed in to the main room. He looked about him curiously, saying nothing.

"Uh, welcome, mister ..." said Arthur.

Mabel had worked fast. When she saw through the window that they were coming, she tossed her and Art's bowls of soup back into the pan, added water, put the pan back in the micro-wave, and exchanged a clean apron for her dirty one.

"We got a guest here for supper, Mabel," Arthur said. "I'll light up the lamp."

"How d'you do?" Mabel said, putting out her

hand to the wrinkled old man. "Welcome to our hospitality."

She said it just right: made it sound welcoming, yet, by slipping in the word "hospitality," let him know she was putting herself out for him. Mabel was educated. So was Arthur, of course. They both read all the seefaxes and magazines. But while Arthur just pored over the engineering or mechanical bits, Mabel studied psychological or educational or etiquette articles. She wanted to know about people. No one was going to put anything over on her.

As she felt the dry, crinkly texture of the stranger's hand, she sighed. This was a wrinkled old man. Mabel wondered if it was male or female.

They sat down at table, the three of them, as soon as the diluted soup warmed, and sipped out of their bowls. The sky outside drowned in stripes of scarlet and orange and yellow, as if someone had tipped sunflowers into it.

"You often through this way?" Arthur asked his visitor.

"Every so often. I haven't got what you might call a regular route."

"Just what model is your truck?"

"You're the boss of the service station, eh?"

Thus deflected, Arthur said, "Why, no, I didn't call myself that, did I? I'm just a mechanic down there, but I'm learning, I'm learning fast." He laughed.

He was about to put the question about the truck again, when Mabel decided it was time she spoke.

"What product do you travel in, sir?"

The long face crinkled like tissue paper, the spectacles gleamed.

"You can't rightly say I got a product," he said, leaning forward with his elbows on the bare table. "Maybe you didn't read the sign on my vehicle:

'Intangibles, Inc.' It's a bit worn now, I guess. Needs repainting."

"So you travel in tangibles, eh?" Arthur said. "They grow New Raton way, don't they? Must be interesting crop to market."

"Dearie me!" exclaimed Mabel crossly. "Didn't you hear the gentleman, Art? He said he peddles intangibles. They ain't *things*. Surely you knew that? They're more like—well, like something that isn't there at all."

She came uncertainly to a halt, looking confused. The little man was there instantly to rescue both of them.

"The sort of intangibles I deal in are there right enough," he said. "You might almost say they're the things that govern people's lives. But because you can't see them, people are apt to dismiss them. They think they can get through life without intangibles, but they can't."

"Try a slice of this cheese," Mabel said, collecting their empty soup bowls. "You were saying, sir. . ."

The wrinkled old man cut himself a square of cheese and a slab of home-baked bread. He said, "Well, now I'm here, maybe I could offer you good folks an intangible for yourselves."

"We're mighty poor," Arthur said. "We only just got married and there's a baby on its way for next spring. We can't afford luxuries, that's the truth."

"I'm happy to hear about the babe," the wrinkled old man said. "But you understand I don't want money for my goods. I reckon you already gave me an intangible: hospitality. Now I ought to give you one."

"Well, if it's like that . . ." Arthur said. But he was thinking that this old fellow was getting a bit whimsical and had better be booted out as soon as possible. People were like that. They were either friendly or unfriendly, and unfortunately there were as many ways of being objectionable while being friendly as there were while being unfriendly. He could not handle people like Mabel did.

Chewing hard on a piece of crust, the wrinkled old man turned to Mabel. "Now, let's take your own case, and find out which intangibles you require. What is your object in life precisely?"

"Mabel ain't got no object in life," Arthur said flatly. "She's married to me now."

Mabel was ready with a sharp retort but somehow her guest was there first with a much milder one. Shaking his head solemnly at Arthur, he said, "No, no, I don't quite think you've got the hang of what I mean. Even married people have all sorts of intangibles, ambition and whatnot—and most of them are kept a dead secret. Even from each other. Maybe even from themselves."

He turned to look again at Mabel. His glance was suddenly very penetrating as he continued. "Wives, for instance, can take it into their pretty heads very early on in marriage to run counter to their husbands' wishes. It gets to be their main intangible and you can't shake 'em out of it."

Mabel said nothing to this, but Arthur stood up angrily. The words had made him more uneasy than he would admit.

"Don't you go saying things like that about Mabel!" he said, in a bull-like voice. "It's none of your business and besides it ain't true! Maybe you better finish up that cheese and go see anybody don't thieve your truck!"

Mabel was also standing.

"Arthur Jones!" she said. "That's not polite to a guest. Or a wrinkled old man. He wasn't meaning me personally. You just sit down and listen to a bit of conversation. It isn't as if we get so much of that!"

Arthur sat down, shaking his head. The wrinkled old man's long, crinkled face regarded him closely, compassion shining behind the spectacle lenses.

"Didn't mean to be rude," Arthur muttered. He fiddled awkwardly with the ceramic salt-pot.

"That don't matter. Intangibles can be difficult things to deal with—politeness, for one instance. Why, some folk never use politeness on account of it's too difficult. The only way with intangibles is to use will power on 'em." He sighed. "Will power certainly is needed. Have you got will power, young man?"

"Enough," Arthur said. The wrinkled old man seemed unable to understand how irritated he was, which made the irritation worse. He twiddled the salt-pot at furious speed.

"So what's your object in life?" persisted the wrinkled old man.

"What's that to you?"

"Everyone's happier with an object in life," the wrinkled old man said. "It don't do to have time passing without some object in life, else I'd be out of business. Suns wouldn't rise without an object in life."

This sounded to Mabel very like the maxims she read in her magazines. Pleasure shared is pleasure doubled; a life shared is life immortal. Caring for others is the best way of caring for yourself. Cast your bread upon the waters; even sharks got to live. Mabel was not happy about this little man in overalls, but obviously he could teach her husband a thing or two.

"Of *course* you got an object in life, Art," she said, severely.

Arthur raised his bovine eyes, looked at her, then lowered them again. A wrinkled hand moved across the table to take the fidgetting salt-pot from his grasp. Arthur had a distinct feeling he was being assailed from all sides.

"Sure, I got objects . . . Make a bit of money . . . Raise some children . . ." After a pause, he added, "Knock a bit of shape into the yard."

"Very commendable," the wrinkled old man said

in a warm tone. "Those are fine objectives for a young man, fine objectives. To cultivate the garden is especially proper. But those, after all, are the sort of objectives everyone has. A man also needs a special, private ambition, just to distinguish himself from the herd."

"I'm never likely to mistake myself for anyone else, mister," Arthur said. He could tell by Mabel's silence that she approved of this interrogation. Seizing the pepper-pot, he began to twirl it as furiously as he had the salt-pot. "That yard—always full of chickweed . . ."

"Don't you have any special, private ambitions all your own?"

Not knowing what to say without sounding stupid, Arthur sat at the table looking stupid. The wrinkled old man politely removed the twirling pepper-pot from his hand. Mabel said with subdued ferocity, "Well, go on then, Art, don't be ashamed to admit it if you don't have no aim in life."

Arthur scraped back his chair and lumbered up from the table.

"I can't say any more than what I have. I don't reckon there's anything in your cargo for me, mister!"

"On the contrary," said the wrinkled old man, his voice losing none of its kindness. "I have just what you need. For every size of mentality, I have a suitable size of intangible."

"Well, I don't want it," Arthur said stubbornly. "I'm happy enough as I am. Don't get bringing those things in here!"

"Art, I don't believe you've taken in a word this—"

"You keep out of it!" Arthur told her, wagging a finger at her. "All I know is, this travelling gentleman's trying to put something over on me, and you're helping him. So keep quiet."

*   *   *

They confronted each other, the wrinkled old man sitting nursing the two pots and looking at the husband and wife judiciously. Mabel's expression changed from one of rebellion to anguish; she put a hand to her stomach.

"The baby's hurting," she said.

In an instant, Arthur was round the table, his arms about her, consoling her, penitent. But when she peeped at the wrinkled old man, he was watching her closely. His eyes held that penetrating quality again. Arthur also caught the glance and, misinterpreting, asked guiltily, "Do you reckon I ought to get a doctor?"

"It would be a waste of money," the wrinkled old man said.

This obviously relieved Arthur, but he felt bound to say, "They do say Doc Smallpiece is a good doctor."

"Doctors are no use against intangibles, which is what you're dealing with here . . . Ah, a human soul is a wonderful intricate place! Funny thing is, it could do so much, but the short lifespan—"

Arthur was feeling strong again now that he was holding Mabel.

"Go on, you pessimistic character. Me and Mabel're going to do a lot of things in our life."

The wrinkled old man shook his head and looked ineffably sad. For a moment they thought he would cry. Every crinkle on his face trembled.

"You're not. You're plain not. You're going to do nothing thousands of human folk aren't doing exactly the same at exactly the same time. 'Cause that's in the interests of the gene pool. Too many intangibles stacked up against you."

Arthur banged his fist on the table.

"That ain't true, and you can get to hell out of here! I can do anything I want. I got will power, like I said."

The wrinkled old man also stood, pushing his chair aside. Seriousness attenuated his long face.

He picked up the pepper- and salt-pots and arranged them side by side, so that they did not quite touch, on the edge of the table. He took his time, and Mabel and Arthur watched.

"Here's a little test," he said. His voice, though quiet and dry, was curiously impressive. "I set these two pots here, on the edge of the table. How long could you keep them just so, without moving them, without touching them, even, in exactly that same place?"

Just for a moment, Arthur hesitated as if grappling with the perspectives of time.

"As long as I felt like it," he said. "Naturally."

"No, you couldn't," the visitor contradicted.

"Course I could! This is my place, I do what I like. It's a fool thing to want to do, but I could keep them pots there a whole year if need be!"

"You'd use your *will power* to keep them there, eh?"

The wrinkled old man treated himself to a secret grin.

"Why not?" Arthur asked. "I got plenty of will power, and what's more I'm going to fix the yard and grow beans and things."

"Keep chickens," Mabel said.

The long face swung to and fro, the shoulders shrugged, the wrinkles interwove.

"You can't test will power like that. Will power is something that should last a lifetime. You're not enough of an individual to have that kind of will power, are you now?"

"Want to bet on that?" Arthur asked.

"Certainly."

"Right. Then I'll wager you I can keep those pots untouched on that table for a lifetime—my lifetime. There!"

The wrinkled old man laughed. He took a pipe out of his pocket and commenced to light it. They heard spittle pop in its stem.

"I won't take on any such wager, son," he said, "because I know you'd never do it and then you'd be disappointed with yourself. You see, a little thing like you propose is not so simple. You'd run up against all those intangibles in the blood as I was talking about."

"To hell with them!" Arthur exploded. His blood was up. "I'm telling you I could do it."

"And I'm telling you you couldn't. Because why? Because in maybe two, maybe five, say maybe ten years at most, you'd suddenly say to yourself, 'It's not worth the bother—I give up.' Or you'd say, 'Why should I be bound by what I said when I was young and foolish?' Or a friend would come in and accidentally knock the pots off the table. Or your kids would grow up and take the pots. Or your house would burn down. Or something else. Things just don't stay put. I tell you it's impossible to do even a simple thing if the intangibles are stacked against you. Them and the pots would beat you."

"He's right," Mabel agreed. "It's a silly thing to do, Art, and you couldn't do it."

And that was what settled it.

Arthur rammed his fists deep down into his pockets and stood over the two ceramic pots.

"I bet you these pots will stay here on this table, untouched, all my life," he said. "Take it or leave it."

"You can't—" Mabel began, but the wrinkled old man silenced her with a gesture and turned to Arthur.

"Good," he said. "I shall pop in occasionally, if I may, to see how things are going. And in exchange I give—I have already given—you one of my best intangibles. An objective in life."

He paused for Arthur to speak, but the young man only continued to stare down at the pots as if hypnotised.

It was Mabel who asked, "And what is his objective in life?"

As he turned towards the door, the wrinkled old man gave a light laugh, not exactly pleasant, not exactly cruel.

"Why, guarding those pots," he said. "See you."

Crimson sunset light flooded in as he left.

Several days elapsed before they realised that he drove away without any further trouble from the engine of his ancient truck.

At first Mabel and Arthur argued violently over the pots. The arguments were one-sided, since Mabel had only to put her hand on her stomach to win them.

She tried to show him how stupid the bet was. Sometimes he would admit it, sometimes not. She tried to show him how unimportant it all was. That he would never admit. The wrinkled old man had bored right through Arthur's obtuseness and anger and touched a vital spot.

Before she realised this, Mabel did her best to persuade Arthur to remove the pots from the table. Afterwards, she fell silent. She tried to wait in patience, to continue as if nothing had happened.

Then it was Arthur's turn to argue against the pots. They changed sides as easily as if they had been engaged in a dance. Which they were.

"Why should we put up with the nuisance of them?" he asked her. "He was only an old guy making a fool of us."

"He was a WOM—you know how wise they are."

"Remind me never to ask an alien in the house again."

"You know you wouldn't feel right if you did move the pots—not yet anyhow. It's a matter of psychology."

"I told you it was a trick," growled Arthur, who had a poor opinion of the things his wife read about.

"The pots don't get in your way," Mabel said, changing her line of defence. "I'm around more than you and they don't bug me, standing there."

"I think about them all the while when I'm working," he said.

"You'd think more about them if you moved them. Leave them a while."

He stood glowering at the two little ceramic pots. Slowly he raised a hand to skitter them off the table and across the room. Then he turned away instead, and mooched into the yard. Tomorrow, he'd get up real early, start on all that blamed chickweed, fix the gate.

The next stage was that neither of them spoke about the pots. Mabel dusted round them. Yet the subject was not dropped. It was an icy draught between them. An intangible.

Suns rose and set. Crops ripened and were harvested. Two years passed before the antediluvian vehicle approached Hapsville again. The day was Arthur's twenty-fourth birthday. Once again it was evening as the overalled figure with the long skull walked up to the porch and rang the bell.

"If he gets funny about those pots, I swear I'll throw them right in his face," Arthur said to Mabel. It was the first time for months either of them had mentioned the pots.

"You'd better come in," Mabel said to the wrinkled old man, looking him up and down round the door. "I suppose."

He smiled disarmingly and thanked her, but hovered where he was, on the step. As he caught sight of Arthur, his spectacles shone, every wrinkle animated itself over the surface of his face. He read so easily in Arthur's expression just what he wanted to know that he did not even have to look over their shoulders at the table for confirmation.

"I won't stop," he said. "Just passing through. Thought I'd drop this in on you."

He fished a wooden doll out of his pocket and dangled it before them. The doll had pretty, round, painted light blue eyes.

"A present for your little daughter," he said, thrusting it towards Mabel.

Mabel had the toy in her hand before she asked, "How did you guess it was a girl we got?"

"I saw a frock drying on the line as I came up the path," he said. "Good night! See you!"

They stood watching the little truck drive off and vanish up the highway towards Hapsville. Both fought to conceal their disappointment over the brevity of the meeting.

"At least he didn't come in and rile you with his clever talk," Mabel said.

"I *wanted* him to come in," Arthur said petulantly. "I wanted him to see we'd got the pots just where he left them, plumb on the table edge."

"You were rude to him last time."

"Why didn't you make him come in?"

"Weren't you telling me you didn't want a WOM in this place? Arthur Jones, you're a hard man to please. I reckon you're most happy when you're unhappy. You're your own worst enemy."

He swore at her. They began to argue more violently, until Mabel clapped a hand to her stomach and assumed a pained look.

This time it was a boy. They called him Mike and he grew into a little fiend. Nothing was safe from him. Arthur had to nail four walls of wood round the salt-and pepper-pots to keep them unmolested; as he told Mabel, it wasn't as if it was a valuable table.

"For crying out loud, a grown man like you!" she exclaimed impatiently. "Throw those pots away! They're getting a regular superstitition with you And when are you going to do something about that yard?"

He stared darkly and belligerently at her until she retired to the kitchen.

* * *

Mike was almost ten years old, and away bird-snaring among the sunflower fields, before the wrinkled old man called again. He arrived one morning, just as Arthur was setting out for the service station. As Mabel ushered him into the front room, he smiled his old engaging smile. Even his worn old overalls looked unchanged.

"There are your two pots, mister," Arthur said proudly, as he picked up his lunch-box. "Never been touched since you set 'em down there, all them years ago!"

Sure enough, there the pots stood on the table, upright as sentries.

"Very good, very good!" the wrinkled old man said, looking genuinely delighted. He pulled out a notebook and made an entry. "Just like to keep a note on all my customers," he told them apologetically.

"You mean to say you've folks everywhere guarding salt-pots?" Mabel asked, fidgetting because she could hear the two-year-old crying out in the yard.

"Oh, they don't only guard salt-pots," the wrinkled old man said. "Some of them spend their lives collecting badges or bottles or books, or sticking little stamps in albums, or numbering the Mauve Stars, or hoarding coins, or running other people's lives. Sometimes I help them, sometimes they manage on their own. I can see you two are doing just fine."

"It's been a great nuisance keeping the pots in place," Mabel said. "A man can't tell how much nuisance."

The wrinkled old man turned on her that penetrating look she remembered so well, but said nothing. Instead, he switched to Arthur and inquired how work at the station was going.

"I'm head mechanic now," Arthur said, not without pride. "And Hapsville's growing into a big place now—yes sir! New freeze factory and everything going up. They're going to build a spaceport soon. We've got all the work we can handle at the station."

"You're doing fine," the wrinkled old man assured him. "And I'll be round to see you soon."

Soon was fourteen years.

The battered old vehicle with its scarcely distinguishable sign drew up in front of Arthur's bungalow. The wrinkled old man climbed stiffly out. He looked around with interest. Since his last visit, Hapsville's suburbs had spread out to Arthur's place. Neat little wooden doll's houses surrounded it on either side of the highway.

Arthur's place itself had changed. An extension with picture windows was tacked on to the south wall. The outside had recently been painted avocado and white. A lawn with rose bushes ran down to the front fence. No sign of chickweed.

"They're doing O.K." the wrinkled old man said. He went up the path and knocked on the door.

A young lady in a smock greeted him. She resembled Mabel, although she skipped a bit. She guessed at once who he was.

"My name's Jennifer, and I'm sixteen and I've been looking forward to seeing you for simply ages! You're the WOM! You'd better come on in because Mom's out back feeding the hens. You can come and see the pots because they're just in the same place and never once been moved. Father says it's a million years' bad luck if we touch them, 'cause they're intangible."

Chattering away, she led the wrinkled old man into the old room. It too had changed. A bed stood in it, and several faded photographs hung on the walls. An old man with a face as pink as sunset sat in a rocking-chair and nodded contentedly when Jennifer and the wrinkled old man entered. "That's Father's Pop," the girl explained, by way of introduction.

One thing was unchanged. A bare table stood in

its usual place, and on it, near the edge and not quite touching each other, were two little china pots. Jennifer left the wrinkled old man admiring them while she ran to fetch her mother from the yard.

"Where are the other children?" the wrinkled old man asked Father's Pop, by way of conversation.

"Yes, but it will soon be summer."

"I said, where are the other children?"

"Jennifer's all that's left," Father's Pop said. "Prue, the eldest got married like they all do. That would be before I came to live here. Six years, most like, maybe seven. Wife died. She married a miller called Muller. Prue, that's to say . . .

"Funny thing that, huh?—A miller called Muller. And they got a little girl called Millie. Now Mike, Arthur's boy, he was a young dog. Good for nothing but reproducin' his kind. And when there were too many young ladies that should have known better around here expecting babies—why, then young Mike thieves an automobile from his father's garage and drives off to New Raton and joins the space fleet, and they never seen him since."

The wrinkled old man made a smacking noise with his lips, which suggested that although he disapproved of such carryings on he had heard similar tales before.

"How did Arthur take it?" he asked.

"Business is thriving. Maybe you didn't know he bought the service station downtown last fall? Maybe the fall before last. He's the boss now!" Father's Pop nodded proudly.

"I haven't been around these parts for nearly fifteen years."

"Fifty years, eh? Long time. Hapsville's going up in the world," Father's Pop murmured. "Of course, that means it ain't such a comfortable place to live in anymore . . . Getting a spaceport next year, they say . . . Yes, Arthur bought up the old station when his boss retired."

"Clever boy, Arthur—a bit stupid, but clever in his way."

"No, I'm never in his way. Though I don't get out like I used."

When Mabel appeared, she was drying her hands on a towel. Like nearly everything else, she had changed. Her last birthday had been her forty-eighth. The years and the children had thickened her. The spectacles perched on her nose were a tribute to the persistence with which she had tracked down home psychology among the advert columns of her perennial magazines. Experience like a grindstone had sharpened her expression.

Nevertheless, she allowed the wrinkled old man a smile and greeted him cordially enough.

"Arthur's at work," she said. "I'll get you some coffee."

"Thank you kindly," he said, "but I must be getting along. Only just called in to see how you all were doing."

"Oh, the pots are still there," Mabel said, with a sudden approach to asperity, sweeping her hand towards the pepper and salt. Catching sight as she did so of Jennifer lolling in the doorway, she called, "Jenny, you get on stacking them apples like I showed you. I want a word with this gentleman."

She took a deep breath and turned back to the wrinkled old man. "Now," she said. "You keep longer and longer intervals between your calls here, mister. I thought you were never going to show up again. It's been fifteen years. We've had a very good offer for this plot of ground, enough money to set us up for life in a better house in a nicer part of town."

"I'm glad to hear it." The long face crinkled engagingly.

"Oh, you're glad are you?" Mabel said. "Then let me tell you this. Arthur is turning that very good offer down just because of these two pots sitting here. He says if he sells up, the pots will be moved, and he don't like the idea of them being moved. Now what do you say to that, Mister Intangible, you and your alien thought processes?"

The wrinkled old man spread wide his hands and shook his head from side to side. He looked genuinely concerned.

"Only one thing to say to that," he told her. "This little bet we made has suddenly become a major inconvenience. We must call it off. How'll it be if I remove the pots right now before Arthur comes home? Then you can explain to him for me, eh?"

He moved over to the table, extending a hand to the pots.

"Wait!" Mabel cried. "Just let me think a moment before you touch them."

"Arthur'd never forgive you if you moved them pots," Father's Pop said from the background.

"It's too much responsibility for me to decide," Mabel said, furious with herself for her indecision. "When you think how we guarded them over the years while the kids were small. Why they've stood there a quarter of a century . . ."

Something caught in her voice.

"Don't you fret," the wrinkled old man consoled her. "You wait till Arthur's back. Then you tell him I said to forget all about our little bet. Like I explained to you back in the first place, it's impossible to do even a simple thing with all the intangibles against you. Wait till Arthur's back."

"He's always complaining about his back," said Father's Pop.

Mabel stared bitterly at the wrinkled old man.

"Know what I mean? The whole character of the human race is ranged against the permanence of those pots, you might say."

Absent-mindedly, Mabel began to dry her hands on the towel all over again.

"Can't you wait and explain it to him yourself?"

she asked. "He won't listen to me. He'll be back in half an hour for a bite of food."

"Sorry, Mabel. My business is booming too—got to go and see a couple of young fellows breeding a line of dogs that can't bark."

"What's time to your kind?"

"I'll be back along presently."

He gave her his dusty smile.

And the wrinkled old man came back to Hapsville as he promised. Nineteen years later. There was only one sun in the heavens and snow in the air and mush on the ground, and Arthur's place was hard to find. A big theatre showing a solid called "Bang-Bang" loomed over the modest home on one side, while a new six-lane toll shuttled trucks along on the other.

"Looks like he never sold out," the wrinkled old man commented to himself as he trudged up the path.

Chickweed grew patchily round the front door. He hesitated there, looking about him. The garden, so trim last time, was a wilderness. The roses had given way to cabbage stumps, old tickets and plastine cartons fringed the theatre wall. Grass was springing up where the fence was down. The house itself looked a little rickety. Damp mottled the avocado.

"They'd never hear me knock for all this traffic," the wrinkled old man said. "I better take a peek inside."

In the room where the china pots still stood, an oil fire burned, warming an ancient figure in a rocking chair. He and the intruder peered at each other through the twilight.

"Father's Pop!" the wrinkled old man exclaimed. For a moment he had thought . . .

"What you say?" the old fellow asked. "Can't hear a thing these days. Come nearer . . . Oh, it's you! Mister Intangibles himself. Been a while since you were around!"

"All of nineteen years, I guess. Got more folk to visit all the time."

"What you say? Didn't think to see me still here, eh?" Father's Pop asked. "Ninety-seven last November, ninety-seven. Fit as a fiddle too, barring this deafness. Though I don't get out like I used."

A woman entered the room by the rear door. She was thick-set, aged about forty-five, plain, dressed in unbecoming mustard green. Something bovine in her face identified her as a member of the Jones family.

"Didn't know we had company," she said. Then she recognised the wrinkled old man. She went rigid, frowning. "Oh, it's you, is it? What do you want?"

"Let's see," he said, scratching a cheek. "You'd be—why, you must be Prue, Arthur's daughter, the daughter who married the miller called Muller."

"I'll thank you not to mention him," Prue said sharply. "I saw the last of him two years ago, and good riddance to him."

"Is that so? Divorce, eh? Well, it's fashionable, my dear . . . And your little girl? It was a girl?"

"Millie's married. So's my son Rex. Both living in better cities than Hapsville," she told him. "If that's any of your business."

"Hadn't heard of *Rex*."

"If you want to see my father, he's through here," Prue said, abruptly. She gestured to the wrinkled old man. "He wants to see you. I can't think why."

"We're old friends, missus."

She led the way into a small bedroom. Here curtains were drawn against the bleakness outside and a bright bedside lamp spread cosiness. A pleasant aroma of sunflower seed oil filled the room. Arthur, a copy of "Mauve Mechanics" on his knees, sat huddled up in bed.

* * *

It was thirty-three years since they had seen each other. Arthur was hardly recognisable, until you discovered the old contours of the bull under his heavy jowls. During early middle age he had piled up bulk which he was now losing. His eyebrows were ragged; they all but concealed his eyes, which lit in recognition. His hair was grey and uncombed.

He put out a hand which the wrinkled old man clutched.

Despite the gulf of years which separated their meetings, Arthur began to talk as if it were only yesterday.

"They're still in there on the table, just as they always were. Have you seen them?" he asked eagerly.

"I saw them. You've certainly got will power!"

"They never been touched all these damned years! How . . . how long's that been, mister?"

"Forty-five years, all but."

"Forty-five years!" Arthur echoed. "It don't seem that long . . . Shows what an object in life'll do, I suppose. Forty-five years . . . That's a terrible lot of years, ain't it? You ain't changed much, mister."

"Keeps a feller young, my job," the wrinkled old man said, crinkling.

"You live forever, don't you?"

"Not quite."

After a silence, Arthur spoke again.

"We got Prue back here now to help out. She'd get you a bite to eat, if I ask her. Mabel's out just now."

The wrinkled old man polished up his spectacles on his overalls.

"You haven't told me what you're doing lying in bed," he said gently.

"Oh, I sprained my back down at the service station. Trying to lift a chassis instead of bothering to use the hoist. We had a lot of work on hand.

I was aiming to save time. Should have known better at my age."

"How many companies you got now?"

"Just the one. We—I got a lot of competition from big cartels, had to sell up the down-town business. It's a hard trade. Cut-throat. By-pass makes it worse. Maybe I should have gone in for something else but it's too late to think of changing now ... Doctor says I can get about again in the spring."

"How long have you been in bed?" the wrinkled old man asked.

"Weeks, on and off. First it's better, then it's worse. The spine transplant didn't help. You know how these things are. I should have had more sense. These big nuclear fuel import companies squeeze the life out of you ... Mabel goes down every day to look after the financial side for me. About them pots—"

"Last time I came, I told your lady wife to call the whole thing off."

Arthur plucked peevishly at the bedclothes, his hands shining redly against the grey coverlet. In a moment of pugnacity he looked more his old self.

"You know our bet can't be called off," he said pettishly. "Why d'you talk so silly? It's just something I'm stuck with. It's more than my life's worth to think of moving those two pots now. Mabel says it's a jinx and that's just about what it is. Move them and anything might happen to us! Life ain't easy ..."

The long head wagged sadly from side to side.

"You got it wrong," the wrinkled old man said. "It's just a bet we made one night when we were young and foolish. People get up to the oddest things when they're young. Why, I called on some young fellows just last week, they're trying to breed pig-sized mice."

"Now you're trying to make me lose the bet! I never did entirely trust you and your Intangibles.

Don't think I've forgotten what you said that first time you came here. You said something would make me change my mind, you said I'd go in there and knock 'em off the table one day. Well—I never have! We've even stuck on in this place because of those two pots, and that's been to our disadvantage."

"Guess there's nothing I can say, then."

"Wait! Don't go!" Arthur stretched out a hand, for the wrinkled old man had moved towards the door. "There's something I want to ask you."

"Go ahead."

"Those two pots—although we never touch 'em, if you look close you'll see something. You'll see they got no dust on them! Shall I tell you why? It's the traffic vibration from the new by-pass. It jars all the dust off the pots."

"Useful," the wrinkled old man said cautiously.

"But that's not what worries me. The traffic will be worse when they build the spaceport next year. I'm scared it will get so bad it'll shake the pots right off the table. They're near the edge, aren't they? They could easily be shaken off, just with all that traffic roaring by. Supposing they are shaken off—does that count?"

He peered up at the wrinkled old man's face, but lamplight reflecting from his spectacles hid his eyes. A long silence fell, which the wrinkled old man seemed to break with reluctance.

"You know the answer all the time, Arthur," he said. It was the only time he had ever used the other's name.

"Yep," Arthur said slowly. "Reckon I do. If them pots were rattled off the table, it would mean the Intangibles had got me."

Gloomily, he sank back onto his pillows. The "Mauve Mechanics" slid unregarded to the floor. After a moment's hesitation, the wrinkled old man turned and went to the door. There he paused.

"Hope you'll be up and about again in the spring."

That made Arthur sit up abruptly, groaning as he did so.

"There's something really alien about you. Come and see me again! Promise you'll be round again?"

"I'll be round," the wrinkled old man said.

Sure enough, his antique truck again came creaking back into the multiple lanes of Hapsville traffic. He turned off the by-pass and stopped as close as he could to Arthur's place. Twenty-one years had passed.

"Neighbourhoods certainly do change fast," he said.

The theatre looked as if it had been shut down for a long time. Now it was used as a furniture warehouse. A big pantechnicon was loading up divans outside its doors. Behind Arthur's place loomed a block of ugly flats, grey, windowless. Children shrieked and yelled down its side alley. On the far side of the busy highway was a straggle of anonymous stores, each skirted by vast car parks. There wasn't a sunflower in sight. Jets bellowed by overhead.

He made his way down a narrow side alley. There, squeezed behind a drug store, stood Arthur's place. Nature, pushed firmly out elsewhere, had reappeared here. Ivy straggled up the posts of the porch. Chickweed grew tall enough to look in at the windows. Moss covered the front step. A gutter dripped.

"What do you want?"

The wrinkled old man would have jumped if he had been the jumping kind. His challenger was standing in the half-open doorway, smoking a cigar. It was a man in late middle-age, a bull-like man with heavy, unshaven jowls and grey streaking his hair.

"Arthur!" the wrinkled old man exclaimed. And

then the other stepped out into a better light to get a closer look.

"No, it can't be Arthur," the wrinkled old man said. "You must be—Mike, at a guess?" He took out his battered notebook.

"My name's Mike. What of it?"

"You'd be—sixty-four?"

"What's that to you? Who are you—police? No—wait a bit! I know who you are. You're the WOM. How come you arrive here today of all days?"

"I just got round to calling. How's your father?"

"You just got round to calling." Mike paused and spat into the weeds. He was the image of his father, and evidently did not think any faster. "You're the old pepper and salt guy?"

"You might call me that, yes."

"You better come in and see Ma." He moved aside reluctantly to let the wrinkled old man squeeze by. He threw his cigar stub down and stamped on it.

Inside, the house was cold and damp and musty. Mabel hobbled slowly round the bedroom, tucking possessions into a large black bag. When the wrinkled old man entered the room, she came close to him and stared at him, nodding to herself. She herself smelled cold and damp and musty.

Mabel was eighty-eight. Under her threadbare coat, she had shrunken to a little old lady. Her spectacles glinted on a nose still sharp but worn bone frail. When she spoke, her voice still carried an incisive note.

"I said you'd be here. I said you'd come. I told them you'd come. You would want to see how it ended, wouldn't you? Well—so you shall. We're selling up. Selling right up. We're going. Leaving. And about time."

"Where are you going?"

"We're selling up. Prue's got married again—another miller, too. Mike's taking me out to his place—got a little shack in the fruit country, New Raton way. Ain't that so, Mike?"

"And ... Arthur?" the wrinkled old man prompted.

She shot him another hard look.

"As if you didn't know!" she exclaimed, her voice too flinty for tears. "We buried Arthur this morning. Proper funeral service. I didn't go. I'm too old for any funerals but my own. Shan't live to see the spaceport built."

"I wish I'd come before ..."

"You come when you think you'll come," Mabel said, shortly. "Arthur kept talking about you, right to the last ... He never got out of his bed again since that time he bust up his back down at the business. Twenty-one years in that bed there ... Five spine ops ..."

She put her knuckles to her mouth.

Mabel led the way into the front room where they had drunk diluted soup together, long ago. It was very dark there now, dark and chill with a sort of green darkness, with the dirty panes and the weeds at the windows. The room was empty except for a table on which two little china pots stood.

The wrinkled old man made a note in his book.

"Arthur won his bet all right! I sure do compliment him," he said. He walked across the room and stood looking down at the pots.

"To think they've stood there undisturbed for sixty-six years ..."

"That's what Arthur thought!" Mabel said scornfully. "He never stopped worrying over them pots. I used to pick them up to dust them every day. I never told him. A woman has a place to keep clean. A woman has her own intangibles, same as a man. Like you once said in this very room."

Nodding, the wrinkled old man made one final

entry in his notebook. Mabel showed him to the door.

"Guess I won't be seeing you again, Mabel," he said.

He offered his wrinkled hand but she would not take it.

She shook her head at him curtly, for a moment unable to speak. Then she turned into the house, hobbled back into her dark bedroom, and continued to pack her possessions.

The wrinkled old man started up his truck. He knew it was a long way to the end of the galaxy.

The Rift

A chronicle such as this could be never-ending, for the diversity of Starswarm by an intelligent reckoning is never-ending. We have time for but one more call, and that must be to an ember world floating in the Rift, now seldom visited by man.

Many galactic regions have been omitted entirely from our survey. We have not mentioned one of the most interesting, Sentinel Sector, which adjoins both the Rift and Sector Diamond. It also looks out over the edge of our galaxy towards the other island universes where we have yet to go.

Sentinel is a vast region, and contact with it uncertain. This is especially so with the Border Stars, which form the last specks of material in our galaxy. Here, time undergoes compression in a way that brings hallucinations to anyone not bred to it. The people who have colonized those worlds are almost a species apart, and have developed their own perceptions.

They have sent their instruments out into the gulf between universes, and the instruments have returned changed.

To some, this suggests that other island universes will remain forever beyond our reach. To the optimists, it suggests that awaiting us there is a completely new range of sensory experiences upon which we cannot as yet even speculate.

Within our own Starswarm we can find other sorts

of disturbance in the order of things. A planet can become imprisoned in its own greatness. This fate threatens Dansson, as it has overcome an older world floating in that thinly populated part of space we know as the Rift.

This world, legends say, was once the seed mote whence interstellar travel originated. In the successive waves of star voyages since Era One, it has been all but forgotten. We regard it today—if we remember it at all—with ambivalence, a cross between an emptied shrine and a rubbish dump.

Great experiments once took place there: not only star travel, but a later experiment which might have had consequences even more far-reaching. It was an attempt to transcend the physical; the result was failure, the attempt a triumph.

The planet has been left to stagnate, now nameless on all but the few charts that mapped the sector millennia ago. Yet even in its stagnation one can glimpse a reflection of the abundance and vitality, the willingness to try new things—to dare all—that was perhaps its chief gift to Starswarm.

The road climbed dustily down between trees as symmetrical as umbrellas. Its length was punctuated at one point by a musicolumn standing on the verge. From a distance, the column was only a stain in the air. As sentient creatures neared it, their psyches activated the column. It drew on their vitalities, and then it could be heard as well as seen. Their presence made it flower into pleasant sound, instrumental or chant.

All this region was called Ghinomon, for no one lived here now, not even the odd hermit Impure. It was given over to grass and the weight of time. Only a wild goat or two activated the musicolumn nowadays, or a scampering vole wrung a chord from it in passing.

When old Dandi Lashadusa came riding on her baluchitherium, the column began to intone. It was no more than an indigo trace in the air, hardly visible, for it represented only a bonded pattern of music locked into the fabric of that particular area of space. It was also a transubstantio-spatial shrine, the eternal part of a being that had dematerialized itself into music.

The baluchitherium whinnied, lowered its head, and sneezed onto the gritty road.

"Gently, Lass," Dandi told her mare, savouring the growth of the chords that increased in volume as she approached. Her long nose twitched with pleasure as if she could feel the melody along her olfactory nerves.

Obediently, the baluchitherium slowed, turning aside to crop fern, although it kept an eye on the indigo stain. It liked things to have being or not to have being; these half-and-half objects disturbed it, though they could not impair its immense appetite.

Dandi climbed down her ladder onto the ground, glad to feel the ancient dust under her feet. She smoothed her hair and stretched as she listened to the music.

She spoke aloud to her mentor, half a world away, but he was not listening. His mind closed to her thoughts, and he muttered an obscure exposition that darkened what it sought to clarify.

". . . useless to deny that it is well-nigh impossible to improve anything, however faulty, that has so much tradition behind it. And the origins of your bit of metricism are indeed embedded in such an antiquity that we must needs—"

"Tush, Mentor, come out of your black box and forget your hatred of my 'metricism' a moment," Dandi Lashadusa said, cutting her thought into his. "Listen to the bit of 'metricism' I've found here; look at where I have come to; let your argument rest."

She turned her eyes around, scanning the tawny rocks near at hand, the brown line of the road, the distant black-and-white magnificence of ancient Oldorajo's town, doing this all for him, tiresome old fellow. Her mentor was blind, never left his cell in Aeterbroe to go farther than the sandy courtyard, hadn't physically left that green cathedral pile for over a century. Womanlike, she thought he needed change. Soul, how he rambled on! Even now, he was managing to ignore her and refute her.

". . . for consider, Lashadusa woman, nobody can be found to father it. Nobody wrought or thought it, phrases of it merely *came* together. Even the old nations of men could not own it. None of them know who composed it. An element here from a Spanish pavan, an influence there of a French psalm tune, a flavour here of early English carol, a savour there of later German chorale. All primitive—ancient beyond ken. Nor are the faults of your bit of metricism confined to bastardy—"

"Stay in your black box then, if you won't see or listen," Dandi said. She could not get into his mind; it was the mentor's privilege to lodge in her mind, and in the minds of those few other wards he had, scattered around Earth. Only the mentors had the power to inhabit another's mind—which made them rather tiring on occasions like this, when they would not get out. For over seventy centuries, Dandi's mentor had been persuading her to die into a dirge of his choosing (and composing). Let her die, yes, let her transubstantiospatialize herself a thousand times! His quarrel was not with her decision but with her taste, which he considered execrable.

Leaving the baluchitherium to crop, Dandi walked away from the musicolumn towards a hillock. Still fed by her steed's psyche, the column continued to play. Its music was of a simplicity, with a dominant-tonic recurrent bass part suggesting pessimism. To Dandi, a savant in musicolumnology, it yielded other data. She could tell to within a few years when its founder had died and also what sort of creature, generally speaking, he had been.

Climbing the hillock, Dandi looked about. To the south where the road led were low hills, lilac in the poor light. There lay her home. At last she was returning, after wanderings covering three hundred centuries and most of the globe.

Apart from the blind beauty of Oldorajo's town lying to the west, there was only one landmark she recognized. That was the Involute. It seemed to hang iridial above the ground a few leagues ahead; just to look on it made her feel she must go nearer.

Before summoning the baluchitherium, Dandi listened once more to the sounds of the musicolumn, making sure she had them fixed in her head. The pity was that her old fool wise man would not share it. She could still feel his sulks floating like sediment through her mind.

"Are you listening now, Mentor?"

"Eh? An interesting point is that back in 1556 Pre-Involutary, your same little tune may be discovered lurking in Knox's Anglo-Genevan Psalter, where it espoused the cause of the third psalm—"

"You dreary old fish! Wake yourself! How can you criticize my intended way of dying when you have such a fustian way of living?"

This time he heard her words. So close did he seem that his peevish pinching at the bridge of his snuffy old nose tickled hers, too.

"What are you doing *now*, Dandi?" he inquired.

"If you had been listening, you'd know. Here's where I am, on the last Ghinomon plain before Crotheria and home." She swept the landscape again and he took it in, drank it almost greedily. Many mentors went blind early in life shut in their monastic underwater life; their most effective vision was conducted through the eyes of their wards.

His view of what she saw enriched hers. He knew the history, the myth behind his forsaken land. He could stock the tired old landscape with pageantry, delighting her and surprising her. Back and forward he went, painting her pictures: the Youdicans, the Lombards, the Ex-Europa Emissary, the Grites, the Risorgimento, the Involuters—and catchwords, costumes, customs, courtesans, pelted briefly through Dandi Lashadusa's mind. Ah, she thought admiringly, who could truly live without these priestly, beastly, erudite erratic mentors?

"Erratic?" he inquired, snatching at her lick of thought. "A thousand years I live, for all that time to absent myself from the world, to eat mashed fish here with my brothers, learning history, studying rapport, sleeping with my bones on stones—a humble being, a being in a million, a mentor in a myriad, and your standards of judgement are so mundane you find no stronger label for me than erratic?! Fie, Lashadusa, bother me no more for fifty years!

The words squeaked in her head as if she spoke herself. She felt his old chops work phantomlike in hers, and half in anger half in laughter called aloud, "I'll be dead by then!"

He snicked back hot and holy to reply, "And another thing about your footloose swan song—in Marot and Beza's Genevan Psalter of 1551, Old Time, it was musical midwife to the one hundred and thirty-fourth psalm. Like you, it never seemed to settle!" Then he was gone.

"Pooh!" Dandi said. She whistled. "Lass."

Obediently her great rhinolike creature, eighteen feet high at the shoulder, ambled over. The musicolumn died as the mare left it, faded, sank to a whisper, silenced: only the purple stain remained, noiseless, in the lonely air. Lowering its great Oligocene head, Lass nuzzled its mistress's hand. She climbed the ladder onto the ridged plateau of its back.

They made towards the Involute, lulled by the simple and intricate feeling of being alive.

Night was settling in now. Hidden behind banks of mist, the sun prepared to set. But Venus was high, a gallant half-crescent four times as big as the moon had been before the moon, spiralling farther and farther from Earth, had shaken off its parent's clutch to go dance around the sun, a second Mercury. Even by that time Venus had been moved by gravito-traction into Earth's orbit, so that the two sister worlds circled each other as they circled the sun.

The stamp of that great event still lay everywhere, its tokens not only in the crescent in the sky. For Venus placed a strange spell on the hearts of man, and a more penetrating displacement in his genes. Even when its atmosphere was transformed into a muffled breathability, it remained an alien world; against logic, its opportunities, its possibilities, were its own. It shaped men, just as Earth had shaped them.

On Venus, men bred themselves anew.

And they bred the so-called Impures. They bred new plants, new fruits, new creatures—original ones, and duplications of creatures not seen on Earth for aeons past. From one line of these familiar strangers Dandi's baluchitherium was descended. So, for that matter, was Dandi.

The huge creature came now to the Involute, or as near as it cared to get. Again it began to crop at thistles, thrusting its nose through dewy spiders' webs and ground mist.

"Like you, I'm a vegetarian," Dandi said, climbing down to the ground. A grove of low fruit trees grew nearby; she reached up into the branches, gathered, and ate, before turning to inspect the Involute. Already her spine tingled at the nearness of it; awe, loathing and love made a part-pleasant sensation near her heart.

The Involute was not beautiful. True, its colours changed with the changing light, yet the colours were fish-cold, for they belonged to another dimension. Though they reacted to dusk and dawn, Earth had no stronger power over them. They pricked the eyes. Perhaps, too, they were painful because they were the last signs of materialist man. Even Lass moved uneasily before that ill-defined lattice, the upper limits of which were lost in thickening gloom.

"Don't fear," Dandi said. "There's an explanation for this, old girl." She added, "There's an explanation for everything, if we can find it."

She could feel all the personalities in the Involute. It was a frozen screen of personality. All over the old planet the structures stood, to shed their awe on those who were left behind. They were the essence of man. They were man—all that remained of him on Earth.

When the first flint, the first shell, was shaped into a weapon, that action shaped man. As he moulded and complicated his tools, so they moulded and complicated him. He became the first scientific animal. And at last, via information theory and great computers, he gained knowledge of all his parts. He formed the Laws of Integration, which reveal all beings as part of a pattern and show them their part in the pattern. There is only the pattern; the pattern is all the universe, creator and created. For the first time it became possible to duplicate that pattern artificially—the transubstantio-spatializers were built.

Men left their strange hobbies on Earth and Venus and projected themselves into the pattern. Their entire personalities were merged with the texture of space itself. Through science, they reached immortality.

It was a one-way passage.

They did not return. Each Involute carried thousands or even millions of people. There they were, not dead, not living. How they exulted or wept in their transubstantiation, no one left could say. Only this could be said: man had gone, and a great emptiness was fallen over Earth.

"Your thoughts are heavy, Dandi Lashadusa. Get you home." Her mentor was back in her mind. She caught the feeling of him moving around and around in his coral-formed cell.

"I must think of man," she said.

"Your thoughts mean nothing, do nothing."

"Man created us; I want to consider him in peace."

"He only shaped a stream of life that was always entirely out of his control. Forget him. Get onto your mare and ride home."

"Mentor—"

"Get home, woman. Moping does not become you. I want to hear no more of your swan song, for I've given you my final word on that. Use a theme of your own, not of man's. I've said it a million times, and I say it again."

"I wasn't going to mention my music. I was only going to tell you that—"

"What then?" His thought was querulous. She felt his powerful tail tremble, disturbing the quiet water of his cell.

"I don't know—"

"Get home then."

"I'm lonely."

He shot her a picture from another of his wards before leaving her. Dandi had seen this ward before in similar dreamlike glimpses. It was a huge mole creature, still boring underground as it had been for the last hundred years. Occasionally it crawled through vast caves; once it swam in a subterranean lake; most of the time it just bored through rock. Its motivations were obscure to Dandi, although her mentor referred to it as "a geologer." Doubtless if the mole was vouchsafed occasional glimpses of Dandi and her musicolumnology, it would find her as baffling. At least the mentor's point was made: loneliness was psychological, not statistical.

Why, a million personalities glittered almost before her eyes!

She mounted the great baluchitherium mare and headed for home. Time and old monuments made glum company.

Twilight now, with just one streak of antique gold left in the sky, Venus sweetly bright, and stars peppering the purple. A fine evening in which to be alive, particularly with one's last bedtime close at hand.

And yes, for all her mentor said, she was going to turn into that old little piece derived from one of the tunes in the 1540 *Souter Liedekens*, that splendid source of Netherlands folk music. For a moment, Dandi Lashadusa chuckled almost as eruditely as her mentor. The sixteenth century, with the virtual death of plainsong and virtual birth of the violin, was most interesting to her. Ah, the richness of facts, the texture of man's brief history on Earth! Pure joy! Then she remembered herself.

After all, she was only a megatherium, a sloth as big as a small elephant, whose kind had been extinct for millions of years until man reconstituted a few of them in the Venusian experiments. Her modifications in the way of fingers and enlarged brain gave her no real qualification to think up to man's level.

Early next morning, they arrived at the ramparts of the town Crotheria, where Dandi lived. The ubiquitous goats thronged about them, some no bigger than hedgehogs, some almost as big as hippos—what madness in his last days had provoked man to so many variations on one undistinguished caprine theme?—as Lass and her mistress moved up the last slope and under the archway.

It was good to be back, to push among the trails fringed with bracken, among the palms, oaks and treeferns. Almost all the town was deeply green and private from the sun, curtained by swathes of Spanish moss. Here and there were houses—caves, pits, crude piles of boulders, or even genuine man-type buildings, grand in ruin. Dandi climbed down, walking ahead of her mount, her long hair curling in pleasure. The air was cool with the coo of doves or the occasional bleat of a merino.

As she explored familiar ways, though, disappointment overcame her. Her friends were all away, even the dreamy bison whose wallow lay at the corner of the street in which Dandi lived. Only pure animals were here, rooting happily and mind-lessly in the lanes, beggars who owned the Earth. The Impures—descendants of the Venusian experimental stock—were all absent from Crotheria.

That was understandable. For obvious reasons man had increased the abilities of herbivores rather than carnivores. After the Involution, with man gone, these Impures had taken to his towns as they took to his ways, as far as this was possible to their natures. Both Dandi and Lass, and many of the others, consumed massive amounts of vegetable matter every day. Gradually a wider and wider circle of desolation grew about each town (the greenery in the town itself was sacrosanct), forcing a semi-nomadic life into its vegetarian inhabitants.

This thinning in its turn led to a decline in the birthrate. The travellers grew fewer, the towns greener and emptier; in time they had become little oases of forest studding the grassless plains.

"Rest here, Lass," Dandi said at last, pausing by a bank of brightly flowering cycads. "I'm going into my house."

A giant beech grew before the stone façade of her home, so close that it was hard to determine whether it did not help support the ancient building. A crumbling balcony jutted from the first floor; reaching up, Dandi siezed the balustrade and hauled herself onto it.

This was her normal way of entering her home, for the ground floor was taken over by goats and hogs, just as the third floor had been appropriated by doves and parakeets. Trampling over the greenery self-sown on the balcony, she moved into the front room. Dandi smiled. Here were old things, the broken furniture on which she liked to sleep, the vision screens on which nothing could be seen, the heavy manuscript books in which, guided by her know-all mentor, she wrote down the outpourings of the musicolumns she had visited all over the world.

She ambled through to the next room.

She paused, her peace of mind suddenly broken.

A brown bear stood there. One of its heavy hands was clenched over the hilt of a knife.

"I am no vulgar thief," it said, curling its thick black lips over the syllables. "I am an archaeologer. If this is your place, you must grant me permission to remove the man things. Obviously you have no idea of the worth of some of the equipment here. We bears require it. We must have it."

It came towards her, panting doggy fashion, its jaws open. From under bristling eyebrows gleamed the lust to kill.

Dandi was frightened. Peaceful by nature, she feared the bears above all creatures for their fierceness and their ability to organize. The bears were few: they were the only creatures to show signs of wishing to emulate man's old aggressiveness.

She knew what the bears did. They hurled themselves through the Involutes to increase their power; by penetrating those patterns, they nourished their psychic drive, so the mentor said. It was forbidden. They were transgressors. They were killers.

"Mentor!" she screamed.

The bear hesitated. As far as he was concerned, the hulking creature before him was merely an obstacle in the way of progress, something to be thrust aside without hate. Killing would be pleasant but irrelevant; more important items remained to be done. Much of the equipment housed here could be used in the rebuilding of the world, the world of which bears had such high, haphazard dreams. Holding the knife threateningly, he moved forward.

The mentor was in Dandi's head, answering her cry, seeing through her eyes, though he had no sight of his own. He scanned the bear and took over her mind instantly, knifing himself into place like a guillotine.

No longer was he a blind old dolphin lurking in one cell of a cathedral pile of coral under tropical seas, a theologer, an inculcator of wisdom into feebler-minded beings. He was a killer more savage than the bear, keen to kill anything that might covet the vacant throne once held by men. The mere thought of men sent this mentor into sharklike fury at times.

Caught up in his fury, Dandi found herself advancing. For all the bear's strength, she could vanquish it. In the open, where she could have brought her heavy tail into action, it would have been an easy matter. Here her weighty forearms must come into play. She felt them lift to her mentor's command as he planned to clout the bear to death.

The bear stepped back, awed by an opponent twice its size, suddenly unsure.

She advanced.

"No! Stop!" Dandi cried.

Instead of fighting the bear, she fought her mentor, hating his hate. Her mind twisted, her dim mind full of that steely, fishy one, as she blocked his resolution.

"I'm for peace!" she cried.

"Then kill the bear!"

"I'm for peace, not killing!"

She rocked back and forth. When she staggered into a wall, it shook; dust spread in the old room. The mentor's fury was terrible to feel.

"Get out quickly!" Dandi called to the bear.

Hesitating, it stared at her. Then it turned and made for the window. For a moment it hung with its shaggy hindquarters in the room. Momentarily she saw it for what it was, an old animal in an old world, without direction. It jumped. It was gone. Goats blared confusion on its retreat.

The mentor screamed. Insane with frustration, he hurled Dandi against the doorway with all the force of his mind.

Wood cracked and splintered. The lintel came crashing down. Brick and stone shifted, grumbled, fell. Powdered filth billowed up. With a great roar, one wall collapsed. Dandi struggled to get free. Her house was tumbling about her. It had never been intended to carry so much weight, so many centuries.

She reached the balcony and jumped clumsily to safety, just as the building avalanched in on itself, sending a cloud of plaster and powdered mortar into the overhanging trees.

For a horribly long while the world was full of dust, goat bleats and panic-stricken parakeets.

Heavily astride her baluchitherium once more, Dandi Lashadusa headed back to the empty region called Ghinomon. She fought her bitterness, trying to urge herself towards resignation.

All she had was destroyed—not that she set store by possessions: that was a man trait. Much more terrible was the knowledge that her mentor had left her forever; she had transgressed too badly to be forgiven this time.

Suddenly she was lonely for his pernickety voice in her head, for the wisdom he fed her, for the scraps of dead knowledge he tossed her—yes, even for the love he gave her. She had never seen him, never could: yet no two beings could have been more intimate.

She also missed those other wards of his she

would glimpse no more: the mole creature tunnelling in Earth's depths, the seal family that barked with laughter on a desolate coast, a senile gorilla that endlessly collected and classified spiders, an aurochs—seen only once, but then unforgettably—that lived with small creatures in an Arctic city it had helped build in the ice.

She was excommunicated.

Well, it was time for her to change, to disintegrate, to transubstantiate into a pattern not of flesh but music. That discipline, at least, the mentor had taught and could not take away.

"This will do, Lass," she said.

Her gigantic mount stopped obediently. Lovingly, she patted its neck. It was young; it would be free.

Following the dusty trail, she went ahead, alone. Somewhere afar a bird called. Coming to a mound of boulders, Dandi squatted among gorse, the points of which could not prick through her thick old coat. Already her selected music poured through her head, already it seemed to loosen the chemical bonds of her being.

Why should she not choose an old human tune? She was an antiquarian. Things that were gone solaced her for things that were to come. In her dim way, she had always stood out against her mentor's absolute hatred of men. The thing to hate was hatred. Men in their finer moments had risen above hate. Her death psalm was an instance of that—a multiple instance, for it had been fingered and changed over the ages, as the mentor himself insisted, by men of a variety of races, all with their minds directed to worship rather than hate.

Locking herself into thought disciplines, Dandi began to dissolve. Man had needed machines to help him do it, to fit into the Involutes. She was a lesser animal: she could change herself into the humbler shape of a musicolumn. It was just a matter of *rearranging*—and without pain she formed into a pattern that was not a shaggy megatherium body, but an indigo column, hardly visible . . .

For a long while, Lass cropped thistle and cacti. Then she ambled forward to seek the hairy creature she fondly—and a little condescendingly—regarded as her equal. But of the sloth there was no sign.

Almost the only landmark was a violet-blue dye in the air. As the baluchitherium mare approached, a sweet old music grew in volume from the dye. It was a music almost as ancient as the landscape itself, and certainly as much travelled, a tune once known to men as Old Hundredth. And there were voices singing: "All creatures that on Earth do dwell . . ."

A giant space station orbiting the Earth can be a scientific boon ... or a terrible sword of Damocles hanging over our heads. In Martin Caidin's *Killer Station*, one brief moment of sabotage transforms Station *Pleiades* into an instrument of death and destruction for millions of people. The massive space station is heading relentlessly toward Earth, and its point of impact is New York City, where it will strike with the impact of the Hiroshima Bomb. Station Commander Rush Cantrell must battle impossible odds to save his station and his crew, and put his life on the line that millions may live.

This high-tech tale of the near future is written in the tradition of Caidin's *Marooned* (which inspired the Soviet-American Apollo/Soyuz Project and became a film classic) and *Cyborg* (the basis for the hit TV series "The Six Million Dollar Man"). Barely fictional, *Killer Station* is an intensely *real* moment of the future, packed with excitement, human drama, and adventure.

Caidin's record for forecasting (and inspiring) developments in space is well-known. *Killer Station* provides another glimpse of what *may* happen with and to all of us in the next few years.

Available December 1985 from Baen Books
55996-6 • 384 pp. • $3.50

Here is an excerpt from Cobra Strike!, coming in February 1986 from Baen Books:

The Council of Syndics—its official title—had in the early days of colonization been just that: a somewhat low-key grouping of the planet's syndics and governor-general which met at irregular intervals to discuss any problems and map out the general direction in which they hoped the colony would grow. As the population increased and beachheads were established on two other worlds, the Council grew in both size and political weight, following the basic pattern of the distant Dominion of Man. But unlike the Dominion, this outpost of humanity numbered nearly three thousand Cobras among its half-million people.

The resulting inevitable diffusion of political power had had a definite impact on the Council's makeup. The rank of governor had been added between the syndic and governor-general levels, blunting the pinnacle of power just a bit; and at *all* levels of government the Cobras with their double vote were well represented.

Corwin Moreau didn't really question the political philosophy which had produced this modification of Dominion structure; but from a purely utilitarian point of view he often found the sheer size of the 75-member Council unwieldy.

Today, though, at least for the first hour, things went smoothly. Most of the discussion—including the points Corwin raised—focused on older issues which had already had the initial polemics thoroughly wrung out of them. A handful were officially given resolution, the rest returned to the members for more analysis, consideration, or simple foot-dragging; and as the agenda wound down it began to look as if the meeting might actually let out early.

And then Governor-General Brom Stiggur dropped a pocket planet-wrecker into the room.

It began with an old issue. "You'll all remember the report of two years ago," he said, looking around the room, "in which the Farsearch team concluded that, aside from our three present worlds, no planets exist within at least a 20-light-year radius of Aventine that we could expand to in the future. It was agreed at the time that our current state of population and development hardly required an immediate resolution of this long-term problem."

Corwin sat a bit straighter in his seat, sensing similar reactions around him. Stiggur's words were neutral enough, but something explosive seemed to be hiding beneath the carefully controlled inflections of his voice.

"However," the other continued, "in the past few days something new has come to light, something which I felt should be presented immediately to this body, before even any follow-up studies were initiated." Glancing at the Cobra guard standing by the door, Stiggur nodded. The man nodded in turn and opened the panel . . . and a single Troft walked in.

A faint murmur of surprise rippled its way around the room, and Corwin felt himself tense involuntarily as the alien made its way to Stiggur's side. The Trofts had been the Worlds' trading partner for nearly 14 years now, but Corwin still remembered vividly the undercurrent of fear that he'd grown up with. Most of the Council had even stronger memories than that: the Troft occupation of the Dominion worlds Silvern and Adirondack had occurred only 43 years ago, ultimately becoming the impetus for the original Cobra project. It was no accident that most of the people who now dealt physically with the Troft traders were in their early twenties. Only the younger Aventinians could face the aliens without wincing.

The Troft paused at the edge of the table, waiting as the Council members dug out translator-link earphones and inserted them. One or two of the younger syndics didn't bother, and Corwin felt a flicker of jealousy as he adjusted his own earphone to low volume. He'd taken the same number of courses in catertalk as they had, but it was obvious that foreign language comprehension wasn't even close to being his forté.

"Men and women of the Cobra Worlds Council," the earphone murmured to him. "I am Speaker One of the Tlos'khin'fahi demesne of the Trof'te Assemblage." The alien's high-pitched catertalk continued for a second beyond the translation; both races had early on decided that the first three parasyllables of Troft demesne titles were more than adequate for human use, and that a literal transcription of the aliens' proper names was a waste of effort. "The Tlos'khin'fahi demesne-lord has sent your own demesne-lord's request for data to the other parts of the Assemblage, and the result has been a triad offer from the Pua'lanek'zia and Baliu'ckha'spmi demesnes."

Corwin grimaced. He'd never liked deals involving two or more Troft demesnes, both because of the delicate political balance the Worlds often had to strike and because the humans never heard much about the Troft-Troft arm of such bargains. That arm *had* to exist—the individual demesnes seldom if ever gave anything away to each other.

The same line of thought appeared to have tracked its way elsewhere through the room. "You speak of a triad, instead of a quad offer," Governor Dylan Fairleigh spoke up. "What part does the Tlos'khin'fahi demesne expect to play?"

"My demesne-lord chooses the role of catalyst," was the prompt reply. "No fee will be forthcoming for our role." The Troft fingered something on his abdomen sash and Corwin's display lit up with a map showing the near half of the Troft Assemblage. Off on one edge three stars began blinking red. "The Cobra Worlds," the alien unnecessarily identified them. A quarter of the way around the bulge a single star, also outside Troft territory, flashed green. "The world named Qasama by its natives. They are described by the Baliu'ckha'spmi demesne-lord as an alien race of great potential danger to the Assemblage. Here—" a vague-edge sphere appeared at the near side of the flashing green star—"somewhere, is a tight cluster of five worlds capable of supporting human life. The Pua'lanek'zia demesne-lord will give you their location and an Assemblage pledge of human possession if your Cobras will undertake to eliminate the threat of Qasama. I will await your decision."

The Troft turned and left . . . and only slowly did Corwin realize he was holding his breath. Five brand-new worlds . . . for the price of becoming mercenaries.